P9-ELD-568

Crooked Herring

By L. C. Tyler

Crooked Herring

a&b

Crooked Herring

L. C. TYLER

Allison & Busby Limited
12 Fitzroy Mews
London W1T 6DW
www.allisonandbusby.com

First published in Great Britain by Allison & Busby in 2014.

A CIP catalogue record for this book is available from
the British Library.

First Edition

ISBN 978-0-7490-1668-5

Typeset in 11/16 pt Sabon by
Allison & Busby Ltd.

The paper used for this Allison & Busby publication
has been produced from trees that have been legally sourced
from well-managed and credibly certified forests.

Printed and bound by
CPI Group (UK) Ltd, Croydon, CR0 4YY

*To my wife Ann, who for thirty years
has successfully resisted murdering me.*

AUTHOR'S NOTE

AUTHOR'S NOTE

Some locations mentioned in the book, such as London, are real enough. Others, such as Didling Green, are amalgamations of various places, the originals having proved less convenient for the perfect crime than one might wish. All of the characters are, to the best of my knowledge, completely fictional. The paint colours mentioned in Chapter One do however all appear on the Farrow & Ball chart, an example of fact being stranger than fiction.

'There is no trap so deadly
as the trap you set for yourself'

Raymond Chandler

PROLOGUE

I've never seen the value of prologues.

Most people skip them anyway, thumb-flicking the pages to reach something that is clearly the beginning of a coherent narrative, not the rambling and deliberately obscure perorations of an author trying clumsily to bulk out a thin manuscript. And what else is a prologue for other than to delay the beginning of the real story? The thing you have paid good money to get your hands on?

And yet . . . and yet, having drafted and reread the strange account of my most recent case, I do feel that it requires some sort of introduction. Some explanation, for example, of why Elsie is not my co-narrator in quite the way she has been (since I have never found a way of preventing it) in all of the past accounts of my detective work.

It is with a heavy heart that I take up my pen to write

these, the last words in which I shall ever record the singular gifts by which my friend and sometime literary agent, Ms Elsie Thirkettle, was distinguished. It will never be possible for her to intrude on the narrative again. Since her role in the case in question was, however, significant – and her duplicity vast even by her own challenging standards – she should be heard from. Fortunately Elsie left behind a diary with notes covering roughly the period in question and I have quoted freely from it. She also left a tape of various conversations that she had covertly recorded, and I have transcribed these as necessary. You should read these sections with an open mind and judge her no more harshly than she richly deserves.

As for my own conduct, I have nothing to be ashamed of – even my actions at the very end of the case, which you will see were wholly justified. I think you will agree that I could not have done otherwise. My career as an amateur detective has been strewn with red herrings of one sort or another, but rarely have they been laid as thickly and unkindly as in the case I am about to relate. One crooked herring after another has, you might say, been deliberately laid in my path by people whom I had every reason to trust. Or at least, by people who should have known better.

But what is the point of my making excuses in a part of the book that hardly anyone will read? Very well. There is no avoiding it. Let the whole sorry story begin.

CHAPTER ONE

It is always a mistake to confess to murder while wearing a paisley bow tie.

'You don't believe me, do you?' asked Henry.

'That you have just killed somebody?' I asked.

'That I *might* have killed somebody,' he said. He looked a little sheepish. The genuine murderer – the real pro – tends to keep track of that sort of thing.

And he wasn't dressed for murder. The tweed jacket, the checked waistcoat, and above all the yellow bow tie . . . they spoke of a man who would fiddle his expenses and arrange for his pregnant secretary to have a sordid backstreet abortion. They would have enabled Henry to audition as an extra in a fifties costume drama – a dodgy bookmaker, say, or a ne'er-do-well younger brother destined for exile to one of the more obscure colonies. They were not clothes that you would risk wearing for a murder. Far too stiff. Far too formal. Far too memorable. In any case, Henry was, like me, a crime writer, and was aware of the main objection to a confession, even on a provisional basis.

'This isn't how it's done,' I said. 'The correct order of things is the discovery of a body, the examination of the evidence, a progressive elimination of suspects and then an arrest. Your leaping straight to an admission of guilt is confusing. At least for me.'

Henry's look implied that a lot of things were confusing for me.

'This isn't one of your stupid amateur detective novels, Ethelred. There's no rule that says we have to start with twelve equally likely suspects. It isn't even necessary for us to assemble in the drawing room so that I can break down and admit everything. Anyway, I'm not saying that I *have* murdered somebody – simply that I *may* have done. And I'd rather hoped you would take me seriously. It is possible, Ethelred, that at this very moment there is somebody lying dead out there and that I may have killed him. I need your help. You're a crime writer. I would have thought you would have leapt at the chance to investigate a crime for real.'

'I have investigated crimes for real,' I said. 'I'm crap at it.'

'Call it research, then.'

'I write police procedurals,' I said. 'Not amateur detective novels, which are an entirely separate subgenre, with their own quirks and clichés. And, contrary to what you appear to believe, I do not invariably have twelve suspects. Ten is usually plenty.'

Occasionally I succeed in being funny. Henry's look told me that this was one of the other times.

'For goodness' sake, Ethelred, I said I needed help, not your pathetic attempts at humour. If you came to me and said you'd committed some terrible crime, I'd at least listen with a straight face.'

This was true. I was having great difficulty in taking Henry seriously. And it wasn't just the tie. He was somewhat younger than I am but often affected the manners of somebody considerably older than both of us. Yellow bow ties, for example. And those checked waistcoats with their rounded lapels and multiple pockets. He also had a rather arch manner of addressing me that I frankly resented. Pomposity in the elderly is regrettable, but in the young it is rarely other than ridiculous. Henry was moreover quite short. His face was red and shiny. Of course, none of these things proved conclusively that he was not a murderer. It's just that I knew he wasn't one, however much he might have preferred to the contrary.

I tried to straighten my face as best I could. 'I'm listening,' I said.

'To begin at the beginning,' said Henry, speaking very slowly and carefully, as if to an idiot, 'I had a bit of a skinful on New Year's Eve. We started drinking at the Old House at Home, just round the corner from here. Then we drove into Chichester and drank at some sort of nightclub for people too young to know better. It claimed to be holding a New Year school disco, but the uniforms were unlike any school I have ever been to. Later I remember being in a country pub, but I've no idea how I got there. The only other clear recollection was waking up in the early hours of the morning in my own bed and thinking: "Oh, my God! I've killed somebody!"'

'And then?' I asked.

'I went back to sleep,' said Henry.

I took a deep breath. It did not require much knowledge of criminal investigation to deduce that Henry had gone to bed drunk and had a nightmare.

'You went to bed drunk and had a nightmare,' I said. 'Case closed. Do you fancy a whisky before you go?'

Henry shook his head wearily. 'And the knotted rope?' he asked. 'How does that fit in with it being a nightmare?'

'This is the first I've heard of a knotted rope,' I said.

'I was coming to that when you started on your deranged theories about the number of suspects needed for a murder inquiry. In the boot of my car, I found a length of rope. What do you think of that?'

'The boot of my car is full of all sorts of junk. Like most people, I rarely bother to clear it out. Your boot is probably much the same. You just picked it up somewhere, perhaps months or years ago, to use as a tow rope . . .'

'It was about three feet long and much too thin to tow even a modestly priced car.'

'That still doesn't make it a murder weapon. Most bits of rope never get to kill anyone.'

'And I was covered in scratches.'

'From the rope?'

'Of course not, you idiot. I mean that I must have been in a fight or something.'

'All right, you got drunk, fell over, cut yourself, went

16

to bed, had a nightmare and woke up to discover some superficial injuries. Antiseptic ointment is sometimes helpful under those circumstances. I probably have some in the bathroom.'

I have to make it clear that people *do* sometimes laugh at my jokes, but we had a difficult audience in tonight. Henry's expression was glacial.

'I was scratched – badly scratched – not bruised from a fall. If you like, I'll strip off now and you can examine my whole body.'

I shook my head. I had known Henry for some time, but I felt I didn't know him quite well enough for what he was proposing. I got him to take off his jacket and roll up his shirtsleeves instead. There were one or two minor abrasions on his hands and wrists, consistent with picking blackberries or playing with a fairly small, considerate kitten.

'If you're drunk it's easy enough to get scratched – maybe you went too close to some rose bushes . . .'

'All right, but how do you explain this? When I went out and looked at my car it was covered in mud. It was as if I'd been driving through the jungles of Malaya.'

'Malaysia,' I said. 'For the past fifty years it's been called Malaysia.'

'Has it? Well, I'd clearly been somewhere where they could spare a few buckets of mud for my car and never miss it.'

'I don't know how much this helps, but I doubt that it was Malaysia. It's a long way away. And you don't recall—'

'No. I don't recall a thing. To save time, Ethelred – because otherwise my hunch is that you'll return to this over and over again – let me state categorically that I do not remember anything after the country pub and not much after Chichester.'

For a moment I contemplated the walls of my new study, wondering whether I had been wise to paint them Book Room Red. I think I had been attracted by the literary associations of the name rather than by the precise shade of the pigment. In the bleak half-light of a winter afternoon, the walls looked the colour of dried blood. Of course, dried blood is part of my stock-in-trade, but you can have too much of a good thing.

Henry too was eyeing the walls with a critical air. I had him down as the sort of man who would paint his study Savage Ground or possibly even Clunch. He had a theory that the stranger the name, the better the paint. Clunch it was then.

But I was suddenly aware how little I really knew him – not just his preference for paint, but almost anything. We were, as I say, both crime writers and had met from time to time at conferences and book launches. We had compared sales figures at Crime Writers' Association parties. We had compared agents in the bar of the Swan Hotel at Harrogate and not to my advantage. When I had moved to this side of the county and bought a house in West Wittering, I noticed from the CWA Directory that he lived just a few miles down the road. I'd invited him round to dinner. It was a perfectly pleasant evening, but once we'd explored the coincidence of our being settled in this corner of Sussex we had found we had remarkably little in common. When he said that I must come and have dinner with him, we both mentally noted that it need not be in the immediate future. Then, suddenly, he had arrived on my doorstep, in the very depth of winter, to tell me that he had murdered somebody. It was much too kind of him.

'If you are really worried,' I said, 'why not go to the police? They handle this sort of thing all the time. I bet they'd be quite good at it.'

'I want to find out what happened, Ethelred. But I don't necessarily want to spend thirty years in Her Majesty's Prison on Dartmoor. When I realised that I might have murdered somebody, my first thought wasn't: "Why don't I go and grass myself up?" Anyway, you clearly don't believe me, so why should the police? I'm only guessing, but I think their jokes will be even worse than yours.'

'Hold on!' I said. 'When you started your account, you said "we". You were clearly with somebody else. All you need to do is phone them now and *ask*, for goodness' sake. Who was your drinking companion? Or don't you remember that either?'

'Crispin Vynall,' said Henry.

'Ah,' I said.

Vynall was no friend of mine, and Henry knew it. I don't mean that we had fallen out, but I had never liked his gory, hard-boiled thrillers, with their multiple gang rapes and eye-gougings – and he had pointedly ignored my traditional police procedurals in his monthly round-up of crime fiction for whichever of the Sunday papers he then reviewed for. The only occasion on which he had mentioned me was when he compared the 'fluent, sparkling prose' of some new young author with the 'predictable plots of an older generation of writers such as Peter Fielding'. Peter Fielding is one of the three names that I write under. I'd have missed it, but my agent was thoughtful enough to send me the press cutting. She'd underlined 'predictable'.

Henry also wrote hard-boiled thrillers that were very much in Crispin's style. I often told Henry how much I enjoyed them but that was a lie. I'd read two. They were facile, fast-paced stories with an abrupt twist inserted as a matter of course at the end of every chapter. The need to switch direction every thirty pages or so mean they were full of unnecessary complexity and multiple coincidences. The main characters could look forward to being tied up or tortured every third chapter on average. The stories kept your attention of course, but the endings were somehow contrived and improbable. They left you feeling duped and slightly stupid. It was as if Henry expected people to read them so quickly that they would not notice the gaps and inconsistencies. Perhaps that was what most people did. His sales were undeniably better than mine. There are clearly a lot of readers out there who like detailed descriptions of hideously violent acts. It's not the sort of book I write myself. But Henry and Crispin both wrote them and they both earned a lot more than I did.

'I tried phoning Crispin,' said Henry in response to my question. 'No reply.'

'Try again now,' I said.

He took out his mobile, glanced at it and declared the battery dead.

'Use mine,' I said.

He took my handset from me and dialled a number.

I heard a buzzing from my phone as, somewhere, Vynall's mobile played whatever catchy little tune it was programmed to play. After a while a recorded message cut in. Even without the accompaniment of Vynall's sarcastic grin, the voice grated – a former public schoolboy trying to do Estuary English. But the message was clear. Crispin Vynall was not available to take my or anyone else's call right now. He was writing some cool stuff or chilling with his mates. He'd get back to me if I left a number. Henry left a brief message asking for his call to be returned at Crispin's earliest convenience.

'He's obviously gone out and left his mobile at home. People do that,' I said.

'No, *you* do that, Ethelred. Normal people, by and large, take their mobile phones with them. They're mobile. That's why they call them mobile phones. People like you – people who start like a frightened rabbit every time it rings – do quite possibly leave their phone behind. You'd know better than I do.'

'Well, you'll get him eventually.'

'If he's still alive.'

'Still alive? You're not saying you think you might have killed *Crispin*?' I didn't like Crispin, but I couldn't quite bring myself to wish him dead.

'Don't you think that's possible? I start the evening drinking with him. Then, at some point, he just vanishes from the scene. Now he's uncontactable. Anything could have happened.'

'Or, more likely, nothing happened at all,' I said.

Henry shook his head. 'You've seen me drunk a few times, haven't you?'

I considered. 'Not really. Not compared with most crime writers I know.'

Henry frowned. A hard-boiled crime writer needed to be, as a matter of course, a hard drinker too. 'I'd have said I could put it away with the best of them.'

Fine, if that was what he wanted. 'OK, then – you've been drunk on half of the occasions I've met you. Is that better?'

Henry nodded as if that fitted in with the most recent research, though it clearly still irked him that I didn't have him down as an out-and-out lush. 'Whatever,' he said. 'But think, Ethelred: however much I put away the previous evening, have I ever told you that I had *no recollection* of what I had done?'

'No,' I said. 'You've never told me that.'

This time, at least, I'd got the right answer at the first attempt. 'Absolutely,' said Henry. 'And *that's* why I need your help, Ethelred.'

I sighed. 'Run it all past me again,' I said. 'Leave out no detail, however trivial. Then I'll give Crispin another call so that he can tell us if he's alive or not.'

Henry scowled at me, but I was not to be browbeaten into condemning him as a murderer. He'd need to make the story pretty good.

And this was the complete story as he told it. He and Crispin Vynall had gone out for a drink on New Year's Eve. They had started at my own local pub – no great coincidence since Henry, as I have said, lived close by, while Crispin lived somewhere over by Brighton. They had decided that the village of West Wittering was a little

22

too quiet and, at Crispin's suggestion, had headed into the great metropolis of Chichester, about fifteen minutes' drive away at legal speeds – ten at the sort of speed Henry would have driven in his vintage Jaguar. They had followed some back roads on the outskirts of town. Henry said he didn't know precisely where they had ended up but, listening to him, I had a fairly good idea about which place they had visited.

I remembered seeing the New Year School Disco advertised in the local papers for some weeks beforehand. There aren't in fact that many nightclubs in Chichester. Pubs, yes. Tea rooms, certainly. Garden centres with cafes selling lemon drizzle cake, no problem. Cavernous spaces throbbing with a pulsating beat – not so much. The establishment in question was, as Henry had implied, a club frequented mainly by students and young professionals intent on having a good time. I wasn't a regular there myself, you might say – I usually preferred Russell's Garden Centre – but I was pretty sure I knew where they'd been.

Henry continued that he had found it hot and the music deafening. He had suggested leaving, but Crispin had said he liked the company of young people, by which he seemed to mean young female people. So, Henry had sat a great deal of the time in a corner drinking beer, while Crispin cruised the dance floor, occasionally draping himself around a girl thirty years his junior with an ease that Henry had envied. I nodded sympathetically.

It all fitted in with my recollection of Crispin in the bars of conference hotels. Nobody could deny that he knew how to have a good time if his wife wasn't watching him too closely. There was agreement, at least amongst crime writers, that Crispin resembled an aging rock star, though there was a lack of consensus over which one. One of the Rolling Stones perhaps, or Rod Stewart, or maybe even Howard Marks, if you wanted to widen the circle to friendly, retired drug dealers. He undoubtedly had the sagging face, the leather jacket, the long, unnaturally black hair and a lopsided grin that hung halfway between easy amiability and unabashed lechery. There was no questioning that he would have been more at home at the club than Henry or I.

Sometime after eleven, Henry continued, Crispin had proposed going on by taxi to another place he knew, where the girls were possibly younger still and the music louder. Henry had politely declined and watched Crispin leave on his own. Then there was a complete blank except for two things. First he remembered the chimes of Big Ben sounding and he had noticed he was in a crowded, low-ceilinged room with copious beams and much brass on the walls. He took this to be a country pub and something more to his liking. Later – or perhaps a little before – he was outdoors, apparently in a wood. It was raining gently and water was dripping from the branches above his head. He could see the spire of the church and, dark against the clouds, its weathervane representing a ship in full sail. He had felt tired. He felt in need of a very strong drink, suggesting perhaps that the pub bit came later rather than earlier. Then he was in his own bed. It was still dark, his bedside clock read 03.54 and a nameless dread was creeping over him. He went back to sleep until mid-morning, when he woke again, got up and made some coffee. Then he phoned Crispin Vynall. There was no reply.

'The church,' I said. 'The first time round, you didn't mention the church.'

'Didn't I?'

'Maybe your memory of the evening is returning?' I suggested. 'Is there any more that you can recall?'

'I don't think so,' he said. But this time he didn't reprimand me for repeating my question.

'How did you get to the church?'

'I must have driven, don't you think? Hence the mud on the car.'

'You shouldn't have been driving in that state.'

'Ethelred, I'm saying that I may have murdered somebody. The drink-drive charges are relatively insignificant.'

'But what if what you half-recall is running somebody over?'

'There was no damage to the car – just mud.'

'Very well. You drove back safely in your muddy car. I'm surprised the police didn't stop you, but you would have been just one of many drunks on the road that night. They can't stop everyone. It's an interesting story. I don't see how I can help you, though. I'd love to, but I can't.'

We both knew there was at least one lie in that last sentence.

'I want you to find out what happened,' said Henry. 'To investigate. I need to know where I went and I need to know that Crispin is all right.'

'And there is some good reason why it should be me rather than you who goes poking around West Sussex in the middle of winter?'

'I could do it but . . . and I admit this . . . I'm frightened about what I may discover. Let me be entirely frank and say I'm not sure I have the guts to go through with it. And you are a better writer than I am – or at least your skills are more appropriate. I write thrillers. If we were both chained in a cellar with the water rising rapidly and rats crawling over our hair, then I'd know what our options were. But you, as you say, write dull and painstakingly accurate police procedurals. You know about gathering evidence and making logical deductions.'

'Most of the things that the police have access to – CCTV footage, fingerprinting, trained pathologists and DNA evidence to name but four – are completely unavailable to me. Nor can I walk into whichever pub you were in, flash a warrant card and demand that people answer my questions.'

'I explained why I can't go to the police,' he said patiently. 'Even if I planned to turn myself in, I'd at least like to know first who I murdered and why. Maybe you will draw a complete blank, in which case I'll have to accept your hypothesis that it was all some sort of dream. But I'd still like you to try.'

Philip Marlowe would have narrowed his eyes and growled: 'OK, but it's going to cost you plenty. I hope you've got a rich uncle.' I just said the first two of those words. And the emphasis was on 'but'. My objections were:

1) I wasn't a real detective, just a crime writer who wrote about detectives. Even that wasn't terribly profitable.

2) To the extent that I had tried my hand at being a real detective, it had usually resulted in terror, discomfort and real humiliation. For me. Not for the criminal.

3) My investigations had led to my being arrested three times and released three times. There was a sense in which I could still quit while I was ahead.

4) If Henry had killed Crispin Vynall I was beginning to realise that I honestly didn't care that much. Of course, I cared in a theoretical way, but that underlined word 'predictable' still grated, even now.

I obviously hadn't explained it quite that well to Henry, however, because he was looking at me as though we'd just become blood brothers.

'So, you'll do it?' he asked.

'It would be pointless,' I said. 'I'm not a detective and I have a deadline looming.'

'I thought so,' he said smugly.

'Thought what?'

'You've never really done any research into how crimes are solved, other than read Agatha Christie and Colin Dexter. You lack even the most superficial knowledge of police work. It's exactly what your Amazon reviews say, by the way.'

Fans of Christie and Dexter might have raised their eyebrows at this. Elsie, as my agent, would have simply nodded and said that was the problem she has always had with my work. But I wasn't in the mood for constructive feedback.

'I've already explained—'

'I don't want a DNA analysis or a report on maggots found at the scene of the crime – just that you ask a few questions and find out what happened on New Year's Eve. How difficult can that be?'

'Not difficult at all. You could do it yourself. In any case, with the greatest of respect, we've hardly seen each other for months then you suddenly turn up and expect me to drop everything and be a detective.'

'I actually phoned you on New Year's Eve.'

'You sent me a text saying you were out having a good time. I sent you one in return saying I was watching television on my own.'

'Did you?'

'Yes. I did. I wasn't looking for an invitation to join you, but at the same time I certainly didn't get one. It's a bit late to invite me to join the party now. I am politely declining your offer. You do it.'

'Apart from all of the reasons I've already given, Ethelred, I simply don't have the time. The *Telegraph* and the *Sunday Times* have both asked me to write a monthly round-up of crime fiction for them. It will be a lot of work but it will give me the chance to support mid-list authors who deserve to be known better. Authors who don't normally get reviewed in the national press. Authors who are unfairly rubbished on Amazon. Authors whose sales deserve the real boost that a glowing review from a well-respected crime writer can offer.'

He looked at me significantly.

'What did you mean about being rubbished on Amazon?'

I asked. 'Are you saying I've had some bad reviews there?'

'Don't you check them?'

'Not often.'

'Maybe you should. Of course, the only important reviews are still the ones you get in the press. The quality press. The sort of papers *I* write for. When is your next book out, by the way?'

I paused. He might be bluffing, but could I risk it?

'I'll do what I can,' I said, 'but I'll just try to establish where you and Crispin were on New Year's Eve – after that you're on your own.'

'That's very good of you.'

'If you remember anything else let me know,' I said.

'I'll try,' he said meekly.

'I'll get back to you as soon as I can. In the meantime, don't worry about it too much. I can't imagine you've done anything untoward – let alone committed murder. I'm sure it will all be fine.'

I was aware I sounded a little bit like the presenter of *Crimewatch*, who (for the record) never reassured me in the slightest that serious crime was a rare occurrence. Henry, on the other hand, seemed satisfied.

'Thanks, Ethelred,' he said, and he shook my hand.

'Just out of interest,' I said, 'what *are* my options if I'm chained up in a cellar with the water rising rapidly?'

'Don't worry. The girl you met in chapter three should have worked out where you are and is already on her way with chain cutters,' said Henry.

'And if she hasn't?'

'It doesn't bear thinking about,' said Henry.

* * *

Later I briefly contemplated phoning Elsie to ask her advice. Had I done so, things might have been very different. On the other hand, judging by Elsie's subsequent conduct, things might equally have been exactly the same. Or worse. We'll never know really. Not now.

CHAPTER TWO

Amazon.co.uk

Death in the Cathedral Close
(A Buckfordshire mystery) [paperback]
Peter Fielding (author)

Customer reviews

***** A great traditional mystery 21 April 2009
By Bookworm
I hadn't come across this writer before, but I loved
the book. If you like a straightforward story with no
unpleasant surprises and good grammatical prose,
then this one is certainly for you. An excellent book
to take to bed and lull yourself gently to sleep. No
hesitation in awarding Mr Fielding five stars. Bravo!

**** Very Good Value 3 September 2009
By M Smith REAL NAME
I found this in an Oxfam shop and bought it for 30p.
I've taken the price into account in marking it four
stars. At full price maybe only three.

***** A Fine Police Procedural 12 December 2009
By 'Churchman'
Peter Fielding's latest book is well up to the standard
of the previous ones. Sgt Fairfax is baffled by the
discovery of a body outside the cathedral on
Christmas Eve. Is it a tramp who has died of cold or
is it ritual murder? Fielding allows the plot to unfold
in his usual leisurely manner, with many interesting
diversions into church architecture and history.
Can't recommend it strongly enough.

* Total Rubbish 15 December 2012
By Thrillseeker
Anyone able to stay awake as far as page 7 will
have guessed the denouement of this slim volume
by Ethelred Tressider, writing here as Peter Fielding.
Tressider has been penning the Buckfordshire series
for some years now and must have exhausted almost
every location in the fictional city of Buckford for the
discovery of murder victims. This one turns up by
the cathedral door, though nobody comments on the
similarity with the discovery in an earlier book of a
body in a pew in the same building. In Buckfordshire,

it would seem, cathedrals are the normal place to recycle dead bodies. You can only conclude that Tressider finds his plots as unmemorable as the rest of us do, which is saying a great deal. I do so wish I could give the book no stars, but one is the minimum allowable. One star it is then.

CHAPTER THREE

The Old House at Home is no more than a ten-minute walk from where I now live. It is a large but rather cosy pub situated in the middle of the village, just where the main road from Chichester turns abruptly to the left and, rejecting as impractical the idea of fetching up against the dunes of East Head, elects to wander off toward Bracklesham. It is functional rather than picturesque, a Victorian building modernised so often that it has the air of having been constructed at no particular time and to no particular plan. But it has a bright and well-cared for appearance. It is the sort of place you'd readily stop if you wanted to break your journey for a meal, or that you'd call in on with the family on the way back from the beach. It also seemed like as good a place as any to start asking questions.

I know the barman well enough to call him Denzil and

he knows me well enough to blink a couple of times, frown and call me Mr Treasurer or, on one occasion, Mr Treacle. It's a tricky name.

'Thanks, Denzil,' I said as he pushed a half of bitter across the bar. Then I added casually: 'I suppose you don't remember who was in on New Year's Eve?'

'Now you're asking,' he said, with total accuracy but little elucidation. 'Pretty much everybody was in, as you will have noticed yourself.'

'I wasn't here,' I said.

'Weren't you? I could have sworn I served you.'

'The night before, maybe,' I said.

'Really?'

If I had been hoping for total recall, this wasn't it.

'Do you remember seeing Henry Holiday? He's a writer, like me.'

'You a writer, then?' he asked brightly.

'Yes, I'm sure I've told you that. Maybe you've seen my books in the shops? I write mainly as Peter Fielding, but also as J. R. Elliott.'

'Not really,' he said. 'But I only look in the crime section. What sort of thing do you write?'

'Crime,' I said.

'Just crime?'

'Well, some romantic fiction under another name.'

'That would explain it, then,' he said. 'I don't read romantic fiction.' He was about to turn and go and check on a food order, when I added: 'So, *did* you see Henry then? He was in with yet another crime writer: Crispin Vynall.'

'Henry . . . Henry . . . Let me think . . . I'm not sure,

35

but I certainly did see Crispin Vynall. I've read some of *his* books. They're brilliant – there's one where some kidnappers take this little kid and then video him being made to drink bleach so that the parents will—'

'Sorry, Denzil, could I just stop you there and get you to tell me about Henry?'

'What does he look like?'

I did my best to describe him. Denzil nodded encouragingly.

'I sort of remember him,' he said, probably meaning he had no recollection at all. 'Weren't you with them, though? I can almost picture the three of you over there by the fire, chatting away – the two of them getting on like nobody's business and you slightly out of it, sipping a half of bitter.'

I put my half of bitter onto the counter. 'No, I was at home,' I said.

'Shame. On your own on New Year's Eve. And your friends a few yards away in the pub. You'd have thought they'd have sent you a text or something asking you to join them. You ought to get out more.'

'It didn't bother me. There was a really good programme on meerkats or something. I had all the excitement I needed. You don't remember anything else about Crispin Vynall? What he was talking about, for example?'

'I wouldn't listen to other people's conversations. As a barman you don't. What's said at the Old House at Home stays at the Old House at Home. But it was definitely Crispin Vynall. I'm pretty sure you came over to the bar and introduced him to me.'

'That must have been Henry. I wasn't here.'

'You sure?'

'Absolutely sure. I had meerkats to look after. What time did they leave, then?'

'Mr Vynall must have left around ten or ten-thirty. I'm pretty sure of that, because a family came in and sat over there by the fire, and they'd been there at least an hour or two by midnight. Yes, maybe closer to ten than ten-thirty.'

'And Henry left with him?'

'Well, I don't remember seeing him afterwards – let's put it like that.'

'Though, equally, you don't remember seeing him before.'

'That's very true.'

'Thanks,' I said. 'You've been helpful.'

I wondered whether I should tip him for this information. I was sure that was what Marlowe would have done. A five spot slipped across the bar that would lead to a phone call a couple of hours later with a vital clue. Denzil wasn't really used to tips, and there was a danger that money passed across the counter for no apparent reason would simply unsettle him. As it happened, by the time I'd made up my mind the information was worth around 25p, Denzil had already gone to check on the food. He didn't come back. I replaced the coins in my pocket, finished my drink and went out into the cold, wet day.

As I say, I was pretty sure where they had gone next. There simply weren't that many options. Chichester is better for afternoon tea than nightlife. If Philip Marlowe had gone in search of seedy joints where naive punters are milked of all they have by twenty-year-old girls with world-weary faces and bright-red lipstick, he'd have drawn a complete blank. But I did know one nightclub.

It was more out by the ring road than actually in Chichester, in as desolate a spot as you'll find within a five-mile radius of any prosperous cathedral city. Its concrete exterior blended well with the warehouses and carpet showrooms that were its immediate neighbours. I chose from the hundred or so empty spaces in the car park, slotting my silver Volvo neatly between the white lines, close to one of the other three cars that were already there. Then I picked my way round the puddles and found the only unlocked door into the building.

At three o'clock on a winter's afternoon, the interior was dark and echoing. It succeeded in being both cold and stuffy. The walls were painted a matt black that probably did not feature at all in the Farrow & Ball colour chart and that seemed to close in on you as you watched. A vast and complex array of lighting equipment, which at the moment produced no light at all, was suspended from the black ceiling. A large stage was flanked with massive speakers and topped with turntables that currently did not turn and amplifiers that had nothing to amplify. It was the people and the noise that made this a venue worth coming to. At the moment it was an empty box, awaiting nightfall, when punters would take advantage of the £8 wristband deal and perhaps the offer of four Jägerbombs (whatever they were) for £9.95. The only action on the dance floor was an old guy in brown overalls pushing a broom in a leisurely manner. Nothing suggested that I was welcome. My footsteps echoed accusingly as I crossed the floor.

Of course, I was going to be out of place here at any time of the night or day. The club's website showed a packed room with nobody over the age of twenty-five. At the time when I might have found an establishment of this sort interesting, none of its existing clientele would have even been born.

The assistant manager, once summoned by the man with the broom, looked as though he had qualified only recently as an adult. His chin sprouted fluffy ginger hair that might have been meant as a beard. He shook his head. 'They left hours ago,' he said.

'Who?'

'If you're looking for your son or daughter – we kicked the last of them out at around nine o'clock this morning. Our staff have to get some sleep too.'

'I'm not looking for one of my children. Actually I don't have any children and almost certainly never will have, but that's beside the point.'

'How can I help you, then? We're not serving drinks at the moment.'

I'd pondered on the journey here exactly what I was going to claim to be. I could simply say that my friend thought that he might have murdered somebody shortly after leaving the club, but there are times when the truth, however straightforward, simply has the wrong sort of feel to it.

'I'm a private detective,' I said.

He gave me a resigned nod of the head. I got the impression that the arrival of private detectives on the premises was more or less normal. Not welcome exactly, but not exactly unprecedented.

'My client runs a business in Portsmouth,' I said. 'He thinks his head of finance may not be playing absolutely straight with him – that he's passing confidential information to a rival. We have information that he met up with somebody from the rival firm here on New Year's Eve.'

'Could be. I'm not sure how I can help.'

'Do you recognise either of these faces?'

I passed him two author publicity photos, downloaded from their respective websites. Neither really looked like a typical head of finance, but Crispin Vynall, in his leather jacket and sunglasses, might have passed on a good day for a bent head of finance. Henry wasn't wearing a bow tie but he still had about him the air of somebody who had recently escaped from an Ealing comedy. Allowed access to the petty cash, he would have hot-footed it to Le Touquet with the nearest chorus girl. They would, I realised, have appeared to the average onlooker as a slightly odd couple, for all that they wrote pretty similar types of books.

Fortunately, to the assistant manager, they were just a couple of guys who, being over thirty-five, would shortly qualify for their free bus passes. 'I think there were a couple of older blokes in that night. Might have been them. Might have been somebody else. Might have been you. Difficult to say.'

He raised an eyebrow. Well, I was definitely an older bloke. No getting away from it.

'I wasn't there myself,' I said.

'No?'

'One of them looks a bit like me in some ways, but he's shorter.'

The assistant manager looked again at the head and

shoulders shot and then at me. 'Yes, I can see that,' he said.

'You can't remember what time they arrived or left?'

'Not really. Why should I?'

'You wouldn't have any CCTV footage?'

'The camera over there's broken. It's just for show. But we've got a camera that works out in the car park. We'd have pictures from that.'

'Can I look at them?'

'No, you can't.'

'But you've got it and know how to work the equipment?'

'Of course I can work the equipment. It's only a bloody DVD player. Any idiot can work that.'

'Yes, of course. Why can't I see it then?'

'Data Protection Act.'

We looked at each other. I had no idea what the Data Protection Act said about CCTV and suspected he didn't either.

'There's a little known clause in the Data Protection Act that stipulates that if you don't get caught, then you can't get into any trouble. I promise you I'll keep the information to myself. I just need to know that they were both here. *My client* needs to know they were both here. It's fine to let me see the video. It's a question of law enforcement.'

'No, it isn't.'

We looked at each other again. This would take more than a five spot.

'Fifty quid,' I said, taking out my wallet.

'Well, why didn't you say so before? The machine's in the back office. Do you know how to work it?'

'No,' I said.

* * *

41

Having been given a five-minute tutorial on which buttons to press, I spent an interesting half an hour watching blurred shots of cars arriving and leaving, but mainly just staying where they were. Every now and then some human figure would flit across the screen but it was really just about the cars. White ones. Black ones. Silver ones. Colours didn't show up so well; red and green were much of a muchness. Slightly earlier than Henry had given me to understand, I picked up Henry and Crispin standing by Henry's Jaguar, Crispin in front, Henry mainly hidden behind him, but clearly identifiable. Then there was another shot in which they were almost right under the camera – this time you would have had to have known Henry well to have identified him by his right elbow, but it was a good one of Crispin. Then they were gone. I continued to work my way through the shots, expecting Crispin Vynall to emerge first and perhaps get into a taxi, followed some time later by Henry. It was around eleven-fifteen when Henry appeared and, almost as large as life, walked determinedly across the car park. Moreover it was definitely Crispin Vynall who was with him, following a few paces behind. Crispin's route was slightly less direct than Henry's – he looked as if he was about to trip over his own feet. They both got into the car. In the next shot the car had already gone. I went back to the earlier picture and checked. No doubt they were still together then. Did Henry perhaps drop Crispin at this second club he had mentioned?

The assistant manager looked round the door.

'You got what you needed? It's just that the boss will be back soon. You wouldn't want to have to slip him fifty quid too.'

'Yes, thanks. I've got all I wanted.'

'You're lucky you came in when you did. I was about to wipe the disc clean. We don't have a lot of storage on that machine. And the quality's not great as you will have observed yourself. Boss says we're going to buy a new one soon, but he says a lot of things.'

'I've got all I need,' I repeated. 'You can delete anything you like as far as I'm concerned.'

'Thanks for that. I appreciate it.'

I paused, then said: 'If you do remember anything else about either of the two gentlemen, maybe you could let me know?'

He shrugged. He wasn't planning to phone me but he wanted me off the premises. 'Do you want to leave me your name and a contact phone number?'

I scribbled them on a scrap of paper.

'Thanks,' he said. 'And do you want to let me have the name of the guy you're investigating?'

I could, but he'd only Google him and find out that he was merely a crime writer, and not an accountant of any sort.

'Sorry. Data Protection Act,' I said.

I took a last glance at Crispin Vynall, for the moment following Henry across the car park, but soon to be deleted for ever. Was he lurching drunkenly in Henry's wake, or had he perhaps just stumbled as the picture was taken? I had no way of telling.

I thanked the assistant manager again and splashed my way back through the car park to my car.

Once back home, I tried Crispin's mobile again, redialling the number Henry had called the day before. There was still no reply. I found my CWA Membership Directory and looked up his landline. The phone was picked up almost immediately.

'Hello?' said a woman.

'It's Ethelred Tressider. Is Crispin there?'

For a moment there was no reply. Just as I was beginning to fear we had been cut off, the woman said: 'No. He's out.'

'Is that Emma?' I asked.

'Who else would it be, Ethelred?'

'Sorry. Yes, of course. I suppose you don't know when he will be back?'

'Do you want me to take a message?'

'Could you ask him to call me?' I gave her my number. She did not repeat it back to me.

'Do you want me to say what it's about?' she said.

My mind went blank.

'Just say it's about a book,' I heard myself saying.

'A book?'

I was beginning to wish I'd sorted out my story in advance.

'That's right,' I said. 'A book of short stories I'm editing.'

'I didn't know Crispin ever wrote short stories.'

'I was hoping to persuade him.'

Fortunately her interest went no further than that. 'OK. Cool,' she said. Then she added: 'It's a while since I've heard from you, Ethelred.'

'Yes,' I said.

'Drop by sometime,' she said.

'Yes,' I said.

'Bye,' she said.

'Bye.'

I pressed the red button to end the call.

Crispin had, according to Henry's theory, been dead for about three days, ever since Henry had murdered him. Crispin's wife, however, did not seem to have registered this fact. Throughout our admittedly brief conversation, Emma Vynall had not mentioned the words 'missing' or 'terribly worried' or 'police'. She had not seemed overly concerned – just slightly hacked off at having to take my message. Yet, at the same time, she had not volunteered any information about when Crispin might be back or able to return my call.

Like my discovery that Crispin and Henry had left the club together, the fact that Emma was reluctant to tell me much about Crispin's whereabouts almost certainly meant nothing. But I was left with the feeling that you have when viewing an Escher print – that although everything looked more or less normal, there was a strange anomaly in the picture that I couldn't quite account for. Perhaps the artist had played a trick with perspective. Or maybe a line that appeared straight was in fact crooked. There was some sleight of hand that was making the impossible look normal. But, in this case, I couldn't see how the trick was done, because I still had no idea what the trick was.

CHAPTER FOUR

Amazon.co.uk

Dead Poets
(#5 in the Master Thomas Series) [paperback]
J. R. Elliott (author)

Customer reviews

**** A joy to read! 15 May 2008
By Mary Williams REAL NAME
Another of Mr Elliott's mediaeval mysteries and
well up to the standard of the earlier ones. Master
Thomas is worried that a serial killer is disposing of
promising young poets. His boss, Geoffrey Chaucer,
hampers the investigations as usual. Greatly enlivened
by many pages of verse in authentic Middle English.

***** More please! 1 June 2008
By Mike Jones REAL NAME
I'd read the author's other books, written under the name of Peter Fielding, but none of the historical mysteries featuring Master Thomas, Chaucer's much put upon clerk and amateur detective. Though I've probably started at the wrong end of the series, I quickly got to know the various characters and am now looking forward to reading the earlier books. This looks like a series that will run and run.

*** Not bad 30 January 2011
By Historymysteryfan
Master Thomas investigates the death of some of Chaucer's more obscure contemporaries. Maybe not as good as the first four Master Thomas books. I can see why his publisher has now dropped the series. Still, it's worth looking out if you can find one in a second-hand bookshop.

* Truly, truly dreadful 15 December 2012
By Thrillseeker
Another slim volume from Ethelred Tressider, this time writing as J. R. Elliott. Lovers of great historical crime fiction should steer well clear of this one. Rarely have I cared less who committed a murder. Difficult to say whether it is the weakness of characterisation or the thin plot or the unbelievable dialogue that caused me to fall asleep so often. Or

maybe it was the feeble attempts at sub-Chaucerian verse. Whatever Tressider is, he is not a poet. I stopped reading halfway through, as you probably will, but if you can be bothered to flick to the back of the book you'll discover it was Chaucer himself who bumped them off. (Yawn.)

CHAPTER FIVE

The map of Sussex, south of Chichester, is scarcely crossed by a single contour line. The wind whips in from the pebbly coast across a flat plain, crossed by meandering, reed-choked streams known locally as Rifes. Large areas are too liable to flooding to be fit for any habitation except isolated farms and sewerage works. Along the exposed southern edge of this peninsular you can buy striped windbreaks and plastic buckets and spades and ice creams and fish and chips in paper. You can place your deckchair on the shingle and watch the grey sea wash in under a broad sweep of sky. The sheltered, marsh-fringed northern coast, conversely, boasts flocks of wading birds, samphire-covered mudflats and yacht moorings. Set back amongst the trees, beyond gleaming, emerald-green lawns, are the white walls and red roofs of what local estate agents describe as yachtsmen's residences – substantial homes in spacious grounds that are usually occupied only at weekends, except in the summer months, when the yachtsman's wife and children are banished there while the yachtsman continues to toil in London as a broker or a venture capitalist.

West Wittering lies at the far corner of this rectangle of land – at a sharp angle of the coast where sand dunes replace the pebbles and the large detached houses meet and rub shoulders with the beach huts and ice cream vans.

From my own house on the edge of the village I took the path along the sea wall, with the dunes ahead of me and salt marsh on either side. Above me were trailing lines of Brent geese, flying home to haven in the boggy fields behind the beach cafeteria and the empty car park. The sky was clearing and the sun was starting to set behind wispy banks of pink and pale-grey cloud. I often walked this way when I wanted to think out a particularly complex strand of a book that I was working on. This evening I walked until the light had faded so much that the hawthorns on either side of the path formed two amorphous black walls and the path itself was dark and featureless. And I could make just as little of the case I had been given to resolve. Henry and Crispin had left the club together. But what difference did that make? Henry had just misremembered. Two people can leave a club and get into a car without one murdering the other. And Emma might have all sorts of reasons for not wishing to tell me, or anyone, where Crispin was. The most likely explanation was that I could find nothing because there was nothing to find.

I returned the way I had come, overtaking one of my neighbours out walking her dogs.

'You look preoccupied,' she said. 'I hope it's a good plot you're working on.'

'On the contrary,' I said. 'I have no idea where this one is going. I'm beginning to think the time may have come to drop it and try something else.'

There was however one further stage of that New Year's Eve that I had not investigated for Henry. Back at the house I spent an hour or so poring over a map of West Sussex. There were plenty of churches and plenty of woods, but very few churches *near* woods. Most seemed to be in the centre of villages or situated to provide fine, uninterrupted views of the Downs. And yet Henry's description had been vivid enough. A church spire caught in the moonlight, the ship on the weathervane riding the scudding clouds and, behind it, a dark, spiky mass of branches. Or was I starting to invent details? I needed to talk to Henry again.

At ten-thirty I finally phoned Henry to report back on what I had discovered so far.

'What on earth did you go to the pub for?' he said. 'I told you, I remembered that part of the evening perfectly. Your questioning of the barman was a complete waste of time.'

Well, it was my own time that I had wasted.

'I thought I might as well cover everything,' I said.

'You clearly found out nothing that was remotely useful.'

'You may be right. I was probably being over-optimistic expecting Denzil to tell me anything of value. He actually tried to convince me that I'd been in the pub with you and Crispin Vynall. He said he remembered me, sitting there sadly clutching my half-pint while you and Crispin made merry.'

'Did he?' said Henry.

'Yes, but I clearly wasn't there.'

'Perhaps that was you on another occasion?' asked Henry.

'On no occasion at all,' I said, 'was I the saddo in the corner sipping a small glass of beer. It's not something I do. Anyway, for what it was worth, he remembered Crispin being in the pub. Denzil seems to be a bit of a fan of his.'

'So, Denzil was convinced you were there – that there were three of us?'

'Yes, but he was wrong . . . Or are you saying there *was* a third person there?'

'The pub was full. But, at our table, it was just me and Crispin. No mysterious third man lurking in the shadows. Or nobody that I saw, anyway.'

'Fine. The point is, Denzil confirmed you left for Chichester much as you said.'

'That's all you discovered at the pub, then? That I left at much the time I said?'

'Put like that, I agree it wasn't especially helpful, but the pub is very close to where I live. It didn't delay me that much. I did a bit better at the club.'

'You found it?'

'It wasn't difficult to track down. To be perfectly honest all you needed to do was to Google "School Disco, Chichester". That would have identified it for you.'

'I'm not that great with computers – not like Crispin. Or you.'

'I'll give you a tutorial sometime,' I said, feeling smug

that I was at least ahead of some people in my knowledge of information technology, whatever Elsie might wish to believe. So much for Henry's comments, too, about my iPhone. 'Anyway,' I continued. 'I located it and went and paid them a visit. There's no doubt you and Crispin were there.'

'Thank you, but again, Ethelred, that is not exactly news. Did you come up with anything more than that?'

'Mainly your arrival and departure times – you were caught on the car park CCTV. What was really interesting, though, was this: you said you thought Crispin left before you. In fact the CCTV shows you leaving together. He looked a bit drunk – well, more than a bit. Could you have given him a lift to the other club?'

'I said – I don't remember much about that stage of the evening. I was a bit drunk too. It hadn't occurred to me there might be CCTV . . . Well, let's hope I dropped him off somewhere, because he certainly wasn't at the second pub with me. I'm sure of that. Maybe I left him in Chichester at the station or something.'

'You think he got a train back to Brighton?'

'I don't think they run that late. A taxi, maybe.'

'A taxi wouldn't have been cheap – especially on New Year's Eve – but I guess Crispin could have afforded it. Anyway, at 11.13, you both vanish off into the night. I've noted the time carefully because they said they were about to wipe the recording. It's a good thing I went there today.'

There was a long pause before Henry said: 'And they *did* wipe it? I mean there's no chance of my being able to go back and check for myself whether it was Crispin with me?'

'None at all, I would think. I suppose I could have asked them to keep it, but I doubt if they would. That's the problem with not being the police. The powers of the amateur detective with regard to the retention of evidence are sadly limited.'

'Did you at least *ask* for a copy?'

'No,' I said. 'Sorry. But there isn't any doubt about it – it was Crispin with you.'

'And I suppose it's too late to get a copy now?' His voice was distinctly tetchy.

'I would think so,' I said.

I suppose he was right. I had been remiss in not asking. I just hadn't thought of it at the time.

For a moment neither of us said anything, then I added: 'Well, we at least know what happened up to that point in the evening. I don't know whether Crispin got home safely. Emma just said he wasn't around at the moment.'

'You phoned his wife?'

'Any reason why I shouldn't?'

'I didn't ask you to. I just asked that you should find out where Crispin and I went.'

Again he was far from pleased. I wondered whether to point out that he was not paying me to carry out this work for him – well, not payment in cash anyway – and that I'd already notched up quite a few miles to Chichester and back, plus fifty pounds in bribery and corruption. Fortunately I'm not used to gratitude.

'She didn't seem worried about him,' I said. 'If he'd really vanished, she ought to be a lot more concerned than she was.'

'Did you mention that I was trying to find him?'

'No, of course not. I didn't mention you at all.'

'But you still have no idea where he is?'

'No.'

'Well, I hope you did a better job of locating the pub,' he said.

'Ah, yes, that,' I said. 'The problem is that this part of the world is full of quaint old pubs. For the moment I'm having difficulty in finding one that fits your description.'

'You mean you haven't made any progress on that at all?'

Even before I made the call I had been wondering whether all of this journeying to and fro on Henry's behalf was worthwhile. Now, with his ingratitude laid bare, I knew the answer to that question.

'Look, Henry, I really haven't done that badly for one day's work,' I said. 'I've confirmed which club you went to and that you and Crispin left together. I've established that Crispin's wife hasn't missed him, which is at least suggestive of his being alive. I'm sorry if that is a disappointment to you. I hope you make better progress yourself from now on.'

'What do you mean?' asked Henry.

'I've found out as much as I can. Maybe a private detective – I mean a real one – might be able to help. But I don't have time to go from pub to pub asking, with decreasing probability of anyone knowing the answer, whether you were in there on New Year's Eve. Especially since I'll only be told what an appalling job I've done.'

There was a long pause, then a more reasonable Henry spoke.

'I'm sorry – I didn't mean to imply you'd done a bad job. Quite the reverse, in fact.'

'Thanks. But it makes no difference.'

'I couldn't persuade you . . .'

'That's right. You couldn't persuade me. I quit.'

'I'd rather hoped . . . you see, I'm going to be so busy with all of those book reviews. For prominent quality papers. It's quite difficult for mid-list authors to get noticed by reviewers these days . . . especially those whose work has inexplicably failed to catch the public's attention. So I feel I need to make a special effort to look out those who were really deserving. I sort of hoped, under the circumstances . . .'

I wondered if he thought he was being subtle. But he probably wouldn't have wasted the effort. Not on me. Something told me he probably wouldn't waste review space on me either.

'I've done all I can,' I said. 'I hope you manage to find out what happened.'

'So, you won't help me, then? Ethelred, there may be somebody dead out there and I may have killed them. I may have killed Crispin.'

'Do you remember burying his body in a deep hole?'

'No.'

'Weighting it with bricks and throwing it in the sea?'

'No.'

'Dissolving it in acid?'

'No.'

'Incorporating it into a motorway flyover?'

'I think you're beginning to labour your point . . .'

'As long as you understand clearly what I'm saying, that's fine. If you had the presence of mind to hide your victim, then it means you were probably sober enough to be able to remember some of the surrounding detail. If, conversely, you had murdered somebody in a drunken haze and left them lying around, the police would have already found the body. It would have featured on *South Today* even if it didn't make the national news. I won't say that nobody was murdered over the holiday period – it's one of the things we traditionally do around then – but I honestly don't think you killed anyone, or not this year, at least. If we could track down Crispin, it would help us a lot – he might at least know where you went. But I don't think he's dead. When famous writers vanish, people notice. They might not notice my disappearance, or even yours, but somebody would have missed Crispin by now – and Emma is likely to be the first to do so.'

I put the phone down thinking that might have been my last chance for a review in a quality daily.

I wondered again whether I should phone Elsie. I thought that I might share with her what seemed to be an amusing delusion on the part of one of my fellow authors. But it was almost eleven and she was almost certainly in bed. And I was not especially concerned about Henry's safety or my own. The case was closed.

Of course, twenty-four hours would change all that.

CHAPTER SIX

The note had been put through my letter box during the night. It had certainly not been there when I locked the door at around eleven-thirty. But by seven it was on the doormat. A plain white envelope with my name inscribed in block capitals.

I picked it up, thinking that it might be from the estate management committee, with a bill for my share of the maintenance of the road or a reminder to take in our rubbish bins after they had been emptied. But it wasn't. The letter was also written entirely in capitals, as if by a backward but extremely vindictive seven-year-old. It read:

JUST A POLITE WARNING, ETHELLRED, TO LET YOU KNO TO STOP STICKING YOUR NOSE INTO OTHER PEOPLE'S BIZNIS. YOU'LL STAY OUT OF IT IF YOU KNOW WOT'S GOOD FOR YOU. YOU'RE NOLONGER

WRITING CHEAP AMATEUR DETECTIVE FICTION. IT'S
VERY DIFFERENT WHEN IT'S REAL LIFE AND YOU
DON'T UNDERSTAND ITS INNS AND OUTS. YOU
AREN'T LORD PETER WHIMSY, WHATEVER YOU
MAY THINK. AND YOU WOULDN'T WANT TO BE
THE SECOND BODY THAT SHOWS UP, WOULD YOU?
BE WARNED; WE KNOW ICKSACTLY WOT YOU'RE
DOING. A FREND.

Not from the estate management committee, then.

It was rather as though fate, having built up the tension
for a while, had decided to throw a couple of clowns onto
the stage. Of course, Shakespeare did it all the time in
his plays. It was just that it didn't happen much in West
Wittering. I needed some down-to-earth advice. I decided
it was time I phoned my agent.

'This had better be good, Tressider,' Elsie said before I
had a chance to speak.

'How did you know it was me?'

'Because my phone told me. Jesus, Ethelred, don't you
know that ninety-nine point nine nine nine per cent of
phones tell you who is calling before you pick up? Probably
not. I expect you still have one of those phones attached
to the wall with a little handle that you turn to alert the
operator that you wish to speak to somebody. And not in
an ironic postmodern way.'

'Oh yes, sorry, of course. I think my iPhone does that
too.'

'It does. Trust me. Anyway, it's seven-fifteen. Couldn't
you practise using your iPhone when people are awake?'

'Sorry, I imagined you'd be up and about by now. I

just wanted to talk something through with you. A death threat actually.'

'Against you or me?'

'Me.'

'Office hours are ten to five-thirty, Monday to Thursday, except in cases of emergency.'

'It's a *death* threat, Elsie.'

'When you say "death". . . how specific is it?'

'Well, you could say that it was somewhat provisional – it applies only under certain circumstances – if I do certain things.'

'Can you hold off doing any of them until, say, nine thirty-one?'

'Yes.'

'Then I'll call you back once I've had a shower and breakfast.'

'My mobile number is . . .'

'It's staring me in the face, Ethelred. Shall I explain again about this thing where you can see from the screen who is calling you?'

'No. I think I've got the hang of it.'

'I'll phone you right back. Right-ish back, anyway.'

It was ten-thirty by the time Elsie had cleared her desk of matters more important than my impending death.

'Sorry – it just sort of slipped my mind,' she said. 'You're still alive, anyway, so no real harm done. Now, tell me all about it.'

I told her all about most of it.

'Well,' she said. 'It would be worth trying to get a review in the *Telegraph*. Not easy for a writer like you.'

'I may end up dead as a result.'

'Yes, but you'll have a review in the *Telegraph*.'

'I'll have an obituary in the *Telegraph*,' I said.

'Oh no,' said Elsie, 'I doubt they'd do that. You have to be well known.'

Elsie had frequently explained to me that it was important to have an agent who was your strongest supporter and advocate. Sadly, she probably was.

'What am I supposed to do?' I asked.

'Look, why don't I drop in later today? I'll take a look at that note.'

'Aren't you needed in London?'

'There's another writer I represent in Selsey. I was going to see her. I could call in on you.'

'You don't have any writers in Selsey. It's only a few miles away. I'd know them.'

'Is it? I still might have taken on somebody there without your knowing.'

'But you haven't.'

'I might.'

'Not in real life, Elsie.'

There was a pause as Elsie decided whether she could be bothered to continue lying. She was anxious to interfere in my life and nothing I could say would stop her. Even if I could prove that there were no writers of any sort in Selsey and that there never had been, it would be an empty victory. She was coming to West Wittering. Eventually she just said: 'Thanks, by the way, for your Christmas present. You shouldn't have.'

'My pleasure. I'm glad you found it useful.'

'I didn't say I found it useful. I said: "you shouldn't

have". I might have added that I had no idea they still made them. Quaint. Anyway, I have started using it in an entirely ironic manner. Now, are there any decent restaurants in West Wittering? I shall need feeding.'

'There's the Beach House,' I said, 'that's good. And the Old House at Home does excellent pub food. You can get a nice sandwich or a croissant at the Landing.'

'I'll see you for a late lunch, then. Your choice of venue.'

'Elsie,' I said, 'are you coming to West Wittering because you are concerned about my safety or to meddle in my business?'

'Entirely for your safety. As for meddling in your business, surely you phoned me? I wouldn't describe answering the phone as meddling with anything.'

'I merely phoned you for advice.'

'Which I can give much more easily if I have a chance to discuss it with you properly over a low-calorie meal. There is a danger that without my advice you may get involved in something that would place you completely out of your depth.'

'And with your advice? What might happen then?'

'One step at a time, Ethelred. You decide where you're going to buy me lunch. I'll let you know what happens after that.'

CHAPTER SEVEN

From the journal of Elsie Thirkettle

Friday 4 January Joy! Ethelred has given me a large leather-bound book with ruled pages for Christmas. Suitable, it says on the box, as a diary or perhaps for writing a first novel. With regard to the diary aspect, Ethelred presumably hasn't noticed that, for the past ten years, whenever I've had to record an appointment, I've done so in some neat electronic device. He hasn't investigated his own iPhone sufficiently over the past two years to discover that it has a Calendar function. So, he's given me half a kilo of heavy-duty paper bound in another half-kilo of leather from a cow that most certainly died in vain as far as I am concerned. Or perhaps Ethelred thinks that, like Samuel Pepys, I plan to sit down at the end of every day and write up my deeds, with passing reference to any major fires or plagues that happen to be going on. Bless.

Of course, it's a well-meaning gift in the sense that he

has given me the sort of thing he would love himself – something totally useless but happily reminiscent of the days of his youth, when cricket was much better and the sun shone all summer long. Possibly I should have kept it and given it back to him next year as his Christmas present, but sadly I have now written in it, so that may not be as good an option as it was ten minutes ago.

Anyway, since no plagues happened this morning and the Dutch are not burning the English fleet in the Medway, let me record the one item of news that I have: Ethelred has coincidentally just phoned me to say that he has an interesting new case that he would love to involve me in. It's touching the way he feels I can contribute, adding my experience, intelligence and intuition to whatever it is he thinks he brings to the party.

It is a while since Ethelred and I dipped our toes into a bit of real-life detective work. The only question, to my mind, is why we should help out a supercilious little prat like Henry Holiday. A review in a quality daily is an obvious incentive, but will it be a good review? I've caught Holiday more than once making snide remarks about Ethelred in the bar at the Harrogate crime festival. The fact that they were absolutely true, and we all agreed with him, didn't stop them from being very unpleasant. Holiday could lead Ethelred on with promises of reviews, only to rubbish him or (standard reviewer's excuse) say that he wrote a glowing review but the editor spiked it. Ethelred, who believes all to be as honest as he, tends not to see shit like that coming. Anyway, why should Holiday want Ethelred to help him if his estimation of Ethelred's ability is really as low as he has previously implied? It suggests a degree of desperation or that there is something about the case that even I have missed.

And then there's Vynall. An even nastier piece of work. Slags off anyone he sees as being a rival. Why? He's making pots of money with his latest gore-fest. He's on *Front Row*. His books are everywhere. He doesn't need to be any more unpleasant than he wishes. He can, conversely, be very obliging indeed if you happen to be an attractive and slightly too trusting young girl. He knows better than to try it on with me, of course.

So, I'm off shortly to have lunch with Ethelred and, purely in passing, to advise him on the Strange Affair of the Forgetful Author (as I plan to call it when we write it up). For the moment the only choice I have to make is between a small green salad and soup of the day (no bread).

CHAPTER EIGHT

It was half past two. We were ensconced in the Old House at Home with the death threat in front of us on the table. Somehow, sandwiched between a plate of scampi (mine) and a small green salad and quadruple portion of double-fried chips (Elsie's) the message looked less significant than it had in the half-light of my early-morning hallway.

Elsie's plump frame was squashed into a smoker's chair. Short of stature and well-rounded, she might almost have been Henry's twin. She had chosen a costume that in some ways mirrored Henry's bow tie and waistcoat – a very fifties frock in bright pink with many petticoats supporting the skirt, a short white cardigan and bright-red lipstick to complete the effect. A pair of sunglasses, which she would not need until late April, were perched on her head. It was the Sunday colour supplements' idea of what to wear at the seaside. But not in January.

'Feel free to help yourself to salad,' said Elsie. 'I think I may have ordered too much. A little lettuce goes a long way. Unless you're a rabbit.'

'I'm good,' I said.

'Do you mean that you are leading a blameless life, or are you trying to talk like a young person?'

'Eat your salad and stay away from my chips,' I said.

She looked at my scampi and chips and shook her head at the amount of food I was proposing to eat. To be fair, she had very few chips remaining on her own plate.

'It's an odd letter,' she said.

'Semi-literate,' I said. 'See how they've spelt "wot" and "inn". I blame the abolition of grammar schools.'

We looked at it again.

JUST A POLITE WARNING, ETHELLRED, TO LET YOU KNO TO STOP STICKING YOUR NOSE INTO OTHER PEOPLE'S BIZNIS. YOU'LL STAY OUT OF IT IF YOU KNOW WOT'S GOOD FOR YOU. YOU'RE NOLONGER WRITING CHEAP AMATEUR DETECTIVE FICTION. IT'S VERY DIFFERENT WHEN IT'S REAL LIFE AND YOU DON'T UNDERSTAND ITS INNS AND OUTS. YOU AREN'T LORD PETER WHIMSY, WHATEVER YOU MAY THINK. AND YOU WOULDN'T WANT TO BE THE SECOND BODY THAT SHOWS UP, WOULD YOU? BE WARNED; WE KNOW ICKSACTLY WOT YOU'RE DOING. A FREND.

'Don't you think the spelling mistakes are deliberate?' she asked. 'Whoever wrote it knows the difference between "it's" and "its". And it's one of the few death threats I've seen that includes semicolons. Grammatically it's fine, with a few spelling mistakes added later to throw us off the scent.'

'To throw *me* off the scent,' I said. 'I don't think anyone envisaged your ever being on the scent.'

'How wrong they were, eh?' said Elsie, through a mouthful of my chips.

'And they've misspelt my name,' I said.

'Easily done if you're not terribly familiar with it,' said Elsie. 'So, there are two questions: who wrote it and who are we supposed to think wrote it?'

'I've no idea,' I said. 'The threats, now I reread it, are remarkably vague. But whoever it is is remarkably well informed. Henry must have told somebody he was consulting me – I've certainly told nobody except you.'

'Well, it obviously wasn't me because you didn't tell me until this morning. I'd have sent you the death threat via Facebook, anyway. That's the way it's done now.'

'Somebody out there doesn't like Henry, that's for sure.'

'It's because he's a nasty little toerag,' said Elsie. She selected another chip from my plate.

'Henry's a friend,' I said. 'Well, sort of.'

'I've always found him an irritating shit. Take the way he dresses . . .'

'I can't see anything wrong with the way he dresses . . .'

'He dresses exactly the way you do, Ethelred, but he's thirty years younger.'

'Twenty years younger.'

Elsie shook her head. 'That still doesn't make it *right*, does it? You wear tweed jackets because you were made to wear them when you were in your pram, and nobody has ever explained to you that you are now permitted to go around in a sweatshirt and jeans. But for Henry they are a pure affectation. Then there's all this business with blood sports and the countryside, when everyone knows he grew up in Putney or Pinner or somewhere. He's a cheap replica of you, only six inches shorter.'

That was possibly true. Hadn't the assistant manager of the club said much the same thing?

'You think he sees me as a role model?' I asked.

'I hope not – not if he wants to make a living out of writing. I just think it's creepy.'

'Thank you,' I said.

'My pleasure. Henry does resemble you in one other way, though – he wanted to write a great literary novel.'

'Nothing wrong with that either.'

'The difference though is that he did write one, rather than just talk about it. He apparently penned a brilliant crime novel of great literary distinction.'

'Which one was that?' I asked. I wasn't being facetious. Henry had published his first crime novel only a few years before, but his output since then had been prolific. People admired his ability to churn out page-turning thrillers. But nobody had ever mentioned the word 'literary' before in the same sentence as the words Henry Holiday.

'I don't know the whole story,' said Elsie. 'Somebody mentioned it in the bar at a conference, the way you do. Apparently Henry spent about ten years working on his first novel. Then it got completely trashed by some critic or other.'

'So it was published? I thought—'

'No, it never saw the light of day. He showed the

manuscript to this big-shot critic. The critic told him that his life's work was rubbish, and so Henry destroyed it – burnt the paper, wiped the discs. The following morning he sat down and started to write the sort of garbage that makes him so much money now.'

'So, if it's destroyed how does anybody know it's a great literary work?'

'Because Henry says it was. It seems that God subsequently revealed unto Henry Holiday in a vision that the big-shot critic was actually a tosser who had no idea what he was talking about. The scales fell from his eyes. Henry's tried a couple of times to rewrite it, but it's gone for good – the plot and the characters are there but not the thing that made it the finest book of all time.'

'Who told you all that? Henry?'

'No. I think it was his editor or agent. Or maybe his publicist. At a conference at three o'clock in the morning these things blur a bit – you know that terrible hour when the bar has stopped serving drinks but you can't quite face the task of asking Reception to remind you what your name is and which room number you are in. But the origin was Henry himself who'd told it to this publicist or maybe to a friend of hers or perhaps to her friend's mother on a very similar occasion at a very similar event. He was weeping genuine tears into an empty glass – that much is certain – though you have to allow for a little picturesque exaggeration in these stories.'

'That's sad,' I said.

'In a way. Had the great literary novel been published, then he'd have been scraping a living, getting brilliant reviews and selling a few thousand copies. As it is, he's on his way to becoming the next Crispin Vynall. Not before time, since you say the first one has been murdered.'

'I certainly didn't say that. I think Crispin's absence is only temporary. It's just a bit inconvenient for Henry because Crispin might just be able to tell us what Henry was doing.'

'Only if he's still alive,' said Elsie.

'Henry certainly didn't kill him.'

'But Henry was drunk and thinks he may have killed *somebody*.'

'Yes.'

'And Crispin's vanished.'

'Yes.'

'All of which is consistent with Henry killing Crispin.'

'Yes.'

'Don't keep saying "yes" like that, Ethelred. It's irritating. Say something with more than one syllable.'

'Sorry.'

'That's only marginally better.'

'If Crispin was dead, Emma would have noticed.'

'Not necessarily.'

'I'm not joking.'

'Nor am I. Who knows what Crispin told Emma or where he said he was going? If only half the things I've heard about him are true, he must have been constantly making up stories to explain an absence for a night or two. That she's not concerned doesn't mean that all is well. And if she only half-believed the latest story, it might explain why she wasn't going to make a fool of herself by telling you he'd been at a book fair in Amsterdam for the past week, or whatever lie he'd sold her, when you might know exactly whose bed he'd been in.'

'So, who's the letter from?'

'Did anybody other than Henry even know you were on the case?'

'Nobody at all. I told you that.'

'That's not quite true, in the sense that you've been clumping round the country asking everyone whether they've seen a short, pompous crime writer murdering one of his mates.'

'Fair enough. Denzil at the pub knows I was asking questions. And I did tell the man at the club that I was a private detective, and I did give him my phone number.'

'And Emma. She might have guessed from your clumsy attempts at detective work that something was going on.'

'I scarcely think this was written by Emma. Denzil, maybe, if he can write at all.'

'Could Henry have told anyone else he was employing you?'

'It would be an odd thing to do under the circumstances.'

'Could you have been followed, then?'

'Yes, easily; but how would anyone have known I was worth following?'

Elsie chewed one of my chips thoughtfully. 'You're right. None of this makes sense. To want you off the case somebody has to know you're on it. And even if they did, why would they want you off?'

'Because I might be about to come up with something that would clear Henry and put the blame firmly on somebody else?' I suggested.

'But that would assume they thought you were in some way a competent investigator . . . That's yummy, by the way.'

'Yes, but I wish you wouldn't do it.'

My agent had been assisting her thought train by squirting large amounts of tomato ketchup on my plate and then dipping my remaining chips into it one by one.

'Shame to waste them,' she said, stuffing three chips into her mouth very quickly.

'I wasn't wasting them,' I said. 'I had plans for them that didn't involve ketchup.'

'Prevention is better than cure,' said Elsie vaguely. 'We have to assume that, while you investigate on Henry's behalf, somebody out there who has a very strong interest in the case is carrying out their own investigations, and doing their best to put a spoke in yours.'

'Possibly,' I said.

'Of course, if I were married to Crispin, I'd murder him, then cover things up with an elaborate but foolproof stratagem, almost certainly involving phony death threats.'

'But you're not married to him. Emma is.'

'You know her well?' Elsie paused, chip in hand, scrutinising me more than I would have wished.

'I've met her. Maybe once or twice.'

'So have I. She's quite attractive. Definitely your type.'

'As I say, I might have talked to her once,' I said. 'Or possibly twice. She sometimes goes to conferences with Crispin. You get talking to people in bars. Quite innocently. Anyway, returning to the subject in hand, if Crispin really has vanished, then the police will soon have to be involved. Taking me out of the equation doesn't really help. I don't want any more of that stuff on my plate by the way.'

'Yes you do. They're really good chips and this is really good sauce. I didn't know you got artisanal ketchup this far out of Hampstead. Still, it's true what you say. You'd rather expect the police to be at least as good as you at solving murders. Of course, the entire premise of the amateur detective novel is that the main character has some special skill – a knowledge of local history or Sudoku or quilting, say – that gives them an insight into crime that a lifetime of mere police work can never match. Perhaps that is how we should approach this problem. What special abilities do you have, Ethelred?'

'I'm a crime writer,' I said.

Elsie patted my hand. 'I know,' she said sympathetically, 'but you must have some useful skills.'

'I've developed my proficiency in logical deduction.'

'Not according to the last review I saw on Amazon,' said Elsie.

'Was that one of Thrillseeker's reviews by any chance?'

'Who?'

'I was reading them last night. It's the Amazon *nom de plume* of somebody out there who dislikes my books very much. He seems determined to read all of them so that he can post on Amazon how much he hates them. He doesn't think I can do logical deduction or anything else. He usually gives me one star.'

'That's harsh. Most of them are worth at least two.'

'Thank you.'

'Well, some of them, anyway. Does he actually buy the books?'

'He seems to have read them. All of them.'

'A fan of sorts, then. I'll check him out,' said Elsie. 'So this murder . . .'

'If there has been one, which I still doubt.'

'. . . if there has been one, which you still doubt . . . has been committed for some reason that a crime writer would understand but not a policeman. Hence wanting the crime writer off the case.'

'You're talking as if we're in a novel,' I said. 'You're assuming that the whole thing has been set up in a particular way and that we can draw inferences from every tiny detail. Actually things don't work like that in real life. In an actual murder inquiry, most things are just irrelevant background noise. So, there's no point in looking for the special skills that I have.'

'You don't do quilting, I suppose?' asked Elsie.

'No,' I said.

'Beekeeping?'

'That was Sherlock Holmes.'

'So it was. Well, if you are really determined to help Henry, what we need to do next is to establish where this church is.'

'Hold on,' I said. 'I'm *not* determined to help him – quite the reverse – I've told him I've quit. And somebody is threatening to kill me if I continue.'

'Not specifically,' said Elsie. 'It's a bit vague. Hardly a threat at all. This is designed to mildly frighten you – that's all. Let's remember he – or she – uses semicolons. Who worries about grammar when writing a real death threat? I'd have said there was a forty to fifty per cent chance they were bluffing.'

'And a fifty to sixty per cent chance they are not.'

'Acceptable odds.'

'Only if they're somebody else's odds.'

'Oh, come on! Whoever wrote this note is clearly a nutter.'

'That isn't as reassuring as you seem to imagine,' I said.

She picked up the note and examined it again.

'Ethelred, this note is about as low-tech as you can get. It is not what somebody does if they can really track your every move. It's not what somebody does if they can listen in on your phone calls and follow each keystroke on your computer. It's what they do if they want to frighten you off for the cost of a sheet of A4 and an envelope. They couldn't even be arsed to put a stamp on it, for goodness' sake.'

'I'm done with it. End of.'

'You need the reviews. End of. Anyway, it will be fun.'

'For you.'

'But, in a very real sense, for you too. And we need to show them that they can't scare us.'

'I said to Henry I wanted nothing more to do with it.'

'You are allowed to change your mind. Tell him you've now got me on the case. That will cheer him up. Tell him that adversity only stiffens your resolve or some crap like that. He'll respect you and give you an extra couple of column inches. I'll keep the note for the moment, if I may – I might get further inspiration or at least some innocent amusement. Now, let's go and take a look at that new house of yours. I'd like to sneer at your curtains before I go back to London. Ten pounds says you've got pelmets in the sitting room – or do you refer to it as the lounge?'

* * *

It was early evening before I had a chance to phone Henry. He answered at once, almost as if he had been waiting for my call.

'I'm back on the case,' I said.

'I thought you weren't interested?'

'Something has happened,' I said. 'There's somebody trying to frighten me off helping you. I'm not going to let them.'

'What do you mean?'

'I had a hand-delivered letter first thing this morning. It informed me that I risked becoming the second corpse in the story unless I took no further part in your case.'

'*Second corpse?*'

'I agree that implies there's a first corpse out there somewhere, but it doesn't follow *you* killed the person concerned, still less that it is Crispin.'

'That's what you think?'

Well, Elsie felt it ought to be Crispin, but I decided not to give Henry the other key piece of information: that my literary agent was also on the case in a low-risk capacity. I didn't feel it would cheer him up as much as she supposed.

'Yes,' I said. 'That's what I think. I don't believe you've killed anyone.'

'But the person who wrote the note reckons I have? Who are they, though?'

'I suppose you didn't tell anyone else that you'd asked me to look into things?' I asked.

'Certainly not. I don't want anyone except you to know for the moment.'

'Well, somebody has clearly managed to find out,' I

said. 'And, whoever it is, he or she actually seems to know more about it than we do – if somebody really has been killed.'

'Look,' said Henry, dismissing the issue of my death, 'I may have remembered something else. I told you about that church? Well, I think it may have been in a village called Didsbury Common or Dilling Green or something.'

I thought for a bit. 'Didling Green?' I asked. 'That's a real place, unlike the other two you mentioned.'

'Could be. It's just, whenever I try to recall that picture – the church and the trees – a name like that comes into my head. Did-something. There's another image I can't get out of my head too – a lonely track leading up into the hills. It's tarmac at first, then just mud and rocks. There are hedges on either side and a smell of damp and decay.'

'A track? Leading from Didling Green up onto the Downs?'

'It could be. Do you know Didling Green then?'

'It's right at the foot of the Downs. I'm sure there's a road more or less as you describe it. I can't swear to the damp and decay bit, but the rest sounds right.'

'Are you sure?'

'I'll drive over there and check it out,' I said. Then, following Elsie's advice, I added: 'Nobody's going to frighten me off this.'

I waited for him to say something that suggested I had gained his respect.

'Maybe you shouldn't,' said Henry. 'I don't want to put you at any risk. Not at your age.'

'I'm scarcely senile,' I said. 'I'm as capable as anyone else of staying out of trouble.'

'Well, that's pretty courageous of you,' said Henry. 'Carrying on with the case, I mean. At any age.'

'Not really,' I said. 'I can handle it.'

Because all the time I was thinking: no serious death threat has a semicolon in it. And I needed some decent reviews.

CHAPTER NINE

Amazon.co.uk

A Most Civilised Murder
(#2 in the Buckfordshire Series) [paperback]
Peter Fielding (author)

Customer reviews [newest first]

* Dull, dull, dull 15 December 2012
By Thrillseeker
There are varying grades of crime fiction. At
the top are the genuinely exciting and realistic
accounts of the investigation of a contemporary
murder. Below these are the many competently
written, but slightly out-of-date novels that
make up the bulk of the police procedurals. At

the bottom of the heap are all books featuring amateur detectives and quilt-makers. Sadly this book fails to live up to even the last of these. The police in Buckfordshire clearly follow procedures known only to them and Lord Peter Whimsy. I have to concede that this book was written some time ago, but Sgt Fairfax does not seem to have moved beyond smoking a pipe in his study as his main method of investigation; and surely even then the police must have had access to some sort of computerised records? You get the impression that Fielding (aka Ethelred Tressider) popped into a police station for ten minutes in the late sixties, but has not done much research in the meantime. This is lazy writing by a lazy writer. It is difficult to know why anyone would buy these books when they might be buying Peter James, Chris Ewan or MR Hall. One star is generous.

Fairfax's Way
(#4 in the Buckfordshire Series) [paperback]
Peter Fielding (author)

Customer reviews [newest first]

* Dreadful 15 December 2012
By Thrillseeker
If you enjoy a good detective story, don't bother with this one. It sucks. Fielding tried to pension Fairfax off in the first book in this series. Sadly, he did not

succeed. The lugubrious Sergeant kept his job and so has been able to bore us through a dozen or so sequels. He is probably my least favourite character in any form of crime fiction – make that any form of fiction, full stop. Not that the book is exactly interesting even when Fairfax is out of the picture for a bit. (Inevitably he gets taken off the case at one point, allowing him to go off and do a bit of amateur detection. Yawn.) Fielding (aka Ethelred Tressider) waxes lyrical about the Buckfordshire countryside for whole pages at a time. I could listen to him for hours going on about the lesser spotted wagtail's plaintive call. Not. Then there are the lectures on Norman architecture, ponderously delivered by Fairfax to whichever unfortunate villain he's questioning. It's amazing they don't break down and confess in case he starts on Early English. I've rarely come across such a slow plot. Even the squad cars seem to travel around at 20 mph. Proust (to whom there is a knowing nod in the title – God knows why) is a laugh a minute compared to this guy. I won't give the storyline away. Let's just say if you read page 17 carefully, you'll spot the discrepancy in the witness statement that it takes Fairfax until page 253 to notice. Of course, Fairfax must be about 87 years old by now, so maybe that's understandable. I thought of giving this two stars on the grounds that it isn't the worst book in the series; but then I thought, no, I just can't be arsed.

Thieves' Honour
(#6 in the Buckfordshire Series) [paperback]
Peter Fielding (author)

Customer reviews [newest first]

* Why? 15 December 2012
By Thrillseeker
The more of this series you read, the more you wonder why Fielding's publisher has tolerated this tosh for so long. The plot is in many ways a rehash of at least one of the earlier books in the series. Several passages seem to have been lifted from it almost word for word. The constant wandering from pub to pub in search of evidence – what a cliché! When a writer starts to repeat himself like this, it is a sure sign that the series has gone on far too long. Fielding (aka Ethelred Tressider) may have once had ambitions to write upmarket fiction, but has settled for this nonsense; when there are so many honest ways of making a living – stacking supermarket shelves for example – you have to ask why he does it. Probably, let's face it, his shelf-stacking simply isn't up to it, any more than his books are.

CHAPTER TEN

From the journal of Elsie Thirkettle

Still Friday 4th January, which Pepys would have called the 26th December since they were still on the Julian Calendar then, not to mention Old Style and stuff like that. I'm amazed Ethelred doesn't insist on using the Julian Calendar, thinking about it. He's just about reconciled to British Summer Time, but you can see the look of relief on his little face every autumn when he can set his gold pocket watch back one hour to Greenwich Mean Time. Maybe I'll try to get him a genuine Julian Calendar as a Christmas present next year. One where the year number doesn't change until March, like they used to do until 1752. He'd like that.

Anyway, when I got home from Sussex, I took a look at Ethelred's bad reviews on Amazon because, though I am immensely sympathetic to all my authors' little troubles, illiterate diatribes can actually be very funny and provide an agent with many a relaxing evening.

The first thing I noticed about the Thrillseeker reviews was that they were pretty well put together. He (for it seemed to be a man – he occasionally pulled his punches in a way that a woman would not have done) had certainly read each of the books, if not from cover to cover, then at least up to a point that allowed him to put in some very effective plot spoilers. Many of the criticisms were of course ones that I had pointed out to Ethelred myself, but do authors listen? Some of Thrillseeker's other remarks were heavy-handed, but most had more than a grain of truth in them.

In the old days the only people who wrote reviews were professional critics or other writers. They weren't necessarily polite, but they did it under their own names and if they didn't like something they normally gave reasons. These days any tosser can be a book reviewer by logging on and typing in whatever crap comes into their head. And you don't have to say who you are. Thrillseeker hid like a creep behind his alias. But in one way I respected him. Some reviewers might have occasionally wavered or accidentally given Ethelred two stars, But no. Thrillseeker gave a single lonely star every time.

And, when you thought about it, Thrillseeker had actually put a lot of work into his criticism. He'd read at least twenty of Ethelred's books – no mean feat, I'm telling you. And, the more I read, the more I wondered, as Ethelred had, why anyone would bother to buy (or even borrow from the library) book after book that they disliked so much. What had Ethelred done to upset him so much?

And another question struck me.

If Thrillseeker didn't like Ethelred's books, what the hell did he like?

CHAPTER ELEVEN

Amazon.co.uk

A Bad Way to Die [paperback]
Crispin Vynall (author)

Customer reviews

***** Bloody Brilliant 3 December 2012
By Thrillseeker
Crispin Vynall does it again! It's rare to find an author who combines a fine literary style and the ability to produce page after page of riveting action. Looking at the sad crop of so-called crime writers we have today, Vynall may be pretty much unique in this respect.

In *A Bad Way to Die*, Joe Smith finds himself the only witness to a gang-land killing. Bravely he goes to the police, who promise him protection if he will testify, but a corrupt officer lets the killers know where to find him and Joe is nolonger safe. Soon he is on the run not knowing who, if anyone, he can trust. The plot never ceases to hold your attention, never ceases to produce surprises right up to the immensely satisfying conclusion.

There is a lyricism to Vynall's prose that makes him stand out from any of his contemporaries. Only the nauseating envy of the literary establishment on the one hand and the incompetence of the pathetic clique that runs the Crime Writers' Association on the other prevent him from being hailed as the finest writer of his generation.

Hear No Evil [paperback]
Crispin Vynall (author)

Customer reviews

***** The book of the year! 30 November 2012
By Thrillseeker
The ability of Crispin Vynall never ceases to amaze me. The man is a genius.

In *Hear No Evil*, DI Arrowsmith of the Liverchester Metropolitan Police is asked to look into a complaint against one of his fellow officers. It quickly becomes clear that the policeman concerned was responsible for the death of a drunken football fan and that his colleagues are covering up for him. Soon Arrowsmith realises that he has been given the investigation only because it is assumed he will quietly go along with the cover-up. When he refuses to do this, first he is threatened and then his family are targeted; his daughter disappears on her way home from school. CCTV shows her walking along the main road near the family home, with a white car parked just ahead. In the next shot she and the car have gone. Arrowsmith suspects that the police are themselves involved in her abduction; and the only way to get her back is to take the law into his own hands. What follows is a roller coaster of a plot in which every other page springs a new surprise.

It is a complete mystery to me why this book was passed over for the CWA Gold Dagger, but it is undoubtedly the finest crime novel to appear this year or indeed for a very long time.

Cliffhanger [paperback]
Crispin Vynall (author)

Customer reviews

***** Vynall Does It Again! 29 December 2012
By Thrillseeker
I've been so impressed by Vynall's recent books that I dipped into this gem from the late 1980s, one of his earliest publications. A tourist vanishes, having

last been seen taking a stroll along a cliff-top path. A search of the area by coastguards reveals nothing. Has she fallen or has she somehow been spirited away? A young detective is sent to the small seaside town to investigate and meets a wall of silence. Nobody is willing to admit even to having seen the woman. When a falling boulder narrowly misses him, he begins to fear his own life may be in danger; thus begins the most frustrating and dangerous investigation that DC Christie (DI Christie in later books) will ever have to undertake.

This is a superb early work from a master of his craft, and one that, sadly, received remarkably little attention at the time of its publication.

CHAPTER TWELVE

The phone had possibly been ringing for some time when I stretched an arm from under the warm duvet. I groped for a moment in the icy air and eventually made contact with the handset. The green figures on my bedside clock showed me that it was just after one o'clock in the morning. Only one person in the entire world would think that I would be delighted to take her call in the middle of the night.

'Hello, Elsie,' I said.

'I've been thinking,' she said.

'It's ten past one,' I interrupted. 'I was asleep.'

'No you weren't. You had to be awake to pick up the phone.'

'I was asleep before that,' I said.

'Not *immediately* before that,' she said. 'You also had to be awake to hear the phone ringing.'

'Yes, because the phone woke me.'

90

'There you are, then. You were awake. I don't know why you have to make such a fuss about things. I've been checking up on Thrillseeker's reviews for you.'

'Why?'

'Because it's odd he's reading so many books he hates.'

'His problem, not mine.'

'But interesting. He's reviewed you twenty times and given you one star each time.'

'Yes, I know.'

'You've counted them? That's sad.'

'You've counted them too.'

'It's my job. I'm your agent. Do you know who else he's reviewed?'

'You've checked?'

'Absolutely. It's not difficult to search for other reviews. Would you like me to give you a tutorial on the Internet sometime?'

'No, I can manage quite well, thank you.'

'So, who do you think he gives five-star reviews to? He likes thrillers.'

'Yes, the clue's in the name.'

'So, guess,' Elsie invited me.

I looked at the clock. 01.12. I yawned. 'Could this wait until the morning?'

'Of course it could. So are you going to guess who else he's reviewed?'

'I don't know. Dennis LeHane?'

'One rather grudging four-star review.'

'Dan Brown? Stieg Larsson? Jeffery Deaver? Lee Child?'

'Nope. None of them.'

'Ambler? Harrison? Patterson? Ludlum?'

'Negative. Somebody you know well.'

'Not Henry Holiday?'

'He certainly writes the right type of books. But no reviews for Henry. At least none from our friend Thrillseeker.'

'Who then?'

'Who does Henry imitate slavishly?'

'Crispin?'

'That's right. Crispin Vynall. Thrillseeker really loves Crispin Vynall.'

'Well, I suppose there won't be a lot of people who like my work and his.'

'There aren't a lot of people who like your work full stop, Ethelred. But that's a discussion for another day. My point is: isn't it a bit weird that of all the writers in all the world, the one he likes is precisely the one whose disappearance you are investigating?'

I gave this some thought. In a darkened room in the early hours of the morning a lot of things seem weird. I could hear the wind blowing in the trees and, in the distance, I thought I could make out the sound of the coal-black sea, breaking on a bleak and lonely shore. From inside the house I heard a creaking sound: perhaps the last contraction of still-cooling copper pipes, as the central heating system finally settled down for the night. Or perhaps . . .

'How many reviews from Thrillseeker for Vynall?' I asked.

'About the same as for you. All five star. Vynall's the finest writer of his generation, it would seem.'

'Where does Thrillseeker live?'

'London, so he claims.'

'Any other details? Blog? Website?'

'Nope.'

'And it's just me and Vynall he's reviewed?'

'LeHane, as I say. And a five-star review for an old John Le Carré. But it's mainly just the two of you.'

'A coincidence,' I said.

'But a weird coincidence.'

Out of nowhere rain suddenly lashed against the window, making me jump. I pulled myself into a sitting position and switched the light on.

'Are you still there?' Elsie was saying.

'Yes,' I said. 'I'm just switching the light on.'

'Why?'

'Because it's quarter past one and it's dark down here in Sussex. There's still one thing that puzzles me—'

'Quarter past one?'

'Yes.'

'I'm sorry, Ethelred, but I really have to go to bed. It's been a long day and, unlike you, I have to do some work tomorrow. I need my beauty sleep, even if you don't.'

I was left feeling that I had in some way disturbed her by taking her call. When we next spoke she would probably chide me gently for it.

I carefully replaced the phone, switched the light off and tried to go back to sleep. I lay there listening to the rain on the window glass and the sea crashing onto the dark, unloved beach. The minutes passed. When I next looked at the clock it was one-thirty and I was still wide awake.

I somehow doubted that Elsie was.

CHAPTER THIRTEEN

The sky was low and grey, and the drizzle was constant. The land, sodden after weeks of rain, was now flatly declining to soak up any more. Puddles on either side of the main road had broadened in places into gently rippling sheets of unknowable depth that stretched from verge to verge. The fields were starting to resemble lakes, contained only by skeletal hawthorn hedges and dark poplars.

The first part of my journey to Chichester crossed countryside as level as any in England. But I was driving towards the chalk hills. In the distance, the South Downs appeared as a low and misty line on the horizon. I motored though Birdham at a cautious thirty-nine miles an hour, aware of both the speed cameras and the standing water; then, reaching slightly drier road, I put my foot down on the accelerator for a couple of gently winding miles.

But the whole time I was glancing at the rear-view,

checking which cars were behind me. A large black Nissan had tailgated me as far as the Itchenor turn-off, oblivious of the spray that I was throwing up. But he was a little too close and a little too obvious to be somebody trying to follow me unobtrusively. Then a white Peugeot seemed to appear from nowhere; but, having driven patiently behind me for a mile or so, it had suddenly performed a dangerous, semi-aquatic overtaking manoeuvre just before the Birdham roundabout, sending a shower of water about ten feet into the air. It hung a right, as they say, and sped off towards the nurseries and market gardens of Earnley. But once beyond Birdham, and for a long time afterwards, I was alone in my watery world.

Of course, the fact that I wasn't being followed didn't mean that nobody wanted to kill me. There was quite possibly somebody out there visiting the same places and asking the same questions as I was. Was I the first to take the road to Didling Green or was my shadow already there? It was lonely on the Chichester road, but at this time of year the Downs would be lonelier still. I turned up the heating in the car a notch or two, switched the radio to Classic FM and drove on. The drizzle turned to steady, unrelenting rain. Only Vivaldi thought that spring was on the way.

I had been to Didling Green a few times before but, even if it had been my first visit, I would have known where I was the moment I entered the village. The main street, with its thatched cottages framed by the gently rounded bowl of the Downs, has featured in many calendars with titles such as Beautiful Sussex or Picturesque England or Colourful

Britain or perhaps even Inconveniently-Arranged-but-Ridiculously-Expensive-Cottages. It's an image that seeps subliminally into your stock of memories, so that chancing unexpectedly on the real thing can be a genuine shock. Many casual visitors probably do a double take as they get out of their car and wonder in which of their past lives they lived there.

But I had been there before, so I simply parked my car by the church and walked across the green, trying to get a view of the steeple from underneath some trees. There were lilacs in the gardens of the houses on the other side. It was possible that Henry could have stood under those. It would certainly have given him the view he described – the weathervane, the clouds. But it would have scarcely felt like a proper wood, however much Henry had had to drink.

At the far corner of the green, however, a narrow lane led off towards the Downs, more or less as I had remembered and approximating to Henry's own description. I walked back to my car, started the engine and set off in that direction. The steady rain had become a heavy downpour. Water cascaded down both sides of the road in two brown torrents, carrying leaves and twigs before them.

For a few hundred yards it was a passable carriageway, then, just beyond what proved to be the last house in the village, I found myself driving on what was no more than a farm track, leading muddily upwards towards an undefined destination. No signs gave a clue to where I was going. I slowed to about five miles an hour, and continued on my way in first gear, the car's suspension audibly protesting every few feet, weaving to and fro to avoid the stones and the potholes. Ahead of me though, viewed through my windscreen with the aid of the wipers going at full speed, was an undoubted mass of trees, the rain swirling around them. Just before we reached them was an impromptu car park – really a widening of the road big enough to take half a dozen or so cars belonging to people setting off on walks over the Downs. On a cold, wet January day, I had it all to myself. I swung the car into the middle of it and cursed as the wheels started to spin helplessly in the soft mud. I'd be lucky to get it out on my own.

But I was at least here now. I waited for a couple of minutes, listening to the drumming of the rain on the car roof. Then, with reluctance, I opened the door and breathed in the smell of damp leaves. There were plenty of old car tracks rutting the surface of the road, but nothing new as far as I could tell. Of course, there were plenty of other ways of getting here. I tried to work out where I would have concealed myself if I wanted to spring a surprise attack on an unsuspecting victim – a crime writer investigating a murder, say. Actually, there were too many places to easily count. For a good five minutes I stood perfectly still, watching the bushes and the trees for any sign of movement. Not a squirrel was stirring on a day like this. I carefully locked the car door and set off up the hill.

A hundred paces or so took me to the edge of the wood, from where I could look down on Didling Green. There was the church and its weathervane, but from this angle he would have seen fields and hedges behind it, not clouds. Still, that didn't mean he hadn't come here. Perfect recall was not to be expected. Water dripped copiously from the bare branches above my head, dampening my shoulders and running down my neck. I had stayed here long enough. With the mud sucking at my boots, I pressed on into the gloomy woods.

For a while the path twisted between the trees. I trod alternately in soft, creamy-coloured goo and sodden black drifts of leaves before finally emerging onto a broad, grassy track that crossed the open Downs. The downpour had slackened. Everything up there was enveloped in a vapour that was neither exactly mist nor objectively rain. Small diamonds of water hung on the sheep-cropped turf. I pulled my collar up and wondered what Henry was doing just now and exactly how high he had turned up his central heating.

But I was not, I discovered, entirely alone. A figure emerged over the brow of the hill just in front of me. She wore a brown hat with a broad brim and a matching cape-like waterproof, which flapped damply around her. Her dog, oblivious of everything else, dashed backwards and forwards, its nose a fraction of an inch above the ground. If I was to do my work as an amateur detective in private, then I'd have to wait until she had passed on her way. So, I did wait as patiently as I could, trying to pretend that standing motionless on a windswept hill in January was not in any way unusual.

'Good morning,' I said as she approached.

I'd expected her to say the same and press on, but she stopped abruptly and peered at her watch before nodding a reply. She regarded me suspiciously.

'Not a great day for walking,' I said.

'You don't have much choice when you own a dog, do you?' she replied. 'If I don't take her out, she's whining and scratching at the door. Where's yours gone? Off after the rabbits, I expect? There won't be many out in this weather.' She turned the way I had been looking a minute or so before as if hoping to catch sight of him.

'I don't have a dog,' I said.

'No dog?'

'Not of any sort.'

'What on earth are you doing up here, in that case?'

'I felt like a walk,' I said.

She shook her head and tactfully refrained from telling me that I was an idiot.

'Well, I'd better get on,' I said, as if my walk was the first stage of an ascent of Everest.

'Where are you off to?'

I decided not to say that, as soon as she was out of the way, I would be going back down the hill to look for dead bodies. I realised, however, that I had no idea what lay over the ridge that I was apparently heading for.

'South Downs Way,' I said ambiguously. It ran all through Sussex parallel to the coast. I had to be close to it.

'You're going in the wrong direction,' she said. 'You need to go back down to the village and take the path by the pub.'

'Ah,' I said.

She waited, maybe expecting me to accompany her and her dog back along the path.

'I'll check the map,' I said.

'Are you saying I don't know where the South Downs Way is?'

'I mean, I was going roughly that way. I might press on a bit up this track, then circle round.'

'That won't work. You need to go back the way you came. I walk this way almost every day, summer and winter, and I'm not a total fool.'

'Thanks,' I said. 'I'll check the map first.'

'Suit yourself. Molly!'

The retriever, which had strayed some way from us, glanced briefly over its shoulder and continued sniffing.

'MOLLY!'

This, at the top of the woman's voice, gained reluctant recognition, and the dog loped slowly towards us, its tail wagging.

'Bad dog,' she said to it.

The dog put its head on one side, as if giving this suggestion its most careful consideration.

'Bad dog,' she repeated.

The dog wagged its tail even harder and then, giving a sudden bark of defiance, ran off down the hill. The woman shook her head as if this were in some way my fault. Then she too set off, though at a much slower pace.

'Molly!' she yelled. 'MOLLY! BAD DOG!'

Just as they entered the trees, the woman gazed back at me, still standing where I was. For about ten seconds she seemed to be taking in every aspect of my appearance, or perhaps she was just checking that I was safe. She clearly regarded me as a complete fool, scarcely responsible enough to be allowed out alone and an unfortunate influence on other people's dogs. Then she and Molly vanished into the wood. Her low opinion of me was not unreasonable. If I had explained what I was actually doing, it would probably have been lower still.

I had told Henry that I was going ahead with the

investigation because I wasn't going to be scared off the case. That sounded good. Actually, I'd have dropped the case in an instant if I'd felt there was any real danger. What had happened was that I'd just drifted slowly round to the view, which was not unlike Elsie's, that spending a day out in the rain in order to get a glowing review in a national newspaper – an increasing rarity as editors cut the space they allocated to book reviews – was as good a use of my time as any. It was legitimate PR and that consideration overrode even Henry's patent ingratitude. I was surprised that Elsie, having done the same calculation, hadn't got me emailing every reviewer in London to ask whether they had any little murders that needed investigating. Of course, it was fraudulent in the sense that I had no chance at all of bringing back any useful information to Henry but that wasn't my problem.

I must have felt slightly guilty at my own cynicism, however, because I dutifully put in time checking the undergrowth on either side of the track as I walked back down through the woods and towards my car. Where paths led off into the trees, I even followed them for a bit until they petered out. On one path, very close to the car, I did detect recent footprints; and somebody more fancifully inclined than I might have made out the signs of a heavy object having been dragged along. I walked up and down that one a couple of times, wishing that I had brought a stick with which to probe the brambles on either side. As it was, I caught no glimpse of a bloody corpse, and this did not surprise me greatly. There was no corpse to find. Crispin Vynall was also probably by now back home and enjoying a coffee in front of the fire.

It was the sound of the church clock striking twelve that brought me to my senses. I gave up being an amateur detective of any sort and returned to my car. There was no evidence that anyone had tampered with it in my absence. And, contrary to my fears, I was able to back it slowly in a quarter circle, leaving me facing downhill with a clear if muddy road ahead.

My final duty was to visit the pub. I ordered a sandwich and a pint of shandy.

'Fairly quiet today,' I added.

The barman looked up from his order pad. 'It's early,' he said.

'You were probably packed for New Year's Eve.'

'Yes,' he said. Not a great conversationalist.

'A friend of mine was here. He said it was a good evening.'

'Did he? Yes, it wasn't bad. Do you want any chutney with that?'

'Please. That would be good. His name's Henry Holiday. He's a writer.'

The barman nodded sympathetically. 'You get all sorts round here.'

'You wouldn't remember seeing him?'

Sympathy was replaced by puzzlement. 'If he said he was here, I'm sure he was, but there were quite a few customers I didn't recognise. It's like that on New Year's Eve. We've just pinned up a few photos that various people took that evening. They're over there on the board. You might spot your friend. I'll get this order to the kitchen, then.'

With every table in the pub to choose from, I elected to sit by the fire, but first I took a look at the noticeboard. Pinned to it, as promised, were various photographs taken of events at the pub. They must have accumulated over the number of years. Different landlords do different things to please their customers; this one apparently had put together a small display of the regulars enjoying themselves and encouraged people to contribute their own pictures. Some were very faded and looked as though they dated back to the eighties and nineties. But one small group was fresh and stood out from the rest. It was the New Year party. I studied the pictures carefully – the images of assorted strangers, glasses in their hands, their befuddled faces red and shining. At first sight, there was no sign of any crime writers amongst the revellers. Either Henry was mistaken about being in a pub or I had located the wrong one. Then I noticed a figure, slumped in a seat in the background of the very last snap. Half-hidden by the main group, who were the real subject of the shot, he was staring in horror in the photographer's direction. He wasn't exactly in focus. Others who knew him less well might not have recognised him. But I did. Tweed jacket. Waistcoat. Yellow bow tie. It was Henry. There was no sign of Crispin with him.

The bar was still empty. I glanced over my shoulder and carefully unpinned the picture and slipped it into my pocket. Henry could hardly say that this trip has yielded nothing of value. This was worth a red-hot half-page review and no mistake.

I took my seat and waited for my sandwich. It was not long coming. The kitchen after all had as little to do as the barman.

'Sorry, I've forgotten the pickle,' he said. Did he glance in puzzlement at the gap on the noticeboard, or was that my imagination?

'Don't worry,' I said. 'I have all I need.'

But even as I bit into my sandwich I was thinking: the photo proves this is the right pub, but why the look of horror? What exactly had I stumbled across?

My phone rang. It was Elsie.

'I don't know what sort of morning you've had,' she said, 'but you'll never believe what I've just discovered.'

CHAPTER FOURTEEN

Elsie had spoilt one of my lunches by eating it. Now she proceeded to spoil another.

'You see,' she said, 'I thought it would be worth following up on Thrillseeker.'

'In the sense that you'd hoped to find more one-star reviews?' I was struggling to cut my sandwich and hold my phone. I needed another hand.

'In the sense that I wondered who he was. So, I had a look at some of the discussion groups on Crispin Vynall's books, just in case he had contributed.'

'You didn't look at the discussion groups on my books?'

'I don't think there are any.'

'And had he commented?'

'Yes. He was fairly active in bigging Crispin up. But there was one contribution in particular that interested me. Somebody had asked in passing whether Crispin was planning to attend CrimeFest this year. What do you think Thrillseeker said?'

'Yes, he is?'

'No.'

'No, he isn't?'

'No.'

'Maybe he'll come?'

'No.'

'OK, I give up.'

'Thrillseeker wrote: "glad you enjoyed the book – *yes, I'll be there* – hope to see you in the bar".'

I let this sink in. 'So, Thrillseeker was pretending to be Crispin Vynall?'

'No, you idiot. Thrillseeker *is* Crispin Vynall. He'd forgotten he'd signed in under that particular alias and just gave a straight answer to the question – he was going to the conference.'

'Which means . . .'

'Crispin Vynall has been giving you anonymous one-star reviews on Amazon.'

'And . . .'

'He has, conversely, also been giving himself anonymous five-star reviews. Thrillseeker is what is known in the trade as a sockpuppet – a *nom de plume* through which criticism and praise can be delivered anonymously. In this case, owned by Crispin Vynall.'

'Untraceable,' I said.

'Except I did trace him,' said Elsie with no discernible pretence of modesty.

'But why would he give me one-star reviews?'

'If he's still alive, you can ask him.'

'And if he's dead?'

'We'll just have to assume that he thought you were crap.'

'I'm shocked,' I said.

'Loads of people think you are crap, Ethelred. It's not exactly breaking news.'

'I didn't mean that. I meant, I'm shocked that Crispin was giving himself favourable reviews.'

'Everyone does it,' said Elsie. 'Why not? There's nothing wrong with it. It's just free publicity when you think about it. It's just the same as your publisher putting on the back cover of one of your books: "another fascinating case for Sergeant Fairfax, which will keep you guessing right up to the last page". Readers know it isn't *really* true.'

'Do they?'

'Well, maybe *your* readers don't realise publishers lie through their teeth, but then your readers are a bit . . . special.'

'Thanks. I'm not sure it's right to criticise other authors anonymously, though.'

'Get real,' said Elsie. 'Most Amazon reviews are anonymous because most of the Internet is anonymous. That's how teenagers get to drive each other to suicide by telling their victims that they are fat or spotty or whatever. Facebook is a more effective murder weapon than cyanide these days. Why should authors have to give their real names on the Internet when nobody else does? And you can't ban authors from writing reviews or from being honest if they don't like somebody's book. What I don't understand is *why* Vynall would want to slag off your books online, however much he disliked them. It's not as though you were any sort of threat to him. It makes no commercial sense to waste that amount of time on that many bad reviews.'

'Malice?' I suggested. 'Spite? Envy?'

'Not envy.'

'No, possibly not.'

'So what have you ever done to Crispin Vynall? Have you ever given *him* a bad review or slept with his wife or blackballed him from the Detection Club?'

'No,' I said. 'I hardly know him. I was once on a panel with him at Harrogate – we debated the merits of cosy versus hardboiled crime. He insisted on an audience vote at the end, which he won easily. We were also both judges for a CWA crime award – but we really only met for the final shortlisting discussion. I've talked to him once or twice in the bar at the Bristol CrimeFest. That's probably a total of five hours in his company in my entire life. He's mentioned me in passing in one or two of his reviews of other writers. I've never reviewed any of his books anywhere. Actually, I've only ever read one of them.'

'Did you fall out over which book was to win the CWA award?'

'Quite the reverse. I think we were in complete agreement over the shortlist and the winner.'

'Were there any other judges or was it just the two of you?'

'Janet Francis was the other one,' I said.

'Crispin's agent?'

'Yes,' I said.

I was aware that Elsie did not particularly like Janet. In the event, her response was relatively mild. 'Very cosy,' she said. 'You'd have been outvoted even if you had disagreed with Crispin.'

'But I didn't disagree,' I said. 'It was fine. A unanimous decision.'

'Did you sleep with his wife, then?' There was a note of accusation in her voice. 'You said that you knew her. And you said it in quite a suspicious way.'

'I met her at Harrogate one year. I give you my word that we never even discussed the possibility of sex. Crispin on the other hand was busy chatting up every woman in the bar under the age of forty. I doubt that he notices what his wife is doing.'

'As we have observed before, he has a bit of a reputation, though my understanding is that he'd have been chatting up every girl under the age of twenty-five. So, even if you haven't slept with his wife, did you sleep with one of his fresh-faced floozies? No, forget I asked that question. Your Facebook status is permanently stuck on Single, isn't it?'

'I don't do Facebook,' I said. 'As for my recent love life . . . Well, that's my affair. But I'm pretty confident in saying that I haven't slept with any of Crispin's floozies over the past two years.'

'Meaning you haven't had sex with anybody at all.'

'If you say so.'

'Of course,' said Elsie, 'it's quite possible that Thrillseeker wasn't his only sockpuppet and that you are not the only one he gave one-star reviews to. There could be dozens. In which case one of the maligned authors might have found out and . . .'

'It's a motive, I suppose. But it's only of any relevance if Crispin is dead.'

'What if Crispin had also been giving Henry one-star reviews and Henry found out? That would be a motive for murder, wouldn't it?'

'Not in my book.'

'But maybe in Henry's book, which sells many times what your book does.'

'The thing that Henry has done, if he has done anything at all, seems to be a random drunken act – not calculated revenge, which he ought to know about. I suppose I could check if he does indeed have a string of one-star reviews. But Henry says he never reads Amazon reviews anyway. He doesn't do the Internet very much.'

'He really is your Mini-Me, isn't he?'

'I use the Internet all the time, Elsie. Most writers do.'

'You didn't know what a sockpuppet was.'

'I'm delighted to say that I've never needed to know.'

'Still, if Crispin makes a habit of trashing people's careers, there may be dozens of people out there who want him dead.'

'We don't know that Crispin is dead, just that he's missing.'

'Why are you whispering?'

'I'm in a pub. I don't want to be overheard.'

'You didn't mind everyone hearing that you hadn't had sex for two years.'

'Did I say that?'

'More or less.'

'Wherever Crispin is, he doesn't seem to be buried in a shallow grave up on the Downs. I'm sure that in a couple of days' time he'll just show up.'

'So what are you going to do in the meantime?'

Clearly I didn't need to do anything, but there was something that I needed to follow up.

'I'm going to talk to Crispin's wife,' I said.

'Again? You think she may have killed him? I can't say I'd blame her.'

'Of course not. But, as you say, Crispin must have told her he was going somewhere – even if she suspects he's somewhere else. There's a good chance he's actually gone exactly where he told her he'd gone. So, almost certainly, I'll be able to get hold of him and confirm he's safe. That doesn't necessarily help us find out what Henry did that night after Crispin left him, but it will at least rule out the possibility that Henry killed Crispin.'

'She might also know why Crispin has been giving you all of those one-star reviews.'

'That's not why I'm going to see her.'

'No?'

'No.'

'Of course, she's very attractive,' said Elsie.

'That also has nothing to do with it,' I said.

'While the cat's away—' Elsie began.

But I hung up before she could complete whatever fatuous remark she was about to make.

Crispin and Emma lived not too far away – just on the other side of Brighton and about an hour's drive. A quick visit would almost certainly clear up everything. And yet I paused for a moment before dialling. Of course Henry could not have killed Crispin. It was too fanciful to be worth considering. And yet, blurred though the snapshot was, there was no mistaking the horror on Henry's face as he realised he was about to be photographed.

I punched in the number. What I was hoping for, above everything, was that, this time, Crispin himself would answer. But deep down I knew that wasn't what was going to happen.

CHAPTER FIFTEEN

It was Emma who answered the phone with a simple 'Hello?'

'It's Ethelred Tressider here, again,' I said. 'Sorry to disturb you.'

'Hi, Ethelred,' she said. 'I wasn't doing anything else of interest. Fire away.'

'Is Crispin back by any chance?'

'Not at this precise moment,' she said. 'I said I'd give him your message, whatever it was.'

'It was just to phone me.'

'Was it? Great. I'll pass it on. So he needs to phone somebody . . .'

'Me.'

'You. Got it. Bye then.'

For some reason I was failing to hold her attention.

'Emma!'

'Yes?'

'Don't put the phone down. There was something else. I'd promised to drop off a couple of books for Crispin when I was next over your way. I'm going to be in Brighton later this afternoon, so I'll call by at about four if you are likely to be in. Or if he will be.'

'Just drop them through the letter box if I'm not here.'

'They're quite big. That's why I thought I'd check whether you were around.'

'Four should be fine.'

'You'll be there?'

'Hang on, let me check. Where am I? Yes, I'm there all right.'

Was she being funny at my expense? Or was she genuinely unsure where she was? I thought that, on the whole, she just sounded tired and a bit pissed off. I'd find out shortly if it was me she was pissed off with.

'I'll see you in about an hour,' I said.

I went into the study and took down the first two books I saw. Then I grabbed my car keys and set off.

It was in fact about four-thirty by the time I located Crispin's house. I'm not that good with satnav to be perfectly honest. And I was still glancing too often in my rear-view mirror to concentrate properly on the road ahead. The voice giving directions sounded slightly despairing by the time that, on the third attempt, I took the correct turn off the main London road and then the second right into a road lined with trees and large red-brick houses. Crispin's residence proved to be a large Edwardian detached villa with much cheerful ornamentation around the windows and an overgrown garden full of glossy laurels and rhododendrons. Rain had started to fall again as I had crossed the Downs and the trees dripped on everything as I walked up the path. I tucked the books inside my jacket to protect them from the water that was beginning to soak me.

Emma Vynall opened the door to me within seconds of my ringing the bell. If she was cross with me, it wasn't immediately apparent. 'Come in, Ethelred,' she said. 'You'll get pneumonia standing there. I'm so sorry, but you've had a wasted journey. It was really stupid of me.'

'I don't understand,' I said.

'Oh dear . . . I'll explain. But come into the kitchen and have some tea. It's the least I can do under the circumstances. You'll have to excuse the mess, I'm afraid.'

Elsie often points out that my own kitchen is a mess, meaning that the breakfast things are still in the sink at lunchtime. Emma Vynall's kitchen was in a different league. Once the sink was full, plates and dishes had spilt out onto the draining board, marble work surfaces and the butcher's trolley. That morning's cereal bowl and mug (or perhaps the day before's) was on the French cherry wood kitchen table. The rubbish bin was overflowing, as witnessed by several tea bags on the floor close by. 'House-proud' isn't a phrase people use much now; I doubted it had ever been in Emma's vocabulary.

'The cleaning lady comes in tomorrow,' she said over her shoulder as she rinsed out two mugs. She peered into one of them and gave it a quick wipe with a grubby dishcloth. 'Would you like some cake?'

'If you've got any,' I said.

She looked inside a tin. 'Sorry,' she said. 'I'm sure I did have some. It would have probably been stale. Tea it is, then.'

It was a large table in a large kitchen and we were able to find enough space at one end of it to accommodate two mugs of tea. Emma rubbed her eyes. Though dressed in jeans and a sweater, she somehow gave the impression of having just got out of bed – that she had thrown these clothes on minutes before I arrived. Her hair was tied back in an untidy blonde bunch. She wore no make-up. Even so, she was as attractive as I remembered her. She sat on the chair, one foot girlishly tucked up beneath her, the other swinging gently to and fro.

'I've been stupid,' she repeated. 'I tried to phone you back but you must have already left the house. I don't think you ever gave me your mobile number, so I couldn't try that. Anyway, there's no point at all in your leaving the books here.'

I thought for a moment that she was about to tell me that Crispin was indeed missing or even that he had been found dead, but nothing at all in her tone suggested she was leading up to that.

'You mean . . .' I began.

Emma took a deep breath. 'Crispin moved out before Christmas,' she said. 'He . . . he and I . . . well, he's gone. He's left me.' She waved her hand in the direction of the sink as if that explained things in some way. Perhaps it did, as some sort of allegory of blighted hopes. We both looked at the piled-up dishes for a moment. It took egg some days to dry out that much on a plate.

'I'm sorry,' I said.

'No, I'm sorry. I just said come round without thinking. At some point he will have to come back and pick up his stuff. But it was only after I put the phone down that I realised that there was no point at all in your bringing the books to me if Crispin needed them urgently. So, you'll have to hang onto them. Unless you want to leave them here until he needs some clean socks or something.'

'But you *are* expecting him back?' I said. 'He's OK?'

She looked at me oddly. 'OK? What do you mean? Why shouldn't he be OK? He walks out on me and you're worried about *his* emotional state?'

'I didn't mean anything.' Not a convincing response. Spoken words always mean something. As a writer's wife she would have been told that. I wondered how much I could explain to her about Henry. He obviously was not in any sense a client because I was not in any sense being paid. Arguably, therefore, client confidentiality was not an issue. Still, I felt that some discretion was required. 'It's just that I've been trying to get in touch with him on his mobile. I was just a bit worried . . .'

Elsie always tells me that she can tell when I'm lying. Emma looked as though she could as well. I wondered briefly whether it wasn't easier to tell her everything, even if that did land Henry in it. But landing Henry in it would measurably diminish the chances of the book review.

'Yes, you said you were trying to contact him. But why were you worried?' she asked.

'No reason.' I still didn't sound convincing. I just sounded as if I had some minor psychiatric disorder that made me over-anxious from time to time. I decided to change the subject. 'Where did Crispin go . . . when he left here, I mean?'

'To another woman, I would imagine. You see, Ethelred, he doesn't treat women well, but he does need us. Fortunately there's usually a good supply so, when he breaks one, he can lay his hands on a replacement fairly quickly.'

'Do you know who he might have gone to?'

'Excellent question. With Crispin you can't really be sure whose harbour his prow will nudge into. Some fifteen-year-old tart probably.'

'Are you serious?'

'No, of course not. I'm just being a bitch. This one may be sixteen for all I know.'

'But you knew he was having an affair?'

'An affair? What a quaint old-fashioned term to use about a sleazy bastard schlepping his dick from bed to bed. Nothing so respectable or permanent, I suspect. Look, Ethelred, I honestly don't know where he went. I also don't much care where he went. And if I did know who he went to, it probably wouldn't help you track him down. Whoever he was sleeping with on Christmas Day, I doubt if it was still the same woman on New Year's Eve. Sorry – picturesque exaggeration. He'll occasionally stay with the same tart for months, if he's comfortable and he can't be bothered to move on. But he always ditches them eventually. You know, I used to think it touching the way he took such an interest in new up-and-coming writers, until I worked out that they were all young and blonde and female. You're not telling me you never noticed?'

'Not really,' I said.

'He gave that CWA debut award to one of them.'

'Mary Devlin Jones?'

'Unless he also gave an award to one of his other young slappers. Don't look so shocked. These things happen.'

'I suppose so . . . her book was very much in his style, of course.'

'*In his style?* Good God, Ethelred – he practically *wrote* most of it for her. Then he got her to enter it for a competition in which he was a judge. Which in turn got her a three-book deal with her first publisher, Atkins and Portas.'

'But surely—' I began.

'You're not saying this is news to you?'

'I'd heard rumours that the novel was plagiarised, but I didn't really believe it . . .'

'It was all over the Internet for months.'

'I do use the Internet – honestly, I do.'

'Not that much, I'd have said. For a while it was actually trending on Twitter. That means—'

'Yes, I know what that means.'

'I suppose in the end the sex-for-ghost-writing wasn't such a bad deal for either of them. Mary got her book and her contract. Crispin got what *he* wanted, by which I don't just mean sex – he likes the unquestioning adulation too. And the prize had to go somewhere. You could call it win-win. Of course, Crispin dumped her by the time she was halfway through the second book. Atkins and Portas were reportedly a little puzzled by the falling off in the quality of her later work. The third book was however quite interesting in the sense that it was about a woman who gets betrayed by a best-seller crime writer and then tracks him down and gets her revenge. It was so gory they almost didn't bring it out. It takes from page 173 to page 349 for him to die. Then the plagiarism rumours started to circulate and Atkins and Portas went cold on the whole Mary Devlin Jones thing. After that she switched to writing cozies for another publisher entirely. They're about an octogenarian amateur detective with half a dozen cats who help her in her cases. You occasionally see them in bookshops. I actually read one. You really have to like cats to see any point in it all. One of the cats is called Hercule by the way. He spends a lot of time purring and licking his own arse. Crispin would have been a better name.'

'You don't have any cats yourself?'

'I might have to get one or two. We'll see how it goes. I'm a crap tea-maker by the way. Why don't we switch to red wine. I've got a bottle open. And if I haven't, I've got a corkscrew.'

I realised that her appearance was not so much of somebody who has just got up as somebody who has been drinking steadily and carefully since shortly before breakfast.

'Coffee might be better for both of us,' I said. 'Shall I get us some?'

Emma laughed. 'That's exactly what you said to me at Harrogate,' she said.

'When?'

'In the bar of the Old Swan, when I tried to pick you up.'

'You tried to pick me up?'

'You didn't realise I was asking you to come to bed with me? Good grief! There was me thinking how gentlemanly you'd been about the whole thing, chatting away in the bar and resisting the temptation to accept my offer – whereas in practice I'd just been too drunk to make it clear I was an easy lay.'

'But Crispin was there in the bar . . .'

'I was scarcely expecting to see him back in his own bed when there were other beds to go to. I doubt he even noticed us ensconced there in the corner, or registered you seeing me back to my room.'

'So I did. I'd forgotten that. Just a peck on the cheek, then, after I made sure you'd got the right bedroom?'

'You got me a nice cup of coffee. Then we chatted for a bit in a quiet corner of Reception – all very cosy and promising, as I thought. Then you saw me back to my room. I believe we shook hands in the corridor. Or maybe I'm making that bit up. I can't recall. Perhaps it's as well I can't. It clearly wasn't my finest performance as a seductress.'

'I remember it as a very pleasant evening.'

Emma burst out laughing. 'Very pleasant? If you say so. Just out of interest, would you have slept with me, if I'd communicated better?'

That seemed a question fraught with all sorts of dangers.

'Do you think Crispin did notice us? Did he think maybe that we did sleep together?'

'It wouldn't have bothered him.'

'You don't think he might have resented it?'

'Not a chance.'

I pondered this for a bit.

'Did he ever mention me at all? I mean, in any context?'

Emma frowned. 'Ethelred, you spurned my advances

but you seem very concerned about whether you were constantly in my husband's thoughts. I'm not quite sure what to make of this but I have to warn you that Crispin is as heterosexual as it is possible to be. And you're about thirty years too old for him anyway.'

'Oh sorry . . . I didn't mean . . .'

She raised an eyebrow. It was time to change the subject.

'Do you know a writer called Henry Holiday?' I asked.

Emma turned and looked across the room at the unwashed dishes. For a moment I thought she hadn't heard my question, then I saw she was frowning, as if trying to recall something. 'Sort of . . . I mean, I've spoken to him . . . He's a drinking buddy of Crispin's in a minor way. I don't think they're great friends, exactly, but they tend to occupy the same bit of the bar at conferences and confide in each other, the way you do at three o'clock in the morning.'

'And they saw each other down here in Sussex? Henry lives close to where I do in West Wittering.'

She shook her head. 'I don't think they met up much other than at Bristol and Harrogate or Crime in the Court. But, as you will gather, I didn't always know exactly where Crispin was.'

'No. I suppose not. You implied that Crispin was . . . well . . . into underage girls. Is that really true?'

'That was probably the booze talking. The booze has a very low opinion of my husband. Crispin's other women have all tended to be on the young side, but even I wouldn't want to accuse him of being a paedo. Crispin's general technique, you see, was to offer whichever silly girl it was some sound middle-aged advice and assistance with their careers, while nudging her gently towards his bed – or any other reasonably flat surface. You don't get many teenage writers, so most of them tended to be in their twenties or early thirties, often from one of the creative writing courses he taught on. Anyway, I may be drunk, but I have noticed you're asking a lot of questions for somebody who is supposed to be dropping off a couple of books.'

'Sorry,' I said. 'It's none of my business. I'm probably just being tedious.'

'On the contrary,' she said. 'It's good to have somebody to talk to in an open and grown-up manner. Until I can buy a couple of cats, it's great to have human company of any sort, even another crime writer. Why don't you stay for dinner? You can help me finish up some of this wine. Crispin left quite a stash of it.'

'I'm sorry,' I said. 'I need to get back.'

I paused, wondering why I had said that. I had nothing to go back to. Not even a cat. Maybe there were some good wildlife programmes on television. But it seemed right. Under the circumstances.

'Let me know if you hear from Crispin,' I said.

'OK. And I'll pass on . . .' She checked the covers. '*Murderous Sussex* and *The Book of the Gun.*'

I slightly regretted the loss of the latter book – an illustrated history of firearms up to 1900 – but they gave me an excuse to go back if I needed one.

'Thanks,' I said.

'My pleasure,' she said. 'I suppose I can always spend the evening washing up.'

She didn't show me out.

* * *

It was a miserable journey home. Sometimes the rain was so heavy I could scarcely see where I was going. Every now and then, I glanced in the rear-view mirror. Occasionally a car would follow me for a few miles at a distance of twenty yards or so. Sometimes I would deliberately slow down and the car would then swish past in a cloud of spray. Sometimes I would speed up, leaving the following vehicle way behind. Not once did anyone show any sign of responding to my change of pace. I was as certain as I could be that nobody had either followed me to Brighton or tailed me on the way back. Whoever was planning to kill me was frankly doing a shit job.

CHAPTER SIXTEEN

'Where are you now?' asked Elsie.

'Back in West Wittering,' I said. I'd been explaining over the phone what I'd found out at the Vynall residence. Elsie was no more impressed than she needed to be.

'Why didn't you stay for dinner?'

'I'm not sure.'

'If she was drinking as heavily as you say, then she'd have let slip a few things as the evening went on.'

'I don't think that would have been very fair.'

'What's fair got to do with anything?'

'It's just that I didn't drive all the way to Brighton in order to behave in an underhand manner.'

'Actually – and this point has only just occurred to me – why *did* you go over to Brighton? You could have talked to her on the phone and saved yourself two hours' driving along the A27.'

'I just thought it would be better to talk to Emma face to face.'

There was a long pause as the person with whom I was not talking face to face did some thinking.

'You do actually fancy her, don't you?'

'Elsie, we are not in the playground and I'm not thirteen years old. Random assertions that I fancy somebody are juvenile.'

'True. Bet you do, though. And you knew Crispin wouldn't be there. Nice work, Tressider, other than your screwing it all up at the end by not staying for dinner. Actually, she's exactly your type – blonde, quite tall, a bit bossy – probably head girl at her school.'

'Is that right?' I'm not as good at sarcasm as Elsie is, but I try from time to time. On this occasion, though, what I intended as a put-down came out as a simple question.

'You know it's right. Think back to all your previous wives and girlfriends. Were they or were they not blonde? Did they or did they not call the shots? Who did they have more respect for – you or the fluff under the sofa? Are you sure you didn't sleep with her in Harrogate?'

'I'd scarcely forget that I'd slept with her.'

'How sweet and old-fashioned of you. You'd have probably written her a thank you note the morning after. Well, that would explain Crispin's antipathy towards you if he thought you had been shagging his missus. That would be worth a few one-star reviews.'

'But I hadn't. And Emma says it would have made no difference. So there must be some other reason why Crispin wrote the reviews.'

'Just because Emma says it, it doesn't make it true. Any of it.'

'Anyway,' I said, 'what's really interesting is that Crispin had moved out well before New Year. On New Year's Eve he went to the Old House at Home from the residence of his teenage mistress and then, quite possibly, returned to it afterwards.'

'Or, if he didn't return, his teenage mistress doesn't seem to have noticed yet. Possibly she's focussing on her GCSE retakes.'

'He still hasn't been reported missing,' I said.

'Precisely. When Agatha Christie vanished, back in the twenties, the hunt was on within hours. Nobody has seen fit to report him lost.'

'Which suggests that he isn't lost, but is alive and well – with whichever woman he went to.'

'Or that crime writers are worth less than they used to be.'

'That too,' I said.

'And Emma Vynall gave you no name?'

'No.'

'That's odd too. I mean, a woman chucks a man out of the house – it's usually for something specific – she's discovered her best friend's knickers in the glove compartment of the family car, for example. She may be misguided. She may be wrong. She may have had one bottle of red wine too many. These things happen to all of us. But she will have a *reason*. She will have got a name out of her husband if nothing else, because that's something women can do.'

'I think she said Crispin had left *her*. She didn't tell him to go.'

'Even then, wouldn't he say, I'm leaving you for so-and-so? Or, if not, wouldn't she ask? There's a strange lack of curiosity on her part. He leaves. She gets permanently drunk and considers buying a cat. But she never tries to find out who he's left her for.'

'What are you saying?'

'I'm saying that, on all of the generally accepted scales of weirdness, this scores seven and a half to eight.'

'Is that high?'

'It's out of ten. It means it's difficult to credit. Your not having had sex for two years scores one and a quarter.'

'That's helpful,' I said.

'Don't mention it.'

'She did give me one name,' I said. 'Mary Devlin Jones.'

In the silence that followed, I wondered if I had been wise to mention this at all. It was a long time ago and had no relevance.

'She used to be with Atkins and Portas?'

'Yes,' I said.

'But they dropped her. I remember that.'

'Yes,' I said.

'There were rumours floating around that her first book was plagiarised. It did her a lot of damage. Atkins and Portas weren't happy, since it would have been a clear breach of contract. It also caused problems with her agent.'

'It wasn't plagiarised, exactly,' I said. I retold the story as I had heard it from Emma.

'Sounds like plagiarism to me,' said Elsie. 'She didn't write it herself.'

'Emma may not have got it quite right.'

'You have other inside information that contradicts Emma's version?'

'No,' I said. 'Not really.'

'Are you sure? There's this strange note in your voice that happens only when you are lying.'

I said nothing.

'So you are basically bullshitting, then.'

'I thought I'd made a lying noise, not a bullshitting noise.'

'They are very similar,' said Elsie. 'So, what will you do next?'

'I need to see Henry to report back. It is, after all, Henry's lost weekend that I'm supposed to be investigating, rather than Crispin's current whereabouts.'

'Unless Henry killed Crispin.'

'Yes, but I don't think he did.'

'Why not?'

'Well, the lack of any possible motive, for one thing. And if he had killed him, I honestly don't believe that he would forget about it. And if he remembers killing him, why get me to investigate?'

'But he was the last person to see Crispin alive,' said Elsie.

'Crispin's not dead.'

On the other hand, there was the photograph. I wouldn't tell Elsie at the moment. She was apt to jump to false conclusions, and even I had no idea what to make of it yet. Perhaps I should ask Henry. I needed to do some shopping – the supermarket in East Wittering would still be open. I could call in on him on my way back.

* * *

'It's not one you'd want to use as your author photo on the inside of the book jacket,' I said.

Henry squinted at the picture and held it out at arm's length. 'I agree that it's not exactly flattering, but I'm clearly not trying to avoid having my picture taken. The flash made me jump – that's all. You can't read much into it. Still, it does show that I was at that pub on New Year's Eve. Thank you.'

'But you don't remember the picture being taken?'

'Not really. Was that the only shot I was in?'

'There was just the one photo of you, which you now have, and none of Crispin. I guess that shows he had already moved on elsewhere.'

'And the landlord didn't notice you had taken this away?'

'He may see that it's gone and put two and two together – the pub wasn't exactly crowded. But I doubt he'll call the police to investigate. He can presumably print another one off. And it will be sometime before I'm in Didling Green again, if ever. I'd hesitate to say I'd committed the perfect crime, but it's pretty close.'

'And you also went up the hill?' asked Henry.

'Yes. There was a track leading up onto the Downs, more or less as you described it. But, in the end, there's not much up there, to tell you the truth – just a muddy track and a wood and then a footpath over the Downs. There are plenty of brambles around – if you'd tripped, say, you'd have ended up with all sorts of scratches. So that fits too. Could you have just taken a wrong turning after you left the pub, got out for some reason?'

I paused. It sounded unlikely. If you drove up there on a

rainy night, thinking perhaps that the track led somewhere, wouldn't you just turn round and go back down once you saw it was a dead end? Or might you need to get out and see if you had enough space to turn in, scratching yourself on some brambles in the dark?

'I'm not absolutely sure I went up there at all,' said Henry.

'Not many people do – at least at this time of year. I met a woman walking her dog. She seemed to think it was pretty odd I was up there on my own.'

'She said that to you?'

'More or less, though the dog took most of the flak.'

Henry looked again at the photo, then stuffed it casually into his pocket. If I'd been hoping for praise I might have to wait a little longer. Some things clearly didn't change.

'Then I went over to Brighton to talk to Crispin's wife,' I said.

'Good grief! What did you do that for? I thought you'd already phoned and got as much information as you could?'

'I couldn't understand why she wasn't telling me where Crispin was. I needed to check where Crispin had been that evening.'

'And you told her that I thought I might have killed her husband?'

'Of course not. I scarcely mentioned your name.'

'Scarcely? So, you did mention it?'

'Only in passing. If it helps, she said that she thought you and Crispin only ever met at conferences. She doesn't know you and he were out on New Year's Eve. She actually thought that the two of you didn't get on that well, though she did say she thought you both confided in each other.'

Henry's expression showed that he would rather I hadn't mentioned his name at all.

'You know that Crispin and his wife have split up?' I asked. 'I mean, I'm assuming he confided that much?'

'I'd heard something,' he said.

'He didn't talk about it on New Year's Eve?'

'No. Why should he? I knew already.'

'He didn't say who he was staying with?'

'Not a word.'

'Really? That's odd. He didn't let slip a name or anything?'

'Ethelred, on my honour, not once that evening did he mention where he was staying. And I didn't feel it necessary to ask. Do you want me to swear an oath on the Bible?'

I conceded that that might be excessive. 'You met him at the Old House at Home . . . did he leave his car there, by the way?'

'No. We drove to Chichester in my car because he hadn't got his. I think he said it was in Brighton.'

'Then he probably walked to the pub. If so, there's a good chance he was staying close by.'

'I suppose he could have been. This may or may not be relevant, Ethelred, but a bus stops right outside the pub and there would have been plenty of taxis.'

This was true. I should have thought of it myself. I drive past the pub often enough. Buses pass every half-hour or so in each direction. They run until almost midnight.

'It's just odd the way he has vanished without trace,' I said. 'It's also odd nobody at all has reported him missing. Wherever he was staying, somebody should have alerted the police if he'd failed to show up after going out for a quick drink on New Year's Eve.'

'And?'

'And that means he probably did show up wherever he was supposed to be. It's just that none of us knows where that is. Though there's another thing that's slightly odd, now I think about it.'

'What?'

'Well, Emma says Crispin cleared off to his mistress. But on New Year's Eve he was clearly trying to pick girls up at the club.'

'That's Crispin for you.'

'So, had he dumped this new woman too?'

'Could be.'

'In which case, she might not be too happy with him either?'

'Lots of women weren't.'

'That's what worries me. I'm beginning to wonder if we shouldn't report Crispin missing ourselves. Let's see if the police can trace him.'

'You just said he's probably alive and well.'

That was true. I had said that. But what if I was wrong? A writer is last seen staggering drunkenly across a car park. Then he vanishes and fails to answer any calls or respond to voicemails. How many days was it now?

'You could be right,' I said. 'But even so . . .'

'Maybe hold off another twenty-four hours? We could look a bit stupid if he did show up. It probably counts as wasting police time or something.'

'I suppose so,' I said. 'But—'

'Anyway,' said Henry, 'you're meant to be concentrating

on what I did, not on Crispin. Tell me again about Didling Green. Where exactly did you search?'

I described my investigations as best I could to somebody who said they had no knowledge of the area.

'I think I should go and take a look myself,' said Henry.

'I thought the whole point of sending me was so that you didn't have to?' I was aware of a note of irritation in my voice. There was again an implication in Henry's proposal that I was not a competent investigator, that I was wasting Henry's precious time. But I'd done my best. It wasn't my fault that he hadn't left a body up there.

'Best to be thorough,' he said.

I tried not to show my annoyance more than I had to. 'I'll lend you my map, if you like.'

'I have satnav, Ethelred. It's you that I need – to show me where you looked and where you didn't.'

'You'll find it from what I've told you.'

'I'd be really grateful if you'd come along too. Really grateful. And it would be good if you could drive me.'

I looked into his eyes to see if I could discern what form that gratitude might take. He was certainly anxious that I helped him. So maybe . . .

'Bring a stick,' I said.

I arranged with Henry we should go the following day. To be quite honest, I'd pretty much given up on the idea that I might get any recognition of my selfless acts on his behalf.

But I was wrong.

CHAPTER SEVENTEEN

From the journal of Elsie Thirkettle

5 January. I've just had a long conversation with Ethelred about Emma Vynall. Why didn't I realise before? Some people might describe Ethelred as an unreliable narrator, but I prefer the term 'liar'. From the moment I first told him that Crispin had it in for him, I could tell that he knew there might be a good reason for it. He just took her back to her room and left her with a chaste kiss on the cheek, did he? Yeah, right. I'd noticed something in Ethelred's manner in West Wittering over lunch – a sort of jauntiness that comes over him whenever, usually against my advice, he has allowed himself to become ensnared by some predatory female. And he couldn't wait to get over to Brighton. That he failed to follow it through and stay the night – well, that was Ethelred all over. Letting 'I dare not' wait upon 'I would' like the poor cat in the adage.

Though Emma claimed that Crispin didn't give a toss, I wasn't so sure. The fact that he allowed himself to go off with anyone he fancied didn't mean that he extended that right to Emma. That isn't the way that men like Crispin think. If Crispin imagined the two of them had been up to something, it would more than explain why he took to Amazon as Thrillseeker and rubbished each of Ethelred's books in turn.

But it doesn't help at all in understanding why Crispin has disappeared. Or why Henry Holiday has commissioned Ethelred, the most incompetent amateur detective in England, to investigate New Year's Eve on his behalf.

Unless Ethelred actually knows far more about things than he is letting on. He wasn't entirely honest with me about his relations with Emma Vynall. And he certainly knows something about the Mary Devlin Jones plagiarism business that he hasn't told me yet.

This needs thinking about.

Sunday the 6th. At the present rate I'll have used up this diary by July, so I'd better not do anything interesting from August onwards.

Still, something fairly interesting has just happened. I went down to the local newsagents as usual on Sunday morning and bought a copy of the *Sunday Times*. I'd worked my way through the Style section, which seemed to be predicting that nice clothes would be designed this year mainly with tall, thin, attractive people in mind. Of course, I keep myself pretty fit just thinking about going on a diet, and I always reckon if you pay your gym subscription promptly, you are morally entitled to the occasional bar of chocolate. So I lingered over the section on this season's pencil skirts. I did however eventually turn to the book reviews, just in case there was a stinking review for somebody I didn't like. And there it was. Half a page by Henry Holiday devoted entirely to Ethelred's *oeuvre*. I now copy some of it down for posterity to read:

> The Buckford series by Peter Fielding (one of the three names that Ethelred Tressider writes under) is one of the most highly regarded in the genre. Praised for their accuracy and attention to detail, the books have an international following and have drawn praise from readers and critics alike. Those who only know the Buckford books are, however, missing a rare treat. The mediaeval series (written as J. R. Elliott) are amongst the finest historical works being written today. They are universally acclaimed as crime novels of the highest literary merit.

Universally? Henry wasn't counting Thrillseeker, then. And it continued in this vein paragraph after paragraph. There was occasionally a vagueness to Henry's literary criticism, suggesting that with some of the books he might have just read the blurb on the back of the cover or maybe just got the title off Amazon and winged it from that point on. Every now and then he spelt the name of one of the characters wrong because he couldn't be arsed to flick open the book and check.

Still, you couldn't fault his sycophancy. His general position was that Ethelred could do no wrong. Even the romantic novels, which Ethelred hasn't dabbled in for a couple of years at least, came in for their share of adulation. And those really are crap.

Time to phone Ethelred, then.

CHAPTER EIGHTEEN

'It's eleven o'clock, Elsie,' I said. 'Of course I'm up.'

'It's Sunday,' she pointed out.

'When you're a writer it makes very little difference,' I said. 'One day is much like another.'

'The thickness of newspapers varies, though. Have you seen the *Sunday Times*?'

'Henry's piece? Yes, it's very good.'

'Good? It reads like a Nobel Prize citation.'

'If you say so. He said he'd give me a good review if I helped him. Virtue is occasionally rewarded.'

'But you haven't helped him,' said Elsie. 'You've farted about and failed to get Emma Vynall to sleep with you. That's worth a cursory mention in "Recent Paperback Releases". If you'd rescued his daughter and her cute little puppy from a gang of flesh-eating zombies, I can see that he might owe you one – but this would be a bit over the top even then. Do you know, Ethelred, I've spent my life trying to bribe and blackmail critics. The best I ever got out of blackmail was "another interesting book from this strangely neglected author". When I read the review, I was *that* close to telling his boyfriend what I'd caught him doing.'

'Well, it was kind of you to threaten a critic on my behalf,' I said.

'Oh, good grief, I wouldn't have wasted perfectly good blackmail on one of *your* books,' said Elsie.

'So, you are ruling out that Henry might genuinely like my work?' I asked with all the sarcasm I could muster.

'Yes,' she said. 'I am. There is something very, very odd about the whole piece. People will know it's overdone.'

'Will they?'

'If they've read your books, yes. Though obviously that will be only a tiny minority of *Sunday Times* readers.'

'I thought Henry had some fairly insightful things to say. He says that Sergeant Fairfax's interest in church architecture gives him greater depth.'

'Except it doesn't really, does it? It just gives you a chance to spend days in the British Library reading up on Norman fonts, when you should be typing out another five thousand words. Saying he's interested in church history is really a bit like saying his shoes are brown or he likes Abba. You know a bit more about him but not enough to actually like him.'

'You don't like Sergeant Fairfax?' I asked.

'Is he supposed to be likeable?'

'I'd always hoped so,' I said.

'He's a tedious, middle-aged alcoholic, who smokes

fifty a day and grunts at his colleagues when they wish him good morning. Even in Book One his workmates were looking forward to the day he retired. Since then he's trodden on the toes of pretty much every one of them.'

'That doesn't mean he isn't loveable.'

'Yes it does.'

'DC Wendy Hobbins likes him.'

'She's *fictional*, Ethelred. You can make her like anything. Anyway, I've always thought that her admiration for Fairfax was completely improbable. She's a lot younger than he is. She's good company. She's attractive in a bookish sort of way. It's difficult to see why you think she would go for somebody like Fairfax, other than to pander to some middle-aged male fantasy that this sort of thing ever happens. Are you actually trying to build her up into a genuine love interest or something?'

'Maybe,' I said guardedly. It was in fact central to the plot of the next book but I hadn't yet told Elsie.

'Fairfax is just a lonely, middle-aged man,' said Elsie. 'Things don't work out like that for lonely, middle-aged men. It's their lot in life to be lonely and middle-aged. They don't get beautiful young women throwing themselves at their feet.'

'Don't they?'

'No.'

'Thank you for that clarification,' I said.

'I didn't mean you, of course,' said Elsie.

'It hadn't occurred to me until this moment that you did,' I said.

'Obviously you are a bit middle-aged . . . and you're a man . . . and . . .'

There was a pause, which I initially took to be embarrassment on Elsie's part, but she proved, in fact, to be opening a packet of biscuits.

'Sorry,' she said. 'These wrappings are really tricky. The first one's all broken.'

There was another pause. Then a crunching noise.

'The fourth one's fine. What were you saying?'

'We were just talking about the plot of my next book. DC Hobbins gets moved to another police force and Fairfax drowns himself in a Norman font.'

'Would there be enough water for that?'

'It was a joke,' I said.

'It's a good plot, though. Are you working on that today?'

'I'm driving over to Didling Green again,' I said. 'Henry thinks I'm not doing a thorough job. He's checking my work for accuracy. How about you?'

'I need to go to the shop for some more biscuits,' said Elsie. 'I'm about to run out completely. I'll call you tomorrow.'

The review was, however, only the first surprise of the morning.

I receive so few texts that it took a moment or two to identify the buzzing noise that announced the arrival of a message. I located my phone and tapped on the Messages icon. 'Bloody hell,' I said.

The new message was from Crispin Vynall.

CHAPTER NINETEEN

As I read the message a wave of relief flooded over me.

> Hi. I think that there may be some concern that I
> haven't been in contact lately. This is just to let you
> know that all is well but I can't tell you where I am
> at present, except that I am nolonger in England.
> Sorry to be a bit mysterious. All will be revealed in
> due course, as they say. In the meantime, please tell
> nobody about this text unless you have to. Crispin.

Then, almost immediately, the relief started to trickle away
into the metaphorical sands and very real doubt set in.
Anyone could send a message and sign it Crispin. And why
was Crispin sending the message to me anyway? Surely
he would contact Henry or even Emma. I would be way
down the list, after many other, much closer friends, his

agent, his editor, his publicist, his builder . . . There would be dozens of people for whom this information would be more important. Unless he knew I was looking for him. I checked the mobile number that the message had come from. It was unfamiliar to me. But I had Crispin's number on my phone from when Henry had tried to contact him. It was relatively quick work to scroll back through the calls. I had just verified the number as being Crispin's when Henry showed up in person.

'I've heard from Crispin,' I said, as Henry got out of his Jaguar. 'Just a text. He says he's out of the country and not to worry.'

'A text?'

'Yes.'

'But it's really him?'

I read out the number. Henry immediately took out his own smartphone and ran through his address book, as if unwilling again to accept my word that the job had been done properly.

'That's Crispin's mobile, all right,' said Henry. 'So, whoever I may have killed, it wasn't Crispin.'

'So, it certainly sounds as if Crispin really is alive,' I said. 'But why is he texting me? I mean, how does he even know I'm aware he's missing?'

'I agree it's slightly odd, but the message does seem to be genuine – I mean, it's from his phone. It sounds like Crispin.'

'I'm also not sure why I have to keep anything a secret. Why contact me at all if I can't let anyone know? You don't suppose that somebody else could have got hold of his phone?'

'A complete stranger? But how would they have known

144

to contact you? I doubt you're in his phone book. It's more likely that it is actually Crispin. Perhaps Emma told him you had been looking for him?'

'Yes, of course. Actually, that's almost certainly it.'

'Well, it's a good job you didn't tell the police he was missing,' said Henry. 'It sounds as if he's just gone off somewhere, after all.'

We both thought about that for a bit, then Henry said: 'OK. We have to assume he's alive. But I still have no idea what happened on New Year's Eve and I'd still like us to go and take a look at Didling Green as arranged.'

'Fine,' I said. 'Thank you, by the way, for that write-up in the *Sunday Times*. It's a while since I've had a review there at all. I'm really grateful.'

'My pleasure,' said Henry.

'I hadn't realised you had read so many of my books,' I said.

'Life is full of surprises,' he said.

'But you genuinely liked them?'

'You read the review.'

'Of course,' I said.

I paused to see if he would expand on this.

'Thank you,' I said eventually.

'My pleasure,' he repeated.

We got into the car.

It was raining again. I peered through the misty windscreen and checked the traffic in both directions before pulling onto Rookwood Road. My foot pressed down on the accelerator and we were soon out of West Wittering and on our way north to the Downs.

'Why do you keep looking in the rear-view mirror?' asked Henry. From his position in the passenger seat he couldn't easily see the road behind. He half-turned, constricted by the seat belt, then slumped back again.

'I was just checking whether anyone is following us,' I said. 'You remember that death threat?'

'Of course. But it didn't seem very serious. I'm not sure it even said specifically that you were to be killed.'

'I suppose not. It was clearly intended just to frighten me off the case. But whoever it was knew that I was doing some detective work on your behalf. Look, Henry, I have to admit that, at the beginning, I was pretty sceptical that anything much had happened on New Year's Eve. But I'm beginning to wonder if somebody is out there pulling our strings – sending us haring round the county for reasons that completely escape me – unless the person concerned *has* killed Crispin and is trying to pin it on you and to stop me discovering the truth. In which case that text from him is certainly a fake – just another deliberately planted red herring.'

'But who would want to kill Crispin?'

'Lots of people, I would think, many of them women. And we know he's attacked me on the Internet, so probably there are other writers too who've been sockpuppeted by him. I knew he had a talent for annoying people, but I'm only just discovering how comprehensive it was. If this were an Agatha Christie novel, they'd probably all band together to commit the crime. In real life, it would take just one of them.'

'And where do I fit in? Why am I the one to be fingered?'

'You were in the wrong place at the wrong time. Perhaps

you were both followed on New Year's Eve. Somebody slipped something in your drink, then abducted Crispin while you were out of it, leaving Crispin dead and you with no recollection of the latter part of the evening other than a nagging feeling that something dreadful had happened.'

'That's interesting,' said Henry.

For the first time I got the impression that Henry thought I was onto something important. Except I wasn't.

'The problem is that it's not terribly likely,' I said.

'No?' said Henry. He had clearly rather liked the idea. I suppose the whole business of doping somebody to abduct their friend was one of his standard plot devices. The death threat too and the strange text message – he'd have used those. But even as I had spoken the words, I had realised how improbable it was that anything like that could have taken place. But then what had happened?

'Or maybe the text *is* real and it's all some bizarre game of Crispin's,' I said. 'Agatha Christie's disappearance was after some row with her husband. Maybe Crispin's playing the same sort of game. He and Emma were not getting on well.'

Henry nodded thoughtfully, staring at the wet road ahead.

'Emma throws him out and he tries to get one back at her,' he said.

'I think he just left her,' I said. 'I don't think she threw him out.'

'But maybe something like that,' said Henry. 'A faked disappearance for whatever reason.'

'In which case,' I said, 'today's trip is unlikely to yield much by way of evidence. Still, Didling Green is said to be the prettiest village in West Sussex, so our journey will not be wasted.'

'Absolutely. And it's possible that walking over the Downs will bring back all sorts of memories.'

'Though it's more likely we'll just get soaking wet. I hope that Barbour of yours is waterproof.'

My smile was confident, but I still glanced again at the mirror. There was currently a large black Mercedes right on our tail. It stayed there all the way to the Chichester ring road, when it shot past us and vanished off into town. We went left at a more cautious pace and continued on our way to Didling Green and whatever evidence it might hold.

The track that rose steeply to the top of the Downs was no better than last time – if anything the rain had made it more softly glutinous and hidden the giant flints more cunningly. Once or twice the wheels spun alarmingly in the creamy mud and we almost ended up in a hedge. But we bounced and slid our way up to the small car park, where we got out and breathed in the cold, damp air that is peculiar to remote hillsides in the dead months. The winter landscape smelt of decay – black and bitter. The grass, long-since flattened by the wind and the frost, lay lifeless and still. The tree branches waved only half-heartedly, as if calling for help that would never come.

Henry stood in his Barbour, surveying the scene. The coat, I noticed, was too big for him. Perhaps when buying it he had forgotten his relatively modest size; or maybe he simply liked to wear a roomy topcoat over multiple layers of clothing. Sherlock Holmes would doubtless have looked at it and made instant conclusions about his profession or his state of mind. But I am not a real detective. To me, he was simply a small writer wearing a large coat. I turned my attention to more important matters. My last trip here had been to hunt for dead bodies; this one was apparently to jog Henry's memory.

'Do you remember that area of woodland?' I asked.

Henry shook his head. 'I do remember the village,' he said.

'It's on lots of postcards,' I replied.

'Yes, but I remember the green and the cottages on the far side. I also remember the row of council houses on the outskirts, which wouldn't feature in most guidebooks. Even without the photograph of me in the pub, I'd be certain I'd been here before.'

'It would have been pretty dark.'

'There was a moon.'

I looked at the landscape, dark green and burnt ochre under a winter sky. It was, if nothing else, remarkably peaceful.

'Look, Ethelred, would you mind terribly if I strangled you?'

'Sorry?' I said, emerging from my reverie and wondering if I had misheard.

Henry took out of his Barbour pocket a length of rope, holding it at about the height of my neck. Just for a moment the jacket seemed not ridiculously large but rather a practical and well-designed means of concealing a range of lethal weapons. Then Henry laughed. 'This is the rope I found in my car boot. If I really did use it up here, then perhaps re-enacting things might help me recall what happened . . .'

I took the rope from him and examined it. It was about as thick as my little finger, originally white with a blue fleck, but now grubby and bleached by the sun – the sort of thing you might find washed up on the beach. I grasped it firmly in both hands and gave it a tug. It was old but still strong enough. Even so, the idea of Henry strangling somebody up here on New Year's Eve was ridiculous.

'You could try it on your own neck if you're that interested,' I said, handing it back.

'That clearly would not have been what I did.'

I sighed and allowed Henry to wander round behind me, gathering up the rope in his hands as he did so.

'Now,' he said, 'if I creep up behind you like this and give the rope a double twist . . .'

The rope was cold and slightly damp round my neck. I felt it rasp against my skin as he pulled the ends. I could scarcely breathe. The rope tightened again. Of course, if I resisted now, I had little doubt I could overcome Henry, but could I still do so in another thirty or forty seconds? How long until I passed out? I'd told him he could do it. Was I going to die because I felt that it would now be impolite to ask him to stop?

'Don't worry,' I heard him say behind me, 'I'm not going to pull it really tight . . .'

Actually it already seemed tight enough. It occurred to me that my face must be turning an interesting shade of red. I doubted that I could speak even if I wanted to. It struck me that Henry had more strength than I had given him credit for. Of course, he was twenty years younger than I was. Then at last I felt the rope slacken and slip from my throat.

I suddenly realised how relieved I was. It was a lonely spot. Today even the woman with her dog was absent. Nobody would have heard my final frantic call for help.

'Did that assist in some way?' I asked, rubbing my neck gently.

Improbably Henry said: 'Yes. It did. Thank you very much.'

'And you recalled doing it before?'

'Quite the reverse. If I murdered somebody, it wasn't standing here.'

'You're sure of that?'

'Absolutely.'

'What now?' I asked. I hadn't hoped for much from the trip, but I had hoped for more than this: a bit of pointless play-acting. I waited for him to do something else with the rope – make it vanish up his sleeve, say. But his attempt to strangle me was the only trick he had.

'Perhaps I should have a stroll round,' he said. 'Which bits of the wood did you check before?'

'There and there . . .' I indicated two broad areas with a wave of my hand.

'Fine – I'll take a look along that path there if you would very kindly check around those holly bushes.' But, as I approached the bushes, Henry changed his mind and sent me off to inspect a more promising patch of brambles. All in all, we spent a fruitless half-hour poking into the vegetation, with several abrupt changes of strategy on Henry's part. Had I been expecting to find anything, I might have objected to the randomness of his approach, but it was always clear to me that this was going to be a waste of time. By the end of it, we were both wet and muddy and one of us was distinctly fed up. Only the memory of that review kept me from terminating the search much earlier. Henry finally seemed satisfied, but I had no idea what we had achieved today that I had not accomplished earlier.

Henry had thoughtfully removed his Barbour and flung it into the boot of my car to stop it soiling the seats. I kept mine on as I climbed into the car by his side. A bit of mud would brush off. My Volvo descended the hill with due caution and no alarms.

Henry declined my suggestion that we should visit the pub in the village. He said that the photograph was enough proof that he had been there. I looked at the warm, yellow glow shining through the leaded windows on a grey world outside and sighed inwardly. Then we set off again on the long drive home.

The feeling that it had indeed been a completely wasted day was reinforced by Henry's abrupt farewell as we reached my house.

'Thanks, Ethelred,' he said, opening the passenger door. 'I owe you one.'

I watched him sprint over to his Jaguar as if expecting imminent sniper fire from the bushes of April Cottage. He was driving away within thirty seconds or so of our return.

I got out of my own car and walked slowly over to the

house in the cold drizzle. I unlocked the door. There was no post on the mat and there were no messages for me on the answerphone.

As I say, a tedious afternoon completely lacking in incident, if you don't count my strangulation. And yet, while I didn't realise it at the time, I had done things that would place me in greater danger than I had ever known. All of the warning signs had been there. It was just that I hadn't noticed them.

CHAPTER TWENTY

'So, Crispin appears to be alive and well,' I said to Elsie. 'If that's a genuine text message.'

I had travelled up to London that morning to do some research in the British Library. Relevant stuff – not Norman fonts. Having mentioned it to Elsie, she had told me that by a strange coincidence she too would be in the library that morning. We could have coffee together and I could consult her on my investigations.

We were now sitting in the cafe, surrounded for the most part by students, lolling over their computers with half-drunk lattes dangerously close to the keyboard. Elsie had ordered a cappuccino and a *pain au chocolat*, claiming that she could not remember if she had had breakfast.

'You think it wasn't really him?' she asked. She looked again at the message. 'That's not how you spell "no longer", she said. 'As a writer he ought to know that.'

'It's only a text message.'

'He would have had to obstinately ignore his spellchecker.'

'It's still only a text message.'

'So you said.'

'It was genuinely his phone – whoever sent it.'

'You're certain of that?'

'Henry said it was the right number.'

'And you just took his word for it?'

'No. I lent my phone to Henry a few days ago to make a call to Crispin. He didn't get him obviously – he just left a voicemail. So I also checked my call records. I've sent a text back to Crispin, by the way, but I've had nothing more from him. I suppose he'd said all he was planning to.'

Elsie had been thinking.

'You signed your reply "Ethelred"?'

'I usually would.'

'You don't think that Crispin thought that your number was Henry's, since Henry had used your phone to leave a voicemail? In other words, that was a text for Henry rather than you? If so, he might not reply to the text from you because he hadn't intended to contact you in the first place.'

'It's possible. And the message began "Hi", not "Dear Ethelred".'

'Ethelred, nobody begins text messages "Dear Ethelred".'

'Don't they?'

'No. Nor do text messages end: "I beg to remain, sir, your most obedient servant".'

'If you say so. But, thinking about it, that does seem

more likely, doesn't it? It's a real message for Henry and Crispin is alive, albeit that he can't spell.'

'That's my guess.'

'I'll tell Henry.'

'When you do so, you can also thank him for the latest glowing commendation of your *oeuvre*. Did you see the *Telegraph* this morning?'

'Another review from Henry?'

'Another review from Henry.' She took the paper from her bag and passed it to me. 'You have a fine literary style, apparently. It's on page twenty-seven. He is turning into your biggest fan – not a high hurdle to jump, but he's making the effort.'

I finished reading and placed the paper back on the table between us, trying to avoid the croissant crumbs.

'That will be worth quoting on the cover of my next book,' I said.

Elsie nodded. 'If playing at murderers up on the Downs gets you this sort of publicity you should do it all the time.'

'I don't think it was just that. Henry said he genuinely liked my books.'

'Really? Are you sure?'

I tried to remember exactly what Henry had said. Maybe not quite that, but something that undoubtedly implied it. 'Yes,' I said.

'OK, you've made some progress, but you're no closer to knowing where Crispin actually is or what Henry did on New Year's Eve.'

'Crispin said he's no longer in England.'

'That leaves a lot of the world where he could be.'

'True. You're right, though. Each discovery we make

simply raises more questions. I don't know why Crispin seems to have gone into hiding. I don't know what Henry did after leaving the club, except that he went to the pub in Didling Green. And I don't know who threatened to kill me.'

'A nutter.'

'A well-informed nutter. There are so many things that almost fit together but don't quite. There's a letter from somebody who clearly knows what is going on and who tries to sound threatening, but succeeds only in being weird. There's the text from Crispin that says almost nothing – whether it's intended for me or Henry. One moment the tension is being ratcheted up – the next we're back to where we were before. It's as if I'm living in a badly plotted novel.'

'You should feel right at home then.'

'But that *is* what it feels like,' I persisted. 'Even the weird bit of play-acting that Henry went in for on the Downs. I think I'm about to be murdered then, no, I'm not. And the story just moves on.'

'That's just Henry,' said Elsie. 'But I agree somebody seems to be having a laugh at our expense. The question is: who do we trust?'

'Maybe I should go and talk to Emma again,' I said.

'Do you really need to go to Brighton? Couldn't you phone?'

'I have questions that it would be better to put to her face.'

'I understand completely.'

'No, you don't.'

'Yes, I do.'

'It's not what you think.'

'If it's not what I think, why should you think I'm thinking that?'

'I just need to see her in person.'

'Planning to shag the information out of her this time?'

'I'll ignore the fact that you said that.'

'It was a serious suggestion. It's an old and trusted technique. Think of Mandy Rice-Davies.'

'I'm not sure that's a good precedent.'

'Ethelred, there are literally billions of good precedents for having sex with somebody. If you have sex, trust me, you won't be the first to do it.'

'But I have no intention of doing so. And, for the record, I never have had sex with Emma Vynall.'

'No? Well, you would say that, wouldn't you?'

'I was in Brighton signing some books and I remembered that there were, in fact, three books I'd promised to lend Crispin. So, I thought I'd just drop in. That's OK isn't it?'

'As long as it's not urgent,' said Emma. She looked at me over the top of her wine glass. There was a smudge of lipstick on the rim. My glass, in front of me on the kitchen table, was as yet untouched. I couldn't afford to get too drunk if I was driving home. I knew, of course, that I ought to be driving home. I knew that if I didn't drive home my life was going to get a lot more complicated. But then, as Elsie had said, what was I doing here?

'You've heard nothing more from Crispin?' I asked, picking up the glass.

'Not since he flounced out of the house just before Christmas, leaving me with a family-sized turkey in the fridge. You?'

'A text,' I said.

I watched her face carefully. She showed no surprise and strangely little interest.

'There you are, then,' she said. Her words were slightly slurred. She was taking her post-break-up drinking seriously.

'I suppose so. It was just that it was a slightly odd message. I wasn't sure whether . . . well, maybe somebody had got hold of his phone . . .'

'Why on earth would he let anyone do that?'

'I mean, hackers can do anything, can't they?'

'No idea. I've never knowingly met one.'

Emma topped her glass up in what was almost a reflex action. She put the bottle down then, realising that she wasn't drinking alone today, picked it up again and nodded towards my glass. I shook my head.

'You're not implying that I sent that message, are you?' asked Emma.

'Of course not,' I said.

'I haven't seen him or his phone since he walked out.'

'I still don't understand why Crispin left,' I said.

'You don't have to. It's not your problem, Ethelred.'

'Sorry – I don't mean to pry.'

'No, pry if you want to. I suppose it will all come out eventually. Crispin's likely to tell all his mates, after all. I'd better give you the full story, even if I don't come out of it as well as I might. It's like this. On the day concerned I'd accused him of sleeping with one of our friends – you don't have to know who. Crispin denied it and, in the end I sort of believed him; but the whole Crispin infidelity thing had gone just a bit too far for me to want to drop it. So I didn't.

Well, you don't, do you? Eventually he said if that was how I felt, he was clearing off. So he marched noisily upstairs and started packing – throwing stuff around the bedroom just in case I hadn't noticed. Anyway, after another couple of glasses of wine, the thought occurred to me that it would really screw up his plans if I decided to go off in the car. So, I drove round the corner to the friend I'd accused him of sleeping with and we got completely drunk. The following morning I drove back and Crispin was gone. As far as thwarting his plans were concerned, I'd left taxis and buses out of my calculations, though hopefully I'd really pissed him off when he dragged his cases downstairs and found no BMW on the gravel drive. But the downside was that I missed out on the bit of the break-up where he says I'm going somewhere where I don't have to put up with this shit – here's the address of that particular place if you are interested to know. Of course, I expected him to be back. I wrapped his presents and put them under the tree. I actually cooked the turkey on Christmas Day. But there wasn't even a phone call. On Boxing Day I took his presents to the Oxfam shop and ate turkey for breakfast, lunch and dinner. You've no idea how big a turkey is until you have to eat the whole thing yourself. It's obscene.'

'So you did throw him out?'

'I suppose so. Why?'

'Just something Henry said.'

'Did he?' Emma topped up her glass.

'You've tried to ring Crispin?'

'It seemed polite to do so. I've found that under circumstances like this you can annoy somebody even more by being very civilised and reasonable – phoning them to see how they are, for example. Being concerned for their bloody welfare. But I just got voicemail. I thought he'd be bound to come back in time for New Year's Day. We'd invited a couple of friends round for lunch. I phoned them late that morning and claimed Crispin was under the weather.'

'Might they have known where he was?'

'If they did, they didn't express surprise that I was claiming he was asleep in our bedroom, and they certainly didn't tell me he was somewhere else.'

'But you weren't worried?'

'He'd said he was leaving and he left. Anyway, he'd got form, you might say.'

'Meaning?'

'He's gone off in a huff before. No communication then, either.'

'Like Agatha Christie?'

'Not one of Crispin's literary heroes. I don't think that would have motivated him. Of course, the whole nation holding its breath while the police searched high and low for the missing author would have appealed to him. So, for all I know he may have even been hanging out in Agatha's room at the Old Swan in Harrogate. I never asked. He never told. After about a week, he just pitched up at home and we never spoke of it again.'

'But you think he might have done the same thing this time?'

'Maybe. Who cares? I just mean he's capable of it. And this time there might have been the sort of publicity he liked.'

I thought of the fake reviews he'd given himself on Amazon. Perhaps it was all beginning to fit together – Crispin slipping something into Henry's drink, then stealing away, then (for whatever reason) setting up a series of strange 'clues' for reasons as yet known only to himself.

'He wouldn't have told you what he was doing, though? To stop you worrying?'

'Worrying? Who's worrying? He'd made it clear that it was no longer any of my business. He's gone wherever he's gone.'

She was looking at me over the top of her glass again, one eyebrow raised. There was a sort of sleepy cosiness, a soft vulnerability about her.

'You're right. I'm sure he'll show up when he wants to be found.'

'Well, when you do find him, you can tell him to go to hell as far as I'm concerned and he can take his teenage bitch-whore with him. Sorry – I should have said, in addition to being infuriatingly polite and reasonable, I'm also being a venomous harpy. It's called multitasking.'

'It must be tough for you,' I said.

I reached out my hand across the table and placed it on hers. She looked at my hand for a moment, her head on one side.

'Ethelred,' she said. 'I really wouldn't want you to get the wrong idea. Crispin's gone but that doesn't mean . . .'

I also looked at my hand, then slid it very slowly back to my own side of the table.

'I'm sorry,' I said. 'I didn't intend to . . .'

'I know I said that I would have slept with you at Harrogate, but I also thought that I'd made it clear I was terminally drunk. Anyway, it wasn't the sort of offer you could take a rain check on.'

'No, of course not. I didn't mean anything . . .'

'I was pretty drunk too when you were last here. As for my current sobriety . . . I'm more in remission than actually cured, you might say. If we sit here at the table drinking until about ten o'clock I may suddenly find I can't tell you from Brad Pitt – but equally I may have already passed out on the floor in a pool of vomit. It's not worth hanging around on the off chance.'

I picked my glass up then put it down again. It looked as if I'd be driving home quite soon.

'I'm sorry . . .'

Emma reached across the table and quickly patted my hand. 'It's fine. You're a man. You're basically programmed to make a pass at any unattended female. I thought it was odd last time – dropping off two books nobody would want at a place they weren't planning to return to. I thought it was even odder this time – adding another book to the pile and asking me all sorts of questions about when Crispin would be home. If I could give you some advice, "here are some books for your husband" isn't a great chat-up line. Most girls wouldn't even let you into the hallway with that one, let alone the bedroom. Still, no hard feelings, eh? Do you want some dinner before you go? That's not a euphemism for anything else, by the way – it's just that I still have a lot of turkey stew in the freezer. You look as if you need feeding up.'

'It's getting late,' I said.

'Your call,' said Emma. 'You may as well take the books with you. I can't promise I'll be able to give them to Crispin any time soon. And you never know when you'll need them as an excuse to visit somebody else.'

She was looking at me oddly, as well she might. Perhaps Elsie was right. There had been no reason at all for me to visit Emma. She had told me nothing that she wouldn't have told me on the phone. I had only succeeded in making Emma think I was slightly weird. There was little doubt that, the more she thought about my two visits, the more inexplicable they would become in the context of normal human behaviour. And all for nothing.

'Just one other thing,' I said as I gathered the three volumes together. 'Why did you suspect Crispin was seeing somebody else?'

'Oh, that's easy,' she said. 'Henry Holiday phoned me up and told me.'

CHAPTER TWENTY-ONE

'I'm not interrupting anything?'

'No,' said Elsie.

'It isn't biscuit time?'

'Not quite, but thank you for the reminder. You have my full attention.'

'I've just got back from Brighton.'

'But that's *much* too early. It's scarcely seven minutes to biscuit time.'

'I know what time it is.'

'If you're going to spend the night with somebody you have to stay where you are. You can't just keep bouncing backwards and forwards across Sussex.'

'I'm not going to spend the night with anyone.'

'Did you make a clumsy and ineffective pass at her, after which she told you to piss off back where you came from?'

'That has nothing to do with you.'

'I thought so. Well, it's clearly too late to phone for my advice now.'

'That's not what I want your advice on. Emma Vynall had a row with her husband after she'd been tipped off he was having a relationship with somebody.'

'Crispin was always having a relationship with somebody.'

'Yes, but guess who the tip-off came from?'

'Her best friend?'

'Henry Holiday.'

'Henry didn't think to mention that to you?'

'No.'

'Of course, he may not be proud of snitching on Crispin.'

'No.'

'But didn't you say that Emma hardly knew Henry?'

'She said she'd talked to him once or twice.'

'Well, if one of those occasions was when he phoned her with the glad tidings . . .'

'His act of kindness wasn't inspired by his close friendship with Emma Vynall.'

'In which case,' said Elsie, 'he must have hated Crispin Vynall's guts big time.'

'Yes,' I said.

'Or Emma's lying,' said Elsie. 'Maybe there's something between Emma and Henry.'

'I don't think so,' I said. 'She said she hardly knew him.'

'Ethelred,' said Elsie. 'Basic lesson in human nature for you. It is perfectly possible for a beautiful woman with access to blonde hair dye to tell the occasional fib. You may find it difficult to believe, but it happens. Think back to your first wife.'

'My only wife,' I said.

'That's true. Why do I think of you as having a string of failed marriages?'

I wondered if I should explain to Elsie that I did not regard my marriage to Geraldine as a complete failure and that we had both enjoyed several happy years together. It was true that she had never shared my interest in crime fiction and I had never shared her interest in shagging my best friend, but in other respects we were as compatible as most couples are. But Elsie's agile mind had moved on.

'OK, let's go with your theory that blondes never lie. That means that Henry hated Crispin? Why? Could Crispin have been slagging him off on the Internet, not as Thrillseeker but under some other *nom de sockpuppet*?'

'Possibly. But you still have to ask why?'

'I did. I asked it a moment ago. Still, here we go again: why?'

'I don't know. It's like a badly constructed novel. Everything slightly askew. Nothing quite fitting together.'

'Yes, you said that before.'

'Yes, but I've thought about it since then. What if this whole thing is some fiction dreamt up by Crispin? What if he wants us to think he's vanished and that something terrible has happened to him? So he dreams up this scheme by which he can slip away unnoticed on New Year's Eve, leaving Henry looking as if he's a murderer? Then he plants all sorts of clues along the way.'

'Why Henry?'

'I don't know – but there's clearly bad blood there of some sort.'

'OK, but if that's true, why text Henry to tell him that he's alive and well?'

'That's what I mean. The plot is full of inconsistencies.'

'It doesn't sound like a Crispin Vynall novel, then. Say what you like, he can put a plot together. More like one of your own novels, when you think about it.'

'That's a little harsh,' I said.

'Not according to Thrillseeker.'

'You mean according to Crispin,' I said. 'What now?'

'Biscuit time!' Elsie announced.

'Is it?'

'It is in Hampstead.'

'I see.'

'I'll call you tomorrow,' said Elsie. 'It's possible I may have some answers for you by then, though it's equally possible that I won't.'

'OK,' I said.

'Jaffa Cakes or Jammy Dodgers?' she added. But I don't think she was talking to me.

'I've just got back from Emma Vynall's,' I said to Henry.

'You've been there *again*?' There was more than a little concern in his voice.

'There were other questions I wanted to ask her.'

'You could have phoned her. You're phoning me,' said Henry.

'I might not have discovered what I discovered.'

'Which was . . . ?'

'Henry, why did you tell Emma that Crispin was

sleeping with a friend of hers? That's why Crispin walked out. They had an argument over it – except it wasn't even true. It was just something you had invented.'

There was a long pause.

'Is that what Emma said?'

'I'd scarcely be making it up. Why did you do it?'

Another pause.

'I didn't.'

'She says you did.'

'Ethelred, you must have seen how she's drinking these days? She always did put it away, but she must be on a couple of bottles a day now.'

'I suppose so.'

'She gets a bit . . . well, confused. She hardly knows where she is sometimes. You must have noticed that?'

'So you didn't phone her?'

'No, I did phone. Of course I did. It was between Christmas and New Year. I'd been talking to Crispin about New Year's Eve. He'd mentioned that he and Emma had had a row and she'd pretty much thrown him out.'

'I thought you said you hadn't talked to Crispin about that.'

'I didn't talk to him on New Year's Eve about it. This was a few days before. Anyway, it was clear that he wasn't going to contact Emma, so I did – just to say that he was safe, and that she shouldn't worry. She was very, very drunk that evening and it took a while for me to get the message across. *She* kept telling *me* that Crispin was having a relationship with a friend of hers – not the other way round. I wasn't that interested, to tell you the truth. I just wanted her to understand that everything was OK. I obviously failed miserably.'

'Henry, you and Crispin were on good terms – right up to the last time you saw him?'

'Yes, of course.'

'You remember this reviewer, Thrillseeker, who was giving me so many one-star reviews on Amazon?'

'Was that his name?'

'It turns out he was Crispin.'

'Crispin was giving you one-star reviews under an alias?'

'Yes.'

'What did you say he was calling himself?'

'Thrillseeker.'

'Why?'

'It's just how the Internet works. People use these aliases.'

'Gosh! So, how did you work it out?'

'He gave himself away in a discussion group – he forgot he'd signed in under that alias. He said "I" when he should have said "he".'

'That's impressive detection work.'

'I wondered . . . if he'd done the same thing to you?'

'I hardly ever read reviews for my own books on Amazon, so I've no idea. You'll have to show me how it all works – how you do reviews online.'

'Yes, OK. Thanks for your own review of my books, by the way – the one in the *Telegraph*, I mean. I thought you had some really interesting things to say about the way my books have developed since—'

'Yes, of course. Glad you liked it. I've got to go now, Ethelred. Let me know if you come up with anything else.'

'Well . . .' I said. I had planned to tell him that Crispin's text message had really been for him. But I was beginning to wonder if that was so. If Crispin was indeed out there pulling the strings, maybe it had been intended for me all along. Maybe I was being drip-fed information as and when Crispin thought I needed to have it and for reasons I did not understand.

I might have asked Henry what he thought of that theory. But he had long since hung up.

CHAPTER TWENTY-TWO

From the journal of Elsie Thirkettle

Ethelred was right, of course. His marriage to Geraldine had been inexplicably happy. He must have been aware that she was playing away, but he somehow managed to disregard it, the way an oyster coats a bit of grit with nacre until it is in possession of a pearl. Of course, the pearl is sod-all use to the oyster, but there's a limit to what can be done with analogy, metaphor, simile and all the other crap writers use. My point is simply that Ethelred has a great but little used capacity to be genuinely happy. He wasn't always the morose git that he is now. He says so himself. He tells me I'd be amazed how much he enjoyed life in the old days before I knew him.

I've had a theory for a long time about Ethelred's love life. I sometimes think that he feels he doesn't deserve to be happy. Maybe he reckons he let Geraldine down in some way – that if he'd been a better husband she wouldn't have needed anyone else. Maybe he reckons he let himself down – that he should have done more to keep her than just saying: 'are you absolutely sure about that?' when she said she was leaving. These days he has the same relationship with love that a bulimic teenager does with food. He'll bolt it down, but half an hour later he's throwing it all up again and looking sorry for himself.

Or, if that's overanalysing things a bit, let's just say he's a dickhead.

It was the relationship between Henry and the Vynall family that was really starting to interest me, though. If Ethelred fancied Emma, then why shouldn't Henry do the same? Of course, Emma was too old for him, but then so were his bow ties and waistcoats. I could see Henry getting a bit of a crush on her the same way as Ethelred, and maybe feeling protective towards her, the same way that Ethelred usually felt about this or that bitch who wanted to get her claws into him. The difference was that Henry would actually notice that Crispin was not treating the lady right.

I also still wondered if Crispin was reviewing Henry under a different alias. I decided to check Henry's reviews and see if there were any patterns there and – hey, what do you know? – there were no trolls after him but he had an admirer. Somebody calling themselves Sussexreader thought he was brill.

Here's an example of what Sussexreader thought of one of Henry's books, and posted only a day or so ago:

Henry Holiday is emerging as one of the most exciting talents of his generation of crime writers. With an older cohort of authors nolonger delivering the goods, young wordsmiths such as Holiday are stepping up to the mark in what is rightly being described as a new Golden Age of crime. Though he has been compared to Crispin Vynall, Holiday's work actually has much greater depth and subtlety. The characterisation in his novels is excellent. In this book, the complex relationship between the young artist, Zak Holbein, and his mentor is carefully delineated. The murder of the mentor, skilfully described in just the right amount of detail, sets off a chain of events that drags Zak into a world of gangs, drug dealing and prostitution. Katja, the drug baron's daughter and Zak's ally, is as brilliantly drawn as any character I can think of in any book in the past twenty years.

And so on and blah-de-blah-de-blah. There were ten reviews in all – much the same as the one above. Sussexreader, a bit like Thrillseeker, seemed to concentrate mainly on one single writer he admired, though that is not completely unknown on Amazon. I checked his reviews for other writers. Nothing for Ethelred, good or bad. Nothing for Crispin Vynall. A couple of nice five-star reviews for Peter James and one each for Peter Lovesey, Joan Moules and Simon Brett, all Sussex-based, suggesting that Sussexreader took the 'Sussex' bit of his alias seriously and also read widely within the genre. Everything suggested he was knowledgeable and literate.

Yet there was something about them that was vaguely familiar – as if I'd read the guy's work before.

I needed to talk to somebody who knew Crispin well,

and I doubted that I could pitch up on Emma's doorstep with a copy of *Murderous Hampstead* (say) and hope to question her without her suspecting anything. Who else would know him well, I wondered?

That's why I have just phoned Mary Devlin Jones, and arranged to meet her in Holborn tomorrow morning.

CHAPTER TWENTY-THREE

Extract from a tape recording. The two people whose voices feature on the tape would appear to be Elsie Thirkettle (ET) and Mary Devlin Jones (MDJ). Diary entries point to the date being on or about 10 January. The background noise and the opening conversation suggest a cafe.

MDJ: . . . that you have there?

ET: No. Absolutely not.

MDJ: I could have sworn that I saw a tape recorder in your bag when you leant across to it.

ET: Oh, that. You mean the tape recorder in my *bag*.

MDJ: Yes.

ET: *That* tape recorder . . .

MDJ: Yes.

ET: I brought it along because I need to record an interview later with one of my writers.

MDJ: But you didn't just switch it on?

ET: No.

MDJ: OK. Because, if you had, it would be a bit weird.

ET: Right. Definitely. So, I think that's everything. Your skinny latte. My hot chocolate with whipped cream and more chocolate on top. Biscuits. Do you think we need more biscuits?

MDJ: I'm good.

ET: Morally or biscuit-wise? Ha, ha!

MDJ: Just biscuit-wise. Thank you.

ET: Don't mention it.

MDJ: It was great to hear from you out of the blue. Obviously I'm very pleased you wanted to meet up, since I've just left my last agent.

ET: Yes, I'd heard that. I've always been a great admirer of your writing, Mary. Could you just talk me through what you've done?

MDJ: But you've read the books, obviously?

ET: Obviously. Still, talk me through it, anyway.

MDJ: Well, *Blood on the Cutting Room Floor* was the first.

ET: That's the one that won the CWA New Writing Award?

MDJ: Yes. They only ran that particular competition for a couple of years, so I was lucky to make it. I first got the idea for it . . .

ET: The book was described as . . . [rustling of papers] . . . a fine debut, very much in the style of Stuart McBride and Crispin Vynall.

MDJ: Is that Marcel Berlins in *The Times*?

ET: Yes. Very much in the style of Crispin Vynall, he says . . .

MDJ: And Stuart McBride.

ET: But also Crispin Vynall.

MDJ: Yes. That's what the review says. Both of those writers.

ET: You knew Crispin quite well in those days. The two of you were pretty close?

MDJ: Close? Oh, I get it. It's back to this business that Crispin wrote the bloody thing for me, isn't it? Is somebody spreading rumours again? I honestly thought I was free of that crap now. Jeez, some people must have very little to do.

ET: So, he didn't write it?

MDJ: Are you sure that tape recorder is off? I think I can see a red light. Or are you running a micro-brothel in your handbag?

ET: Ha, ha!

MDJ: So *is* it turned on?

ET: Ha, ha!

MDJ: Meaning it is?

ET: Absolutely not.

MDJ: [uncertainly] OK. Whatever.

ET: So, did he give you any help? You and he were

a bit of an item . . . I mean, I can see how it might happen. Innocently. Was the book really one hundred per cent yours?

MDJ: I can't believe you asked me that question. Do I actually have to give you an answer?

ET: That's why I asked the question.

MDJ: OK, I can see that, if you are going to be my agent, we need to clear one or two things up. It got in the way of my relationship with my last agent, to be perfectly honest.

ET: Your last agent being . . .

MDJ: Janet Francis.

ET: The same agent as Crispin?

MDJ: Yes.

ET: Just a thought – she wasn't jealous of you and Crispin? I mean, she didn't fancy Crispin herself?

MDJ: I don't think so. I mean, she's much too old for him.

ET: She'd be about the same age as he is.

MDJ: That's what I mean.

ET: So it was just the whole plagiarism thing, then, that caused the problems between you and Janet?

MDJ: Except there wasn't any plagiarism. Let's just get this over, shall we? If it helps at all, I admit it – I mean the infatuated with Crispin Vynall bit. In those days what I was writing was very much Vynall pastiche – a bit the way Henry Holiday now writes Vynall pastiche, only with decent plots. I admired the bloody man – Crispin, I mean. I thought he was the cat's bollocks. I tried to imitate him. It's not that surprising that he liked it as a judge for that competition. I had a bit of an inside track, you might say. And he helped me edit it before it went to the publisher – I didn't have an agent until Crispin introduced me to his – but *that was all*. It was *my* bloody book, OK? Sorry, did I splash you with that coffee?

ET: Only a bit. Maybe if you didn't wave your cup around like that . . .

MDJ: Sorry.

ET: But after the book came out. You and Crispin saw a lot of each other?

MDJ: I'm really, really sorry. I'll pay for the dry-cleaning if you like. Shall I get some more paper napkins for you?

181

ET: No, I'm good. But I mean, why not go out with him? The fact that he's married apart, of course. I'll grant you he's got a few wrinkles, but he has money and he has influence.

MDJ: True. I suppose that's a good summary of why I slept with him. But it had *no connection with the prize*. I won that fair and square.

ET: *Of course* you did.

MDJ: I did discuss the second book with him. A bit. But his suggestions were . . . well, odd. He thought I should introduce elements of the supernatural – cross-over horror and crime thriller. And I did try, but it never felt comfortable. That's probably why that one never really worked out. I don't think he wanted the second book to be a success, to be quite honest. He wanted a dutiful handmaiden, not a competitor.

ET: Then he dumped you.

MDJ: As he had dumped others in the past. One of these days somebody's going to bump him off, just like one of the characters from his books.

ET: One day?

MDJ: Well, at some point in the future. I can't be more specific than that.

ET: He's alive and well now?

MDJ: As far as I know. I haven't actually seen him since last June, but I'd have heard if something had happened . . . or do you mean . . . ?

ET: No. I don't mean anything. But you're certain you haven't killed him?

MDJ: Only fictionally.

ET: Book three.

MDJ: Yes, he was in that, thinly disguised. It's the way we writers get revenge. It's not much, but it's better than nothing. Crispin said he sometimes did the same thing in his books – a thinly disguised caricature of somebody he disliked, clearly identifiable for those who knew, but always just on the right side of libel.

ET: He did a few of those?

MDJ: So he said.

ET: And they'd have upset people?

MDJ: That was the plan.

ET: Can you remember any names?

MDJ: He was always a bit cagey about that for obvious
      reasons. I know the ineffectual blackmailer
      in his third book was supposed to be Johnny
      Rayne.'

ET: His agent before he signed up with Janet Francis?

MDJ: Yes.

ET: He died of a heart attack last year, so it can't
      be him.

MDJ: Can't have been him doing what?

ET: Nothing. Nothing at all. Who is Crispin
      seeing now?

MDJ: In addition to his wife? Or doesn't that count?

ET: They seem to have split up.

MDJ: Wow! I didn't see that one coming. She finally
      gave him the push? Good for her.

ET: So I heard. Who was he consorting with at
      Bristol last year?

MDJ: Nobody really. I mean, all sorts of things go on
      at conferences like that, but nobody likes to

make it too obvious with their agents and publishers and readers all hanging around. You never know who's going to tweet a photo of you chatting in some cosy corner. One moment nobody knows, the next it's gone to 10,000 followers, and that's before the re-tweets. Betrayal's no longer the polite, leisurely thing it once was. Since you ask, however, I did see him in the bar quite a lot with a Swedish writer – Elisabeth Söderling? But I wouldn't want to spread gossip. There may have been nothing in it. That's *Söderling* with a couple of dots above the O.

[Unidentified voice]: You all done with that?

ET: Gosh, did I finish them? Could you bring some more? With chocolate?

[Unidentified voice]: We don't bring them. You have to go up and order them from the counter.

ET: Do I? You couldn't fetch one little packet? No? OK, I'll just grab that . . .

[Obscure noises for some minutes]

[Second unidentified voice]: Two pounds seventy.

ET: For *that*? Two pounds seventy?

185

[Second unidentified voice]: You can put it back if
you don't want it . . . well, no, not if you've
taken a bite out of it obviously.

ET: Fair enough. But two pounds seventy . . .

[Sound of coins being counted out very slowly]

[Second unidentified voice]: Thank you.

[Obscure noises then a thump]

MDJ: You shouldn't have dragged your bag all the
way over there. I'd have watched it.

ET: I didn't think of that.

MDJ: Or were you worried I would fiddle with your
tape recorder while you were away?

ET: No. Of course not. It's off. None of this is being
recorded. I cannot stress that too strongly. I
suppose you don't know where Crispin is now?

MDJ: Why should I?

ET: No reason. If he vanished suddenly, you've no
idea where he might have gone? Where does
Elisabeth Söderling live?'

MDJ: Stockholm. Can we talk about my work for

a bit? And your terms? I assume that's why we're here? Crispin's a bit . . . well . . . in the past. I don't write that sort of thing any more. And, like I say, the story about him writing my book is rubbish. I just wish I knew who'd started that one. I could murder them . . .

ET: Yes, of course. Your current work. So you do cat detectives now?

MDJ: No. My detective owns some cats. Have you actually *read* the books?

ET: You bet! Great books, all of them. I mean the cats help out . . .

MDJ: Only in their capacity as cats.

ET: One's called Hercule?

MDJ: It seemed amusing.

ET: [polite laugh]

MDJ: Yes, about as amusing as that. Certainly not more. So, in principle, would you want to take me on? You represent Peter Fielding, don't you?

ET: Ethelred? Yes. But don't worry – I represent some very successful writers too.

MDJ: It's just that I've always had a soft spot for him – Ethelred, I mean.

ET: Why?

MDJ: Because he's a gent, I suppose. A throwback to a better and more civilised age. I've never heard him slagging off other writers. Or agents. He's a genuinely nice person. Really well liked. And I sort of owe him.

ET: Whatever.

MDJ: So, are you interested in representing me? I understand that you might not wish to say anything on the record but . . .

ET: Good point. Hold on. I just need to check something in my bag. Ah, yes, here it is. Now we can talk properly . . .

RECORDING ENDS

CHAPTER TWENTY-FOUR

From the journal of Elsie Thirkettle

My meeting with Mary Devlin Jones went well. One thing that I am now convinced of is that she was stitched up over the plagiarism. But by whom?

She had omitted one small fact from her account. The most effective witness in her defence might have been Crispin, but he had entered the fray somewhat late in the day with a short and rather bland statement to the effect that he had merely helped her with some editing. Well, that's all you get if you have written the person concerned into one of your novels and then subjected their alter ego to a couple of weeks of excruciating torture over 150 pages.

But it was unlikely, however sore he was feeling, that Crispin would have started the rumour himself. Emma, conversely, was both sufficiently well informed and sufficiently well motivated to screw Mary's budding career.

I was fairly sure that a little more research might trace the original rumour back to her – I was less sure that it would help solve the problem of where Crispin was and whether Henry had killed him.

Back, then, to the death threat letter.

I got the sheet of paper out from the place where I carefully store such things, and re-examined it. It was on cheap A4 of the sort sold in supermarkets pretty well anywhere. I was pretty sure there'd be no fingerprints on it. There'd be mine and Ethelred's, of course, but probably not the writer's. The ink was ballpoint – probably also from a supermarket or a freebie picked up at a conference. The block capitals were neat and without much character. The various spelling mistakes were clearly deliberate – a literate man pretending to be otherwise.

JUST A POLITE WARNING, ETHELLRED, TO LET YOU KNO TO STOP STICKING YOUR NOSE INTO OTHER PEOPLE'S BIZNIS. YOU'LL STAY OUT OF IT IF YOU KNOW WOT'S GOOD FOR YOU. YOU'RE NOLONGER WRITING CHEAP AMATEUR DETECTIVE FICTION. IT'S VERY DIFFERENT WHEN IT'S REAL LIFE AND YOU DON'T UNDERSTAND ITS INNS AND OUTS. YOU AREN'T LORD PETER WHIMSY, WHATEVER YOU MAY THINK. AND YOU WOULDN'T WANT TO BE THE SECOND BODY THAT SHOWS UP, WOULD YOU? BE WARNED; WE KNOW ICKSACTLY WOT YOU'RE DOING. A FREND.

Most of the 'mistakes' were blatant, clumsy things. It was the product of a writer of fiction with too much time on his hands. 'Inns and outs', for example, was an improbable error, coming from somebody who could spell 'amateur'. And, I noticed, it was not only Ethelred's name that was misspelt. Lord Peter Wimsey had suffered the same fate. But there was one error that, for me at least, stood out the most. Most of us grow up with a blind spot for one or two words – however many times our spellchecker puts us right. In an uncorrected handwritten note they are almost a signature. Running together 'no' and 'longer' into a single word looked like one of these. After all, we have 'nowhere' and 'nobody' and 'nothing'. Why not 'nolonger'? I used to do it myself, so I tend to notice it when it does crop up. And I was sure I'd seen it before very recently – and more than once. The question was where?

I made myself a coffee and opened a packet of chocolate biscuits. But the answer to the question was so obvious that I had eaten scarcely three-quarters of them before the answer was revealed. It was Thrillseeker on Amazon:

> *In* A Bad Way to Die, *Joe Smith finds himself the only witness to a gang-land killing. Bravely he goes to the police, who promise him protection if he will testify, but a corrupt officer lets the killers know where to find him and Joe is nolonger safe.*

Well, well, the author of the death threats and Thrillseeker (that is to say, Crispin) both thought there was such a word as 'nolonger'. I went through Sussexreader's reviews too:

> *Henry Holiday is emerging as one of the most exciting talents of his generation of crime writers.*

With an older cohort of authors nolonger delivering the goods, young wordsmiths such as Holiday are stepping up to the mark.

Interesting.

I looked again at the death threat and the other spelling error I had just noticed. Maybe that too would show up in the Amazon reviews? It certainly rang a bell. Another trawl produced this, from Thrillseeker's review of 15 December:

At the bottom of the heap are all books featuring amateur detectives and quilt-makers. Sadly this book fails to live up to even the last of these. The police in Buckfordshire clearly follow procedures known only to them and Lord Peter Whimsy.

So, two very distinctive misspellings made their appearance both in Crispin's Amazon reviews and the death threat. It was almost like a fingerprint.

But I knew I'd seen the 'nolonger' mistake somewhere else. Where was that? I was throwing the biscuit wrapper in the bin when I finally remembered – it had been in the text message from Crispin to Ethelred. That pretty much sealed it.

Of course, I realised that it might not stand up in court, but it was clear enough to me. Crispin had, for reasons best known to himself, set up multiple sockpuppet accounts to praise some authors (such as himself and Henry Holiday) and rubbish others (such as Ethelred). Then he had vanished, having sent a death threat letter to Ethelred that implied that he had been murdered. And leaving Henry under the impression that he had killed Crispin. It was, in its own crooked way, ingenious. But why on earth would he want to do it?

Anyway, why would Crispin big up Henry on Amazon? Even to the extent, if I remembered correctly, of admitting Henry was the better writer. How was that a necessary part of anything? It was true that Henry was a blatant imitator of Crispin's style. But even if Crispin had loved Henry's books to bits, there would surely be better ways of doing it than anonymous reviews on Amazon.

And why then send a text to Ethelred, in effect blowing his cover? Could somebody else have sent the text? The text was, when you thought about it, outright proof that Crispin was alive.

I reread Sussexreader's reviews, looking for the smallest detail that might prove useful. Then I noticed the big detail. The most recent was dated 7 January. So, there was further evidence that Crispin had not died on New Year's Eve. Dead men do not review on Amazon.

I decided to phone Ethelred in the morning. There were unanswered questions, but I was as sure as I could be that Crispin was alive. I'd also cracked the riddle of who sent the death threat. And if Crispin had indeed now fled the country, Ethelred could be sure that he wouldn't be getting any more of them.

CHAPTER TWENTY-FIVE

The envelope was lying on the doormat. It was six-fifteen in the morning. I stood for a moment, clutching the cup of coffee I had just made. Then I picked it up and opened it.

WELL, ETHELRED, YOU DIDN'T HEED MY WARNING AND NOW YOU ARE IN IT UP TO YOUR NECK, AREN'T YOU? I KNOW WHERE YOU'VE BEEN. I NO YOU TOOK HENRY HOLIDAY TO DIDLING GREEN AND I NO YOU DROVE TO BRIGHTON TO VISIT EMMA. BUT SHE'S NOT EXACTLY BIN HONEST WITH YOU, HAS SHE? YOU NEED TO TALK TO HER AGAIN AND GET HER TO TELL YOU THE TROOF THIS TIME. YOU'RE GOING TO DIE ETHELRED, BUT I'M AT LEAST GOING TO GIVE YOU THE CHANCE TO FIND OUT FIRST. SO, WHY DON'T YOU RING EMMA AGAIN. HERE'S HER NUMBER, JUST IN CASE YOU FORGOT IT. GOOD LUCK, MORON.

The number that followed was indeed Crispin's home number.

Again, I was left with the feeling that the various errors in the letter were deliberate. How else could I explain the correct spelling of 'been' on line three, apparently forgotten completely by the time the writer reached line six. Or the inexplicable double misspelling of 'know'. And yet there was not an apostrophe or comma out of place.

I knew I had not been followed to Didling Green. Or to Brighton. The question was whether anyone had needed to. If they already knew Henry had been to Didling Green on New Year's Eve, how far would they have to follow us to guess that was our destination? If they knew I had phoned Emma, it would not take much ingenuity to guess I might have followed it up with a visit? And yet, there was a certainty in the note that contradicted the idea that this was mere guesswork.

I called Elsie.

'I've had a death threat.'

'Yes, Ethelred, I know. I saw it. Actually I've got it in my handbag.'

'I'm talking about a second one. It's just like the first one – I mean it's all in capitals and misspelt. It says I'm going to die.'

'You can't have a second one. I was about to phone you. I'd just worked the whole thing out and a second death threat is impossible. Crispin wrote the first one. And he's now out of the country. Does it have a Swedish stamp or anything?'

'No, it was delivered by hand, like the last one.'

'Then Crispin's lying about having left the country,' she said.

'I don't understand,' I said. 'Anyway, why should he be in Sweden?'

Elsie then explained, with due reference to her unrivalled cleverness, how she had established that the death-threater, Thrillseeker and Sussexreader were all Crispin. I expressed admiration, though perhaps less than she felt was her due.

'So what does the letter say this time?' she asked.

'It says somebody knows exactly where I've been. And I'm going to die.'

'Well, unless you had imagined you were immortal, that won't have come as a shock. The days of our years are three score and ten.'

'I don't think the writer is making either a philosophical or a theological point. He implies he can speed things along.'

'And he's encouraging you to talk to Emma again?'

'Yes.'

'I don't get it. Why does Crispin want you to talk to Emma? Unless he's making the point that the whole thing is revenge for your nocturnal activities at Harrogate.'

'There were no nocturnal activities at Harrogate.'

'I bet there were. You just didn't get your share of them. I'm sure Crispin had plenty.'

'That could be. There and in other places.'

'Does the name Elisabeth Söderling mean anything to you?' Elsie asked.

'A reasonably successful writer of gloom-laden Nordic crime.'

'She was with Crispin at Bristol, apparently.'

'Possibly. Is that why you think Crispin's in Stockholm?'

'That was my theory. The latest letter rather puts a hole in it, though.'

'Well, I don't think it's worth my going out to Sweden just in case,' I said. 'But I do think it's worth phoning Emma to see what it is she hasn't told me.'

'But that's what Crispin wants you to do.'

'I can't see there's any problem in my talking to Emma again,' I said.

'I have a better idea for tracking Crispin down.'

'Really? What?'

'Never you mind. Just be impressed when I let you know where he is. And in the meantime, ignore that letter completely.'

'And not phone Emma?'

'Don't even think about it,' said Elsie. '*It's what he wants you to do.*'

She was right, of course. It was indeed what he wanted me to do. But in the end I didn't need to phone. Emma phoned me.

CHAPTER TWENTY-SIX

'What are you playing at, Ethelred?'

I was used to Elsie beginning conversations with me like this, but not usually other people.

'Sorry, Emma, I'm not sure what you mean,' I said.

For a moment the phone seemed to have gone dead. Then she spoke again. 'Are you saying it wasn't you?'

'Wasn't me what?'

'Wasn't you who reported Crispin missing?'

'Somebody has reported Crispin missing?' I said.

'The police came round this morning. They said he had been reported as a missing person. I felt a bit stupid having to say I had no idea where he was. I mean, if anyone was going to report him, it was really down to me, wasn't it?'

'Anyone can report a missing person.'

'Yes, but if the missing person is married you'd expect

his wife to notice first. Somebody else reporting it suggests a negligent approach on my part.'

'Well, I don't know any more about it all than you do. Somebody else has clearly noticed he's gone.'

'Clearly. Who?'

'I don't know. Emma, perhaps I should have told you all this sooner, but there's something very odd going on. I've had a strange letter . . .'

'Strange in what way?'

'A death threat,' I said.

'A death threat? Saying what?'

'Saying I'd be next.'

'*Next*? Next after whom?'

'They may have implied Crispin . . .'

'You mean you're saying Crispin's *dead*?'

'No, the letter said that. I'm as sure as I can be that Crispin is alive. I had that text. But I think it's possible that Crispin actually sent me the letters himself.'

'Crispin sent you a letter saying he was dead and that he was going to murder you?'

'Put like that it doesn't sound too probable, I admit.'

'And why would he do that?'

'Perhaps because he thought something had happened between us at Harrogate?'

'Don't be stupid, Ethelred. Anyway, you're saying you were told in a letter that Crispin was dead, but didn't think it was worth passing on that information to me? You came over here twice, but that bit skipped your memory?'

I realised that, if Crispin was indeed dead, I had not broken the news of his death terribly well. Of course, he wasn't dead, but from Emma's point of view, I was now somebody who insisted on personal visits when out-of-date textbooks were the issue, but who was quite happy to mention, over the phone and purely in passing, that her husband might possibly have been murdered. I could see why she might find this odd.

'I don't think that anything like that has happened,' I said very quickly. 'I think he has simply gone off somewhere. Perhaps he wants us to think he is dead . . .'

'But he sent you a text message.'

'In confidence. I wasn't to tell anyone.'

'But why should he want the rest of us to think he was dead?'

'I don't know. You mentioned the Christie thing.'

'*You* mentioned the Christie thing. I just said that he had vanished before. Anyway, Agatha Christie didn't send death threats to all and sundry.'

'True.'

'And I said: when he vanished before he was just away for a few days. No fuss. No amateur dramatics. Just a four-day-long sulk. Crispin wouldn't have sent you death threats. Have you told the police?'

'Not as yet,' I said.

'Why, Ethelred? In the name of God, why? You come round here and ask me all sorts of questions. You seem desperately interested to know where Crispin is. But, having been told in writing that Crispin may be dead, you decide to keep it to yourself?'

'Yes' was the simple answer to this question. I took it up one notch from there.

'Sort of,' I said.

'When did you get this note?'

'The first one? About a week ago.'

'You've had more than one?'

'Yes.'

'Both implying that Crispin has been killed?'

'You could say that.'

'And you've reported neither?'

'No.'

'Why?'

Would telling her that Henry had more or less confessed to murdering Crispin make my actions more or less plausible? I could see that it might not stand to my credit in Emma's eyes.

'I can't explain,' I said. 'There are things I can't tell you at the moment. But I think you do know where Crispin is.'

'Ethelred, you are now really trying my patience. I do not know where he is. I've told you that.'

'Are you sure?'

'What do you think? If you ask me any more stupid questions, I'm hanging up.'

'OK. But do you know anything about a writer called Elisabeth Söderling?'

The phone went dead. I decided not to call her back.

I could only hope Elsie had had more success. I tried phoning her and got a recorded message, inviting me to speak after the tone. But I felt I needed to gather my thoughts. I needed to phrase things in a way that didn't make me appear a complete idiot. A text might be better. I sat down and started to compose one that would do this news justice.

CHAPTER TWENTY-SEVEN

From the journal of Elsie Thirkettle

The one person who ought to know exactly where a writer is at any time of the night or day is his agent. Writers are more like dogs than cats, really. You can let a cat out and trust it to come home at dinner time, whereas dogs end up stuck down rabbit holes or helplessly drifting downstream, heading for the weir but still holding firmly in their teeth the valuable stick they plunged into the river to retrieve. There are good arguments for microchipping writers if vets could be persuaded to do it at a reasonable price.

Anyway, it struck me that if anyone knew Crispin's current whereabouts it would be his agent. The only problem was that Janet Francis is a stuck-up cow who, for some reason, thinks I run a tinpot agency on the outer fringes of the literary world where the sun rises only briefly even in midsummer. Just because I answer my own phone, whereas you have to talk to about twenty of her minions just to get to say hello to her, doesn't mean her agency is more important than mine. So, I waited patiently as her receptionist put me through to her secretary and then her secretary, after a ten-minute grilling on my intentions, put me through to her. Finally Janet Francis spoke to me. The temperature in the room dropped about four degrees as she did so.

'Elsie! How delightful to hear from you. We don't seem to move in quite the same circles these days.'

'I don't move in circles at all,' I said. 'I prefer straight lines.'

'Do you? Well, as my secretary will have told you, I'm just dashing out. One of my Swedish writers is over and I have to be at Foyles for a signing. You know what it's like. Or maybe not. Could I call you back later?'

'I'm trying to track down Crispin Vynall,' I said.

'Would you like one of my people to pass him a message?'

'How many people do you have?'

'Enough to take messages. Now, shall I get one of them to do that?'

'No, I want to talk to Crispin myself. Do you have contact details for him?'

'Obviously we do. I'm his agent.'

'I mean recent details. He's not answering his mobile and I can't get him on his Brighton number. You know he's left his wife?'

There was a short silence. She clearly didn't know. One small point to the agent without a PA, then.

'No, he can be difficult to get on his mobile sometimes.

He switches it off when he doesn't want to be disturbed. The landline is usually better. I think he did give us a new contact number – another landline.' There was another pause, then she said: 'Yes, it's here on the card. He gave it to us just after Christmas.'

'So, what is the number?'

'I can't tell you that, can I?'

'You can if you want to.'

'Hmmm, yes, but I don't want to. If you have a query, you could email it to my assistant, Tuesday.'

'I can't wait that long.'

'No, my new assistant is called Tuesday. You can email her today.'

'I need to speak to Crispin myself, not leave a message.'

'Well, good luck with finding his number then. Sorry, Elsie, I really have to go.'

Somewhere in Soho a well-manicured talon rested briefly on top of a gleaming handset. Then, no doubt gathering her handbag and Filofax together, she flew from the room.

Filofax? Yes, I do mean that. Janet's great days had been in the eighties and nineties. That was when she had discovered Crispin and a couple of other best-selling authors. The twenty-first century had proved a bit of a disappointment for her. Deep down I think she still yearned for shoulder pads, eyeliner and frosted lipgloss. I had no doubt that her card index was immaculate, but it would be a card index all the same – not a computer system or an entry in her iPhone's contact list. I counted slowly to 100 then phoned her office again.

'Sorry, she's just gone out,' said the receptionist.

'Could you put me through to her new assistant – Tuesday, I think she's called?'

'That's right. Putting you through now.'

'Hi, Tuesday. Elsie Thirkettle here. I was talking to Janet a moment ago and she said she'd let me have Crispin Vynall's new number. But she's apparently gone out. You couldn't look it up for me on the card index in her room, could you?'

One good thing about New People is that they are touchingly eager to please. Give them a month or two and they'll know all too well why you shouldn't divulge random facts about your authors to complete strangers on the phone. But catch them in those delightful first few weeks and they'll give you anything they can lay their little hands on. Bless.

'Yes, of course. Hold on a moment.'

Either she was very close to Janet's office or (more likely) she ran there and back. She was panting slightly as she read from the card.

'There's a home number, which is Brighton . . .'

'It would be a recent entry,' I said. Then I had a moment of inspiration. Thinking of a remark of Ethelred's that Crispin might have been staying quite close to West Wittering, I added: 'I think it begins 01243.'

'That's right,' she said, brightly. If she had had any worries at all that the Data Protection Act applied to her, I had allayed them. She proceeded to read out a number.

'Thank you, my dear,' I said.

'My pleasure,' she said. And she actually meant it.

She was no longer panting, so she was probably quite fit. Fit, bright-eyed and alert. I briefly imaged her jumping around the office, when not otherwise engaged, like a small hind.

I wondered whether to add that Tuesday should tell Janet how pleased I'd been with her. But then I decided that would be too cruel. Let her skip around in her sunny glade for a little longer before the harsh realities of employment at a literary agency finally struck home.

'Oh, and who was Janet off to see?' I asked.

'Elisabeth Söderling,' she said.

'Of course. So, she's in England?'

'Yes.'

'Not in Sweden?'

'No. She's been over here a couple of days. She's signing books at Foyles this afternoon.'

'How long will she be at Foyles?'

'Until six. Janet has another meeting afterwards, though, if you were hoping to catch her.'

'Thank you,' I said. 'You've no idea how helpful you've been.'

CHAPTER TWENTY-EIGHT

From the journal of Elsie Thirkettle

I hung around outside Foyles until about six-fifteen. I watched Janet Francis leave, looking at her sparkly watch and hobble off down the road. She's too old for skirts that are that tight and has, I regret to say, put on a bit of weight since I saw her last. I hid in a doorway as she passed. It wasn't that I was planning to do anything illegal or unethical, but I still didn't want Janet to stop me doing it.

I could see Elisabeth Söderling standing just inside the door, saying her goodbyes to the Foyles staff. I waited until she had left and set off down Tottenham Court Road, then stepped out smartly from my hiding place, waving a book I happened to have in my handbag. 'Miss Söderling!' I called.

She turned and, doubtless thinking I was a fan after a signature, stood there in a resigned sort of way.

'I was just leaving . . .' she said, half-apology, half-justifiable irritation that she'd spent an hour in the place and I'd waited until now.

'Could I have a quick word with you?' I asked.

She looked down at the book and noticed it was one of Peter James's. It was (to be fair) a well-regarded police procedural, which had been on the best-seller list for several weeks and sold a few hundred thousand. But sadly it wasn't one of hers.

'You want me to sign that?'

'Be my guest,' I said. 'But I'd hoped we could have a quiet chat somewhere. I'm an agent.'

'And that's why you want to talk to me?'

'Yes.'

'Francis and Nowak handle my books here in the UK,' she said.

'What do they charge you?'

'Fifteen per cent.'

'I'll do it for seven and a half.'

'Really? As little as that?'

I'd just given her the first figure that came into my head. If I'd been seriously planning to take her on I'd have suggested fourteen and a half to begin with and negotiated from there, a quarter of a percentage point at a time. There would be no profit in seven and a half. On the other hand, I'd have taken her away from Francis and Nowak.

'You bet,' I said.

'I'm not sure I can—'

'Janet's not taking you out to dinner, then?'

'No, she had another appointment. She's always very busy.'

'So am I, but I've got time for my authors. I know a very good restaurant just up the road from here. Well, it's very good for what they charge.'

'I'm not one of your authors.'

'You've still got to eat, though, haven't you? Anyway, I also want to talk to you about Crispin Vynall.'

'That tosser!'

'Indeed, as you say, that tosser. May I congratulate you, Miss Söderling, on your command of the English language? The restaurant is just up here on the left.'

Judging by how little food she ordered, she was not going to be an expensive client. I ordered a little more for myself so that the restaurant didn't think I was being too cheap.

'That's the jumbo hamburger with extra bacon and double chips for you, madam? And just a small salad for you, madam?'

'Yes,' we said simultaneously. 'And ketchup,' one of us added.

While we were waiting for our food Elisabeth had a glass of Pinot Grigio and I had a cup of hot chocolate with cream and extra chocolate and extra cream. (It was cold outside.)

'I was supposed to be meeting Crispin tonight,' said Elisabeth. 'We'd arranged to see each other when I came over, but since New Year I've heard nothing from him – no confirmation of the date, no apology he can't make it.'

We sat in silence for a while. I was puzzled in that I'd started to assume that Crispin had vanished off the radar so effectively by getting a flight over to Sweden. Even after the hand-delivered note, I hadn't quite abandoned the theory – after all he could have an accomplice in Sussex.

'But he was expecting to see you when you were over?'

'Yes. He said he was looking forward to it.'

'And your relationship was . . . well, ongoing?'

'I had thought so. I was obviously wrong.'

I had also assumed that Crispin's disappearance – wherever he was – had been planned in advance. But it now seemed to be a last-minute decision and one that he had kept a secret from pretty much everyone.

'You know he and his wife have split up?' I said.

'Recently?'

'Just before Christmas.'

'He told me they'd split up ages ago. You can't trust men, can you?'

Well, there was Ethelred, but, like his readers, he's a bit special.

'No,' I said.

My phone beeped. There was a text from Ethelred. Normally under these circumstances I would have ignored a text, but I could see Ethelred there, laboriously typing out the words, with many corrections and deletions and much attention to punctuation, his tongue licking his upper lip all the while, his mouth half-open in wonderment at this strange new technology. Then at the end of twenty minutes or so he would have pressed SEND and collapsed back into his chair with relief.

'Hold on,' I said to Elisabeth.

The message (and I was sure that it had taken him a couple of hours to compose it) read: 'Crispin has been reported as a missing person; the police are investigating.'

'From one of your children?' asked Elisabeth.

'You could say that,' I said.

A waiter approached. Elisabeth smiled at him and shook her head.

'I'll have the banana sundae,' I said.

'Extra cream with that?' asked the waiter, flicking open his notepad.

I just stared at him in disbelief. 'Extra cream?' I said. 'Do you think I'm the sort of person who orders extra cream?'

When he returned he brought a large jug and told me to help myself. Silly tosser. Irony only works if you don't overdo it.

CHAPTER TWENTY-NINE

'Missing?' said Elsie. 'So the police think he's dead?'

'No,' I said. 'The report didn't say that. It's just that somebody has reported Crispin missing.'

'So who reported him?'

'Not me or Emma,' I said.

'What if he reported himself missing?' asked Elsie.

'Could you do that? I mean, anyone can make a report, but the police would surely check on the identity of whoever made it. And it would still be a strange thing to do.'

'No stranger than sending you death threats,' said Elsie.

'You've still got that first letter safe I take it?' I asked.

'Naturally. I won't lose it. What about the second one?'

'I dropped it round to Henry. I told him we thought Crispin was the author and he said he wanted to see it. He said he had samples of his handwriting. He's going to let me know what he thinks of it. I'll pick the letter up again later.'

'Did you get any more out of Emma?' she asked.

'Not really. I just ended up making her think I was weird.'

'No shit? How on earth did you manage that?'

'I'm not sure. I think probably . . .'

'Sorry, Ethelred. That was irony.'

'Was it?'

'Yes. OK, tell me, then – what was her reaction to what you told her?'

'Well, she was cross that I hadn't mentioned the death threats before. Then when I asked whether she knew where Crispin was, she got even crosser and hung up on me.'

'Ethelred . . .' Elsie paused for a moment.

'Still here,' I said.

'You don't think that maybe she did kill Crispin? I mean, let's say that Henry did drop Crispin off in Chichester and that he got a train or taxi back to Brighton. So, he shows up at the family home at one o'clock in the morning, completely drunk. He and Emma argue, as they well might. Emma bludgeons him to death with the left-over turkey or whatever is to hand in the kitchen. But she knows that he was out with Henry – the scumbag who lied to her about Crispin and her best friend. So, she reckons she can pin it on him. You phone her with all your questions. She puts two and two together – you are working for Henry. The next thing you know you've got a death threat on your mat, implying that Henry is the killer.'

'I'm not sure she even had my address,' I said.

'But it's all in the CWA Directory, isn't it? Any crime

writer or agent or their friends and relations could get their hands on that.'

'Whoever wrote the letter would have to live close by – it was hand-delivered in the early hours of the morning.'

'Brighton's close enough,' said Elsie. 'And she kept the BMW.'

'But why does the second note tell me to question Emma more closely if she wrote it?'

'To throw you off the scent,' said Elsie.

'I don't think so,' I said.

'She would also have Crispin's phone to hand to send you a text.'

'She said she didn't.'

'Did I explain that blondes can lie?'

'Yes.'

'Anyway,' said Elsie, 'do you want to know the rest of what I've discovered?'

'There's more?'

'Quite a lot more, but I've just had to take on two additional clients because of you,' said Elsie.

'Because of me?'

'Don't keep repeating what I say like an author trying to pad out a very thin book with unnecessary dialogue. That's also annoying. And don't say sorry. That's even more annoying.'

'I wasn't planning to say sorry,' I said.

'Yes, you were. I'm your agent. I know you better than you know yourself, though that isn't saying very much.'

I wondered how to apologise without saying sorry. It probably wasn't worth trying. Paraphrase probably annoyed Elsie most of all.

'Who have you taken on?' I asked.

'Elisabeth Söderling and Mary Devlin Jones.'

'I don't see how having either of them helps me.'

'It was the price of getting the information that you need.'

'Which is?'

'First, Crispin had arranged to meet Elisabeth on her current trip to London. But he hasn't. Nor has he left a message.'

'In view of your low opinion of men generally, wouldn't you say that was par for the course – just clearing off without a word of farewell?'

'Yes, but my opinion of men is in fact much lower than that. There was clearly no-strings-attached sex on offer and he still cleared off. That means his disappearance is not merely odd but unnatural.'

'Men do occasionally decline sex,' I said.

There was a brief hesitation on Elsie's part, as though she might in fact have discovered the same thing.

'At the very least, I don't think his departure was planned,' she said. 'And I've found out that Crispin was staying close to you around Christmas time.'

'Didn't we know that?'

'You assumed it. I proved it.'

'Where was he?'

She read out a phone number.

'Where did you get that?'

'From his agent.'

Well, of course. Why hadn't I thought of that? It would have been so easy. So very easy.

'But Janet Francis didn't say whose number it was?'

'You could say that the way I got it rather precluded that.'

'And I'm now supposed to track him down from the number?' I asked.

'Yes.'

'The number *is* sort of familiar. I could look through my address book and see if it's there.'

'Phone it, Ethelred.'

'Why don't you phone it?'

'Because I've decided that it's your job. It might prove to be another writer, then I'd probably need to take them on as a client too.'

'So, you want me to cold-call the number and ask whether they know why Crispin has vanished and then reported himself missing? I suppose it beats pretending to be from Microsoft and claiming that whoever-it-is has a virus on his computer.'

'Don't be stupid, Ethelred. You'll need to be a bit more subtle than that.'

'I'll look into it,' I said. 'So, what did Mary Devlin Jones have to say?'

'She said she'd like to kill Crispin.'

'In that case it's hardly likely that she has.'

'Unless it's a double bluff.'

'Which people don't do in real life. Was that all?'

'Sort of. We talked about this business of Crispin having written her first book for her.'

'That's what they say.'

'Yes, but *who* says it?' asked Elsie. 'She claims it's not true. So who started the story? I mean, who told you?'

'I'd heard rumours before,' I said. 'On the Internet.'

'Yeah, right,' said Elsie.

I decided to ignore all of the implications in that. 'Emma filled in a lot of the detail, though,' I added.

Elsie paused and then said: 'Mary said she owed you one. What did that mean?'

'It could mean all sorts of things . . .'

'Ethelred, have I ever explained this thing where I can tell when you're lying?'

'OK. I was one of the judges when she won the CWA award.'

'You never told me that.'

'I must have done. I'm sure I said that it was one of the few occasions when I had met Crispin.'

'That's the one where Janet Francis was the other judge?'

'Yes. She didn't prove a very active judge in the end. She just showed up for the final meeting.'

'So you and Crispin did the shortlisting?'

'Yes. But—'

'But? Either you did or you didn't.'

'I was fairly busy then too. I had a deadline. You were pushing for a completed manuscript. Crispin produced a shortlist. I took a quick look through some of the other stories . . .'

'So, Crispin really was in a position to fix things for Mary? All on his own?'

'Arguably. But all three of us signed off on the final decision.'

'In spite of the fact that you hadn't read most of the stories and Janet probably hadn't read any of them?'

'Yes,' I said.

'Of course!' said Elsie. 'That would also explain why Mary signed up with Francis and Nowak. Janet would have used her position as judge to snap up any promising talent. Except, if Janet was on the judging panel and there was any funny business about who wrote the book, then Francis and Nowak wouldn't have taken her on.'

'If Crispin did write the book, we weren't aware of it at the time. That came later.'

'So,' said Elsie, 'of the very small number of people involved in that award – Mary has had her career pretty much destroyed, you've had death threats and Crispin has vanished.'

'But Janet Francis is OK.'

'Early days yet,' said Elsie cheerfully. 'Let's wait and see, shall we?'

CHAPTER THIRTY

It was pretty much inevitable. Early the following day a police car rolled up in my drive and a sergeant got out.

I had the door open even before he had rung the bell and quickly had him seated with a mug of coffee in front of him on the kitchen table. I had of course nothing to tell him – except possibly for Henry's confession that he had killed Crispin on New Year's Eve. It seemed a good idea to get this over as soon as I could.

'Do you know Mr Vynall well?' the sergeant asked.

'No,' I said. 'We're both writers, but I see him only occasionally. We were judges for a CWA award a few years back. I've been on a panel with him at a crime-writing conference. We were talking about whether crime writers should get police procedures correct or whether it's more important to keep the story going.'

The sergeant took a sip of his coffee and expressed no opinion. 'When did you last see him?'

'Probably at Bristol CrimeFest last year.'

'CrimeFest?'

'It's a festival of crime writing – not of crime.'

'I would imagine not. And that was . . .'

'Late May.'

'So, no contact since then? No phone calls or emails?'

'No. But . . .'

'Yes?'

I wondered whether this was a good idea, but he would certainly have spoken to Emma, so it might seem odd to say nothing.

'I have seen his wife, though. A couple of times. I needed to drop some books off.'

'You dropped books off on two occasions?'

'Yes.'

'When was that?'

'In the last few days.'

'Even though you hadn't seen him since May?'

'Yes,' I said.

'I see. Where were you on New Year's Eve, sir?'

'Here. I was watching a programme on meerkats.'

'All evening?'

'No. There was other stuff on too.'

'Do you have any witnesses?'

'About what I was watching?'

'About your being here all evening.'

I would dearly have loved to have been able to say that I had a witness who could confirm the truth of my statement. I hesitated for a moment.

'No,' I said.

'Are you sure about that?'

'Don't you think I'd give you a name if I could?' I said. Then a thought occurred to me. 'Emma Vynall said that Crispin had left home just before Christmas.'

'Yes, sir.'

'And he is still missing now.'

'Yes, sir.'

'So he's been gone two weeks. Why are you asking me specifically about New Year's Eve? Did whoever reported his disappearance say specifically that that is when it was?'

'That is, if I may say so, sir, none of your business. Unless there is something you'd like to tell me about New Year's Eve? Something you know but are keeping from us?'

'There's nothing I want to tell you,' I said.

'Are you sure?'

'Absolutely sure.'

'You seem to have asked Mrs Vynall a lot of questions about Mr Vynall's disappearance? You were quite concerned about whether he had talked about you?'

'I may have said something like that.'

'For any particular reason?'

'No,' I said. 'I was just making conversation.'

'But you yourself were worried about Mr Vynall's disappearance, well before he was reported missing?'

'Yes. You could say that.'

'Mrs Vynall did say that. She said you were very concerned that you couldn't get in contact with him.'

'Yes.'

'So you were *trying* to get in contact with him, then? Even though you say you hadn't seen him for months?'

'Yes, it was . . .' I tried to remember what reason I had given Emma. A book? 'It was about a short story,' I said. 'For an anthology.'

'And you needed the story urgently?'

'Publishers have deadlines,' I said. 'You know what it's like.' I smiled in the hope of sympathy or at least a vague understanding.

'Not really,' he said.

What else had I told Emma? There was the business of the death threats, but that conversation had surely taken place after she had spoken to the police? The point might come where I had to mention them, but for the moment I could avoid mentioning Henry's confession. On the other hand, if I said nothing now and the police spoke to Emma a second time (and why not?) then the omission might, in retrospect, look odd.

'Have you lived in this part of the world for very long?' asked the sergeant.

'I moved here about a year ago,' I said. 'I lived just outside Worthing until then.'

He nodded and closed his notebook. 'We may need to ask you further questions, sir, but that is all for the moment. Unless you have recalled anything that might be relevant?'

'No,' I said. Then I added: 'Mrs Vynall said that she hadn't reported him missing. So who did?'

The sergeant paused, as if weighing up the advantages and disadvantages of answering my question. 'It was a close friend of his. Another writer, like yourself. Mr Henry Holiday.'

CHAPTER THIRTY-ONE

I watched the police car drive away. What exactly was Henry playing at? How could his own movements on New Year's Eve be kept a secret if he had contacted the police? What had he told them? And why?

I needed to speak to Henry urgently, but first I wanted to find out who owned the telephone number that Elsie had obtained from Tuesday at Janet Francis's agency. I had toyed with the idea of phoning Janet Francis, of course, but I would have had to explain how I'd got the number in the first place. One way or another I'd put off making the call, but it could be deferred no longer.

I dialled. After the phone had rung six times, it switched to an answerphone. Whoever owned it had not had the know-how, or had simply preferred not, to add a personalised message. I was told that the owner of that number was not available to speak. Not wishing to leave a message, I hung up. It would clearly have to wait until after I had spoken to Henry.

I sat down at my computer. The police had questioned me very specifically about New Year's Eve. Had Henry himself told them that that was when Crispin had vanished? Or, contrary to all of the indications that Crispin was still alive, had the police found a body then that they had only just identified as Crispin?

I opened Google and typed in 'body found New Year's Eve'. A body had indeed been found of a New Year reveller who had jumped into a river. But that was at the other end of the country and it had been identified. I tried searching for 'Crispin Vynall' but just found page after page of old interviews and reviews of his books. Next I typed in 'strangled body found Sussex'. Plenty of results there, as you might expect, including some horrifying murders, but nothing recent.

It was time to go and see Henry again.

I left the house and unlocked the car, throwing my Barbour onto the back seat. Even as I did so, the action seemed to recall some unfinished business. I could see Henry very clearly flinging his own coat into the boot on the day we went to Didling Green. But I couldn't remember him taking it out again. Indeed, on our return from the Downs, he had dashed off too quickly for him to be able to retrieve anything. The weather was cold and damp. He must surely have realised that he had mislaid his coat? And yet he had not phoned.

I walked round and opened the boot. There indeed was the Barbour, with the length of rope beside it. I took the coat out and held it up. It would have fitted me quite well – much too big for Henry. Unless . . .

I felt in the pockets. The first yielded only fluff and a few twigs. The second held an envelope with a shopping list on the back: milk, eggs, pasta, shoe polish . . . Nothing too revealing there. I turned it over. It was addressed to Crispin Vynall.

For a moment I just stood there, with the rain falling gently and the Barbour in my hands. So had Henry written a shopping list on the back of an envelope addressed to Crispin? Or, more likely, had Henry been wearing Crispin's Barbour? In which case, why?

I was about to get in the car and drive the mile or so to Henry's house when my mobile rang. I answered it.

'Hello, Ethelred, it's Henry.'

There was a hiatus as both of us waited for the other to speak.

'Yes?' I said.

'You called me,' said Henry.

'When?'

'About half an hour ago. You called my landline but didn't leave a message. I'm phoning you back.'

Even then it took a couple of moments for things to fall into place. Since I was still neither in the house nor in the car, a fine mist of rain was gently soaking into my clothes. It dripped from my hair.

'Crispin was staying with you,' I said eventually. 'He was staying with you after he left Emma. It was your phone number he left with his agent.'

'Yes,' said Henry.

'So, you didn't meet up at the Old House at Home. He was already with you.'

'Yes.'

'And the following morning you knew perfectly well that he hadn't come home.'

'Yes.'

'So, you've wasted my time, then you've reported him missing, exactly as you should have done anyway.'

'Yes.'

'In summary, you've known all along where he was.'

'More or less.'

'And you've killed him, haven't you?'

'I'm coming right over, Ethelred. Stay exactly where you are. I can explain.'

Shortly afterwards he arrived in a new car. A red Fiat.

CHAPTER THIRTY-TWO

'I'm sorry if I have not told you the entire truth,' said Henry. 'But it was necessary.'

'Necessary?' I said.

'Just give me a chance to explain.'

'I don't see what justification you can possibly offer,' I said. 'You did kill Crispin Vynall, and you knew that all along. The whole memory loss thing was a complete fabrication.'

'Yes,' said Henry.

'I just don't understand why you would want to kill Crispin. Still less why you would want to involve me.'

'Yes, you do. Think back, Ethelred. When did you first hear about me?'

'When? I don't know. Sometime after your first book was published. Possibly I read a review. Or maybe I saw you on a debut authors panel at Harrogate or somewhere.'

'No, further back than that.'

'I don't know then . . . were you in publishing or something? Did we meet at somebody's book launch?'

'Publishing? I worked as a waiter while I wrote my first novel. It took seven years – seven years during which I starved for my craft.'

'Starved? In a restaurant? Surely not?'

'I speak metaphorically. Of course, they fed us. I mean the long days spent hunched over a keyboard, deprived of sunlight or the sight of flowers or the sound of children laughing . . .'

'Fair enough,' I said.

'. . . or love or affection or money or friends or the sort of simple pleasures other people take for granted . . .'

'But that's what being a writer is like,' I said.

'Yes, and it's worth it when your book is finally published.'

'But yours was.'

'Not the first one. Not the one that I entered for the CWA new writers' competition.'

'That was the great literary detective novel that you subsequently destroyed?'

'Precisely.'

'You killed Crispin because he awarded the prize to Mary Devlin Jones.'

'He wrecked my career. You all did. You and he and Janet Francis. Crispin's role was at least an active one – he actually read that first manuscript. Much later he joked that he thought that it was simply too good – he'd been jealous of my talent. That's why it was never shortlisted. In fact, he'd simply promised Mary Devlin Jones that she'd win the competition and he was carefully knocking out anything that might stand in her way. His motive may have been wholly dishonourable, but *he had a reason*. But you and Janet couldn't even be bothered to read it . . .'

'Crispin told me I didn't need to,' I said.

'So you didn't.'

'No, I didn't.'

'Of course not. Crispin said not to.' Not even Elsie, at her most sarcastic, could have got the childish whine into that last sentence. Crispin said *not to*. The note of petulance was real. The wound was still raw. 'You were a pathetic, feeble excuse for a judge of a literary award, just as you are still a pathetic, feeble excuse for a writer. Weren't you even curious to see the thing I'd spent seven years working on? You didn't want to just take a peep at it? Just in case your views were a tiny bit different from Crispin's?'

'I was busy . . . there were so many manuscripts to read . . .'

'Don't you think that those of us who had submitted our life-work had also been busy? Don't you think we deserved better?'

'I apologise. Does that help?'

'No.'

'Fair enough,' I said.

I waited to see what Henry would say next.

'It was a bit like that Count of Monte Cristo, really. The black deeds of my enemies had been exposed – yours, Crispin's, Janet's and of course those of Mary Devlin Jones.'

'But Mary was completely innocent,' I said.

'Only legally and morally,' Henry sneered. 'Do you know what total despair feels like, Ethelred? The feeling of utter worthlessness with no hope of anything better? Your soul ripped from your body and tossed aside as worthless dross? Grief such as nobody has ever felt before or will ever feel again?'

'Yes,' I said. 'Actually, most days are a bit like that.'

'No you don't,' he said. 'Not like the grief I felt then. Moral wounds have this peculiarity – they may be hidden, but they never close; always painful, always ready to bleed when touched, they remain fresh and open in the heart.'

'That's good,' I said. 'I'd underestimated you as a writer. Is that from one of your books?'

'It's Alexandre Dumas,' he snapped. 'But he might have penned it for me personally. Crispin wrote to me after the competition. He said that the three of you had read the book and thought it was rubbish. Oh, he presented it as helpful criticism, but that was the general drift. I destroyed the manuscript. I wiped the computer disc clean. I deleted earlier drafts. I tore out the notes I had written on the plot and dumped them in the recycling bin.'

'And then you decided to take your revenge?'

'No. Of course not. I'd assumed your criticism was justified. I admired Crispin as a best-selling author. Janet's reputation as an agent was then at its peak. I even had some sort of regard for you. How could you all be wrong? At first I resolved to write nothing ever again. Then I thought – well, if Crispin sells so many books, why don't I just try to write like him? How hard can that be? And it worked. I sold my second novel to my current publisher and I've never looked back.'

'Except you did look back. You couldn't forget what Crispin . . . what we . . . had done.'

'It was much later, when I saw Crispin together with Mary Devlin Jones, that alarm bells started to ring. I asked around. Some people had raised their eyebrows when he had awarded the prize to her, but the feeling was that you at least were decent and honourable and that you wouldn't have allowed the award to go to her unless you felt that she deserved it. Hah!'

I'm not sure I had ever heard anyone say 'hah!' in quite that way before. There was a depth to his bitterness that was quite remarkable. It was like looking into a well whose sides drop away forever into a dark, ice-cold void.

'Once I realised how I had been cheated, I tried to resurrect the lost novel. I could still remember the plot. I found a list of characters that I had jotted down and forgotten about. I set about rewriting it. I'm pretty sure that I got the action in the first chapter exactly as it had been – but the magic had gone. I pressed on chapter after chapter, but when I reread it, it merely sounded smug and pretentious.'

Henry put his hands to his head as if recalling the anguish anew. One thing that I was not ruling out, because I knew Henry's work reasonably well, was that the original had been smug and pretentious too. Pretentiousness in other writers is always immediately apparent. It takes time and patience to spot it in your own work. Very often you see it when you return to an old draft after a long break.

'But you were a success . . .' I pointed out.

'By your standards, perhaps . . . I was making money, but I was writing books that I despised. I thought that I

231

could write crime novels that would be shortlisted for the Booker Prize.'

'It doesn't happen,' I said. 'It will never happen.'

'*I* could have done it,' he said.

'I've always wanted to write a literary novel myself,' I added.

'Yes, Ethelred. The difference is that I was actually capable of doing so. I've read your stuff, remember? And I've talked to your agent. She's under no illusions – trust me on that.'

Was there any point in saying that I had thought, in all of my novels, that my literary ambitions were there for all to see? Probably not. I was in any case more and more convinced that, in spite of the reviews he had written, Henry had read none of my books.

'Mary Devlin Jones was the easiest,' Henry continued. 'She had blatantly imitated Crispin's style. Once I knew the two of them were an item, it wasn't difficult to start a rumour that the book was really Crispin's. An insinuation here, a word slipped in there. Mary's rise had been meteoric in its way. Her sales had been excellent. Justifiable praise had been showered on her. She had received the adulation graciously and modestly. People were delighted to discover that she was in fact a talentless hack. As for Crispin, my immediate reaction, when his duplicity became absolutely clear, was quite simply that he deserved to die. Of course, it's much easier to say that than to do it. It took a while to go a stage further and reason that, as a crime writer, I ought to be able to bump him off and get away with it. It's all a matter of Motive, Opportunity and Means, isn't it? I had the Motive, so I worked on Opportunity. I got to know him better. I hung around in the bar with him. I got him to *trust* me. I had no specific plan in mind – just that when the chance arose, I would take it. One of the best methods, as you know, is simply to push somebody off a cliff. People fall to their deaths pretty much every week. All I'd have to say was that we were both out for a walk together and that he went too close to the edge and slipped. I tried to save him but unfortunately . . . a terrible scream then a sickening thud on the rocks below. It's just a matter of choosing a time and place where there are no witnesses – a lonely coastal footpath in Pembrokeshire in January, say, if you can persuade the victim to take a bargain city-break in Haverfordwest. Food poisoning too is good – especially if I had been prepared to give myself a non-lethal dose of the same thing to allay suspicion. So, I extended the hand of friendship, you might say and waited for my chance.

'It came quite unexpectedly and not in a way that I would have predicted. Crispin and Emma were not getting on well, for reasons that will have been clear to you. I had said to Crispin that if things ever became too unpleasant at home, he could come and stay with me. Why, you ask, would he choose me rather than anyone else? Because turning up on somebody's doorstep with a suitcase and a broken marriage and then requesting to stay for an indefinite period is a test of any friendship, however long-standing. I knew he would have few choices other than me.'

I nodded. After my split with Geraldine, I'd found much the same thing. I was offered much sympathy but few beds for the night. And nobody suggested that I should move in permanently.

'Having him in my own house seemed to offer up all sorts of possibilities,' Henry continued. 'A badly wired plug, fumes from a faulty boiler, a tripwire on the stairs. But for a while relations between him and Emma seemed to improve. So I decided to speed things up a little.'

'You contacted Emma and told her Crispin was sleeping with her best friend?'

'Exactly. It seemed likely to move things on. To cut a long story short, Crispin phoned me and I collected him in my car, Emma having driven off in theirs. He was not a troublesome guest. He had a book to finish and worked most of the time. His contact with the outside world was limited to the odd call to his agent. He welcomed the seclusion my house offered. But I suggested that we let our hair down a bit on New Year's Eve and hit some of the local nightspots. It was only when we were in the car, with Crispin very drunk, that it struck me that I could probably strangle him there and then without his really noticing. Of course, I'd have a corpse to dispose of, which is awkward, but then an idea occurred to me, because sometimes being very drunk seems to strip out all of the extraneous stuff and allows you to concentrate on the one thing that really matters. I was no longer Henry Holiday. I was Edmond Dantès, I had the Baron Danglars in my passenger seat and he was snoring his head off.

'When we reached Didling Green, I drove straight up the hill – I know the area well – and parked at the top. Crispin was still fast asleep, head back, mouth wide open. I had some rope in the boot. I crept out, got it and had it looped twice round his neck before he knew what was happening. As he breathed his last I whispered in his ear the title of that lost book. I think he understood, but, on balance, I don't give much of a shit one way or the other. Once he was dead, I dragged the body into the woods and concealed it in a mass of brambles. It would be found, of course, but probably not for a few days and by then I would be safe. I drove back down to the pub where the New Year festivities were still in full swing and ordered myself a double whisky.'

'Where your photograph was taken.'

'Yes. It was a stupid thing for me to have done. But my hands were still shaking. I needed that drink. I honestly thought that a pub on New Year's Eve would be one place that I could slip into and out of without anyone remembering me. The flash from the camera startled me, but I still reckoned that I was enough in the background that nobody would notice me. People take so many pictures these days and then scarcely look at them, let alone print them out. Things were so much better in the fifties, weren't they?'

'Much. Colin Cowdrey and Peter May opening the batting for England.'

'Trueman and Statham bowling the Australians out for a handful of runs. Happy days.'

'Happy days, indeed. Then you drove home?'

'Very carefully. Very carefully indeed. I didn't want to kill anyone, after all.'

'And you then came round to me and asked me to investigate the murder you had committed?'

'Precisely.'

'I don't understand why.'

'You will.'

'Shall I? OK. So, you killed Crispin and destroyed Mary's career. You imply you have some revenge planned for me. What about Janet Francis? Or have you forgiven her?'

'Forgiven? Certainly not. Her turn will come. I got her to agree to take on a young niece of mine as an unneeded work-experience assistant. I don't yet know all of the little secrets the agency is hiding but I know some. In fact I've already discovered one very large secret the press would love to know. That will become public before too long. The agency may limp on afterwards with the handful of clients it has left, but Janet will be finished as a force in publishing.'

'Well, I can prevent that at least,' I said.

Henry smiled and shook his head. 'As I say, I already have a great deal of information. In any case, I think you'll find that in the next few weeks that isn't your main priority. It's not as though Janet Francis is anything to you.'

We stood there for a moment, sizing each other up. About five foot four in Henry's case. Unless he was carrying a gun, I didn't rate his chances of stopping me before I got to the phone.

'You can scarcely expect me to forget what you've told me,' I said. 'Crispin was no friend of mine, and I admit we both acted badly towards you, but you can't suppose I'll allow you to get away with murder. I'm sorry, but I've got to tell the police. You can stay or go as you wish, but I'm going to call them now.'

'Be my guest. There would, however, be no point.'

'Why not?'

'Because I have already phoned the police and told them that *you* killed Crispin.'

'But I didn't.'

'Oh, I think the evidence will prove that you did. Let's begin with your own motive, shall we?'

'I don't have one.'

'You were enraged by Crispin's online reviews of your books. And rightly. He was trying to destroy your career, Ethelred.'

'I still don't understand why he did it,' I said.

'That may always remain a mystery. Still, you knew about it and you told me you knew.'

'That's not right,' I said. 'You told me to go and look at Amazon. You said I was getting some dreadful reviews.'

'Did I? I don't recall. I have something of a reputation as a technophobe, so the police may decide not to believe you. But there's no doubt you saw them. The evidence will be there on the hard drive of your computer.'

'But why did Crispin write them?'

Henry smiled.

'Unless . . .' I added. 'Unless you poisoned his mind against me the way you poisoned Emma's against him – the way you poisoned people's minds against Mary.'

'That's altogether possible,' said Henry. 'I mean, that would be quite enterprising of me, wouldn't it?'

'But how?' I asked. 'And how did you get him to write glowing reviews of your own books? Blackmail?'

Henry looked at his watch. 'We honestly don't have time to go into every last detail,' he said. 'And it really doesn't matter. The fact is that you cleverly spotted Crispin was Thrillseeker. You can't deny you told me that, and I have, regrettably, had to pass this information on to the police. You had a motive. Revenge.'

'The police won't believe I killed him for that reason.'

'Some might not agree with you. Some might say it was plenty.'

'Some might. But I doubt that a jury would find it convincing.'

'If you say so. But there's more for the jury to ponder, isn't there? You were also infatuated with his wife. People saw you together in the bar in Harrogate. And Emma herself will testify that you paid her two completely inexplicable visits *once you knew her husband was out of the way*. And you seemed to know he was dead, apparently – you'd said you'd been told. Odd that, isn't it? The book loan was a pathetic excuse for your visit, when you think about it. It was a feeble fabrication. The jury will see that. Your only motive was quite clearly to see Emma and if possible force yourself on her once you knew her husband was out of the way. Your feelings were not reciprocated, of course, but you were unable to control them.'

'That's nonsense,' I said. But Emma had already confirmed a great deal of that in what she had told the police – the sergeant had told me as much. As for what Elsie might say if the police questioned her, heaven forbid, on my relationship with Emma Vynall – it did not bear thinking about. 'He fancied her rotten,' I could hear her saying in her dulcet Essex tones. 'It stood out a mile. Would you like a biscuit with that coffee, Inspector?'

Henry was smiling, like the villain who has just got away with it. But he had missed one vital fact. 'You are forgetting,' I said, 'that on New Year's Eve I was here, at home, watching a programme about meerkats, whereas you were out with Crispin.'

'I think you said that Denzil, the barman at the Old House at Home, was certain you were in the pub?'

'He was wrong.'

'Yes, but he still remembers you clearly. That was a stroke of good fortune that I could not have anticipated. The staff at the club in Chichester may also remember you quite well after your visit there on my behalf. That was as I intended. You left your name, I think. They may find the strange questions you were asking more explicable in the light of the murder charges you will shortly be facing. How unfortunate that the CCTV has now been deleted, but how helpful of you to tell me.'

'But—' I said.

Henry held up his hand. 'We really don't have time for questions. You and Crispin, having visited the club, then drove to Didling Green, where you strangled him and dumped his body in the brambles. When the police check your car they will obviously find plenty of mud matching that of the crime scene, because I made sure you went there. The first time it was clear, from your description of your search, that you had gone nowhere near the body. So, I had to take you back and show you where to tread. The police will therefore find copious footprints of yours all over the hillside, but enough of them close to the hiding place to convince them that you had dumped Crispin there. It is possible, if they manage to track her down, that the police will also be able to talk to a lady who walked her dog there a couple of days after the murder and found you acting in a very suspicious manner. Some people do

239

actually believe that thing about murderers returning to the scene of their crime . . .'

'Hardly proof,' I said.

Henry held up his hand again. 'They will also, when they search your car, find Crispin's Barbour jacket and a length of rope – you will recall that I threw both into your boot the day we were at Didling Green. I assume they are still there?'

'So that *is* Crispin's coat? I thought it was a bit big for you at the time, then I found the envelope . . .'

'After you killed Crispin, you drove back down to the pub for a whisky. A few days later you returned and stole a photo because you were in it. I'm sure the landlord will remember you.'

'None of this matters. I'll obviously still tell the police that it was you who killed Crispin and that you tried to frame me.'

'Frame you? Why on earth would I have done that? Because of some first novel competition years ago? An unimportant prize that I had no need to win? And in any case, I *like* you. I've just written two improbably good reviews of your books.'

'Improbably good? You didn't really mean what you wrote? You didn't think they were masterpieces?'

'As if.'

'But I scarcely knew Crispin.'

'You certainly had his mobile number.'

'Only because you made a call from my phone . . .'

Henry smiled. 'Precisely. There will be a record of the call. From your mobile to his. I have, naturally, deleted the voicemail I left.'

'You kept his phone?'

'For as long as I needed it. In short, Ethelred, you had Motive, Opportunity, Means and the police will have a great deal of evidence that you have subsequently been fannying about exactly where the body will be found . . . probably it is being found at this very moment, because I told the police that you had taken me to Didling Green and then driven me up onto the Downs for no apparent reason other than, perhaps, to check that the body was well hidden. I described where you made me look and which areas you steered me away from. There's no point in making it too difficult for them. And they will find evidence that Crispin was in your car. There should be plenty of DNA transferred to the passenger seat via that Barbour – or enough anyway. It's amazing how little is required.'

'So that's it. Your revenge in full. Crispin is dead and I'll be convicted for the murder.'

'Hopefully,' said Henry. 'I mean, that would be really nice if it all works out.'

'But all I have to do is to say it was you. They'll check your car too . . .'

'Sadly I wrote it off a couple of days ago. My fault. Nobody else hurt. Hardly worth claiming on the insurance policy. It's already been sold as scrap and crushed. I watched it go. Did you like the new one, by the way? Not as impressive as the Jag, but quite nippy and good on these winding roads.'

'Then there's the photo . . .'

'I think it may have been in the car when it went to the crusher. Actually, I'm pretty certain it was.'

241

'The man who took it – he may still have it on his camera or computer.'

'He might. You might even track him down and he might even not have deleted it. It's a bit tricky to see who it is, though – just somebody in a tweed jacket, a bit out of focus – it could even be you. It's a small risk that I'll have to take.'

'But why should the police believe you rather than me?'

'You mean that I killed my good friend, Crispin? To whom I had offered a bed in his hour of need? The man *I reported missing*? The man I reported missing when *you* also knew he was missing but failed to contact the police in any way or even mention your concerns to his wife – an odd fact that she will also probably feel the need to mention.'

'I was going to report him missing but then there was that text from Crispin . . . you sent that as well, didn't you?'

'You'll have difficulty proving it. I obviously haven't been so stupid as to keep the phone. And the police will see that you have been rushing from one side of Sussex to the other covering your tracks.'

'You asked me to.'

'You have that in writing?'

'Of course not.'

'What I asked you to do, will in that case always remain our little secret.'

'I thought I'd been living in a badly plotted novel,' I said. 'It was one of yours.'

'Not as badly plotted as all that,' he said. 'You'll find I've covered pretty much everything – occasionally with your help, but every great writer deserves a competent editor to fill in the little gaps. You might consider a career as an editor, once you get out. Except at your age you may not live long enough to breathe the untainted air beyond the prison walls.'

'You think you've been very clever . . .'

'That's because I have been,' said Henry. 'As for you Ethelred . . . there were times when I could scarcely disguise my exasperation with your incompetence, though I always did my best. Well, I won't have to put up with it any longer. I expect the next time I see you will be in court when I'm giving evidence against you. While I'm perjuring myself, you can contemplate the fact that none of this would be happening if you hadn't been a feeble-minded tosser.'

'Wait!' I said, because Henry was already heading for the door. 'You won't get away with this.'

'Oh really, Ethelred,' he said. 'I'd hoped for better from you than that old cliché! Lots of people get away with murder. I'm going to be one of them. You, sadly, are not. The police will be here very soon. You'd probably better pack a bag or something to take to the police station. Take your Kindle; you'll have plenty of time on your hands. I shouldn't imagine you'll get bail. And don't even think of trying to destroy Crispin's coat or washing the car. Washing won't remove every trace of the mud, even if you had time. And I can swear to the court that I saw Crispin's coat in your boot, along with a piece of rope. I won't even need to lie about that, will I? Because I did see them quite clearly shortly after I placed them there. Goodbye, Ethelred. There's no need to see me out, by the way.'

* * *

'You stupid, moronic, brain-dead arsehole.'

'Thanks, Elsie, but we don't have time for pleasantries. The police will be back in about half an hour to arrest me for Crispin's murder. What do I do?'

'Ethelred, I advise you on contracts, foreign rights, royalty payments and occasionally plot lines and syntax. You need a criminal lawyer, though there may not be one good enough to get you off this. Why couldn't you see how Henry was setting you up?'

'Did you see how he was setting me up?'

'I advise you on contracts, foreign rights, royalty payments and occasionally plot lines and syntax. I do not tell you when you are being framed for a murder charge. Check your contract. It's all in there.'

'So, as my agent, you have no advice?'

'Correct.'

'What would you advise as a friend?'

'As a friend, I'd advise you to pack your Kindle. You'll have a lot of time on your hands in prison.'

'I've just spent ten minutes explaining to you in detail how Henry worked this one. And that's the best you can do?'

There was a long pause.

'Elsie,' I said. 'Are you eating biscuits?'

'I think I just do it when I get bored,' she said. 'You say this video of Henry and Crispin would have cleared you?'

'Yes, but they've wiped it.'

'Are you sure?'

'He said he was going to do it straight away.'

'I've had writers who said they were letting me have the revised manuscript straight away. It turned out they meant next year. Why do writers do that? The whole unwillingness to let go thing, I mean?'

'Elsie, we are drifting from the subject and I'm about to be arrested for murder.'

'Oh yes. Sorry about that. Henry's been busy, then. But I bet he hasn't been as clever as he thought. There must be something else – something really obvious that we've missed.'

'What?' I asked.

'I'll have to get back to you on that.'

At that point I heard the doorbell ring.

'I'm going to have to go,' I said.

And I couldn't even remember where I'd left my Kindle.

CHAPTER THIRTY-THREE

From the journal of Elsie Thirkettle

Of course, I was not worried about Ethelred. After all, he had not committed the murder, Henry had. And there was bound to be stacks of evidence out there to prove it. On the debit side, Ethelred had behaved like a pillock up to and including the twelfth *instante mense*. There was every chance that he would continue to behave like a three-rosette pillock under interrogation.

When discussing the *raison d'être* of the amateur detective with Ethelred, I had pointed out that the main one tended to be that the said detective had skills or knowledge that the regular police lacked. The first piece of knowledge I had was that Henry Holiday was a nasty little toerag. I also knew that he couldn't plot to save his life. His books were full of unnecessary twists and improbable logic. One unlikely red herring after another. Take the 'strangling' of Ethelred up on the hill above Didling Green. Why do that?

Because it provided a dramatic moment when he fancied one was needed, just to keep things ticking over. The one thing I was sure of was that Henry would have slipped up over and over again. And my other special skills and knowledge came from being an agent. I was a dab hand at spotting crap.

I checked my iPhone for messages and news. There was one news item that caught my eye. Following a tip-off, the police had discovered the body of missing crime writer Crispin Vynall in a wood on the South Downs. An arrest had already been made. More was to follow.

I needed a bit of quiet and a little snack containing chocolate or biscuit or both. I checked the cupboard. No biscuits. I took a piece of scrap paper and made a shopping list:

CHOCOLATE
BISCUITS
CHOCOLATE BISCUITS

It was progress of a sort. Once I was properly nourished, I could return to the fray and prove Ethelred's innocence. In the meantime, I could only hope Ethelred wasn't screwing things up too badly at his end.

CHAPTER THIRTY-FOUR

The room was small and bare, apart from a table and three chairs. I had noticed, when I first came through the door, a slight odour of sweat and coffee, recalling for some reason a gym that I briefly belonged to some years ago. There was a mirror on the wall, which might have been a two-way device, for other investigators to view the interrogation, or equally might have just been a mirror. There were no windows, except for an uncurtained horizontal slit, very high up on the wall, which at this hour of the day and this time of the year gave no light at all. In an ideal world I felt that there should be a single light bulb, with no shade, suspended from the ceiling. The room was in fact illuminated by two neon strips, one of which buzzed quietly to itself the whole time. I had ceased to be aware of it after a few minutes. I had now been in the room with my interrogator for almost half an hour. We were not making much progress.

'But I've told you: I wasn't at the pub,' I said.

The inspector was unblinking.

'According to evidence that we have received, Ethelred, you and Mr Vynall and Mr Henry Holiday spent the early part of the evening at a pub in West Wittering. Mr Holiday then went home and you proceeded with Mr Vynall to a nightclub in Chichester.'

'According to Henry Holiday's evidence,' I said. 'But he's lying. You must see that?'

The inspector said nothing.

'I wasn't at the pub,' I repeated. 'I know that Denzil claims I was, but I wasn't.'

'Who is Denzil?

'The barman.'

'Surname?'

'I don't know. But there's only one Denzil there.'

The inspector made a note in his book. 'Thank you, Ethelred. That's very helpful. We shall of course talk to him, now we have that information.'

'And it was Henry Holiday who went to Chichester with Crispin Vynall,' I added.

'You have evidence of that?'

'Well, first, Henry told me.'

'And second?'

'There was CCTV evidence of both of them arriving and departing.'

'We'll take a look at it, then.'

'It's been wiped,' I said.

'You know that?'

'Yes.'

'How?'

'I asked them. At the club.'

'Why?'

'Because, as I told you, I'd been investigating what Henry had done on New Year's Eve. He asked me to.'

'Because you have some special skills in investigation?'

'I'm a crime writer.'

The inspector said nothing.

'I write police procedurals.'

'This is real life, Ethelred. That being the case, didn't you think, if Mr Holiday actually did ask you to do any such thing – which he strongly refutes – that it would have been better for you to hand the whole thing over to the police?'

I wondered whether to correct him over his use of the word 'refute'. Probably not worth it at this stage. 'He said he wanted to know what had happened before he decided what to do next. He didn't want me to go to the police in case he really had killed somebody . . .'

The inspector raised his eyebrows. 'So you are saying that you would have willingly been party to a cover-up if it transpired he had murdered somebody?'

'No. Obviously not.'

'So, why not go to the police straight away, then?'

'I'm not sure.'

'Do you think we're all idiots, Ethelred? Do you think we don't know how to investigate a crime?'

'No. I mean, I don't think you're idiots and you do know how to investigate crimes.'

'So, why not come to us?'

'Henry said he preferred me to investigate.'

'You? That's scarcely likely, is it? And, for the record,

Mr Holiday assures us that nothing of the sort took place. He says he became more and more suspicious of your activities, particularly when you asked him to accompany you to Didling Green. Eventually he formed the reluctant conclusion that Mr Vynall's disappearance had something to do with you. He immediately came to us. Quite properly.'

'I was going to report him missing, but Henry Holiday had kept Crispin's phone and then sent me the text, apparently from Crispin, saying he was alive. So I didn't go to the police after all.'

'And where do you think the phone is now?'

'Henry says he got rid of it.'

'We found it in the bushes near the body.'

'Henry must have thrown it there, after he sent the text, when we both went to Didling Green. It would have been easy enough to do. He had me searching all over the place. I couldn't watch him the whole time.'

'Or *you* threw it there, having previously sent the text to yourself, so that you could persuade Mr Holiday that his friend was still alive. That's equally possible, isn't it?'

'Henry's lying. He actually told me that he'd killed Crispin.'

'Why would he do that?'

'He wanted me to know that he'd set me up – that he'd got his revenge.'

'Even at the risk of incriminating himself?'

'Yes.'

'That's not very likely either, is it? Not in real life.'

'No,' I said.

'You have to admit, Ethelred, that your version of

251

events looks a little contrived. Why should Mr Holiday have reported his friend missing if he had in fact killed him? Why should he have prevented your reporting him missing when he was about to do so anyway? Why should Mr Holiday have told us where to look for the body?'

'There you are! He knew where the body was.'

'Only very roughly. He said you had taken him to the spot – something you more or less admit. He thinks you were unable to resist returning to the scene of your crime. Looking in the boot of your car he'd noticed some rope and what appeared to be Mr Vynall's Barbour. I scarcely need to say that we have recovered both from your vehicle and are having them tested now.'

'I'm not denying I've been to Didling Green. I'm not denying I drove Henry there. I'm not denying it was Crispin's coat or that the rope was used to kill him. But it wasn't me that killed him. Anyway, the coat will certainly have Henry's DNA on it too.'

'He says you lent it to him up on the Downs because it was raining. Later he realised with horror that he had been wearing Mr Vynall's coat.'

'But he was there in Didling Green on New Year's Eve. There was a photo of him in the pub.'

'Where is the photo?'

'I gave it to Henry. He destroyed it.'

'You're saying you let him destroy evidence that he was the killer?'

'Yes.'

'Knowing that it was crucial to the case?'

'I suppose so, but . . .'

'We've also taken a look at your computer.'

'I'd like that back when you've finished.'

'I'm sure you would. In the meantime, could you explain why your last searches are for a body found strangled in Sussex and for Crispin Vynall?'

'I just wondered if a body had been found . . .'

'Where were you on New Year's Eve, Ethelred?'

'I've told you already, three or four times. I was at home. Watching television.'

'On New Year's Eve?'

'Yes, on New Year's Eve.'

'Nobody was with you?'

'No.'

The inspector paused. 'Are you sure?'

'Yes. Why do you ask?'

'There was a suggestion that Mrs Vynall might have been with you.'

'A suggestion? Meaning Henry said that?'

'It was apparently widely known that the two of you . . .'

Well, that was clever of Henry and perhaps explained why the police had pressed this point when they had first interviewed me. Henry was suggesting an alibi of sorts for me, seeming to disprove my contention that he was out to incriminate me. But Emma would of course deny it, leaving me back where I started, except for a lingering suspicion on the part of the police that I did have a motive for bumping Crispin off: an unrequited passion for Emma Vynall that drove me to kill her husband.

'It's not true,' I said. 'She wasn't with me.'

'Mr Holiday implied that you were actually claiming something of the sort.'

'Claiming?'

'Boasting, you might say.'

'What? That I was in bed with Emma on New Year's Eve? Does he have any sort of proof?'

'Of course not. You offered him no hard evidence. It was merely something you claimed to have done.'

'Well, I didn't say anything like that.'

'So when you told him that you had been at home that evening with a lady friend, that is untrue? Maybe some other lady?'

'I told him nothing of the sort,' I said.

I sounded, on reflection, like a Victorian gentleman trying to protect the reputation of some innocent woman that I had inadvertently compromised. Since I wasn't a Victorian gentleman, the inspector would simply conclude that I had repeatedly lied and changed my story concerning what I had been doing. I had to admire Henry's plotting of this particular fiction. He had been thorough. In some ways.

'Anyway, Emma will have told you that she was back in Brighton.'

'She seems to have a certain . . . well . . . affection for you, though.'

'Does she?'

'That surprises you?'

'A bit.' It sounded ungracious, but I was, under the circumstances, surprised she had said it.

'So, you and she had had some sort of relationship?'

'That isn't what I said.'

'She said she'd tried to get you into bed at Harrogate and you'd turned her down.'

I was grateful to Emma for at least trying on my behalf.

But I hadn't turned her down. I'd just missed the signals.

'Are you saying you didn't reciprocate her feelings?'

'I suppose . . . up to a point . . . but it has no relevance.'

'You find her attractive?'

I hesitated. It seemed rude to say 'no', inopportune to say 'yes'. The silence continued for some time.

'Cat got your tongue, Ethelred?' he enquired.

'She's a very attractive woman,' I said. 'But we were scarcely even friends – let alone anything else.'

'But you visited her twice in the last few days. She said you seemed to be trying to find any excuse to do so.'

I sighed. This was much as I had feared. 'And I suppose she said that I seemed to know Crispin was dead?'

'No, Ethelred, she didn't say that. Did you in fact tell her that Crispin was dead?'

'Only inadvertently. I mean, I hadn't intended to say that, but it all came out wrong. She got the impression that I knew he'd been killed. It was only because of the death threats and the reference to a second body.'

'That's the second body that is such a cliché in detective fiction?'

'Yes, I suppose so.'

'And who wrote these death threats?'

'Henry, I suppose. It must have been part of the web of lies . . .'

'Web of lies? Another cliché?'

'If you say so.'

'And he admitted to writing the letters?' asked the inspector.

'No. He didn't.'

'And where are these so-called death threats now?'

'My agent took one of them and I gave Henry Holiday the other one.'

'So we can't see either? How convenient.'

'I can get the one my agent has. I doubt Henry plans to release his.'

'That would be helpful, but not as helpful as letting us have both straight away, if they exist.'

'I realise that you don't believe me.'

'You're right there, anyway.'

'It seems you also had another motive. Mr Vynall had been writing overly critical reviews of your books on Amazon?'

'Under an assumed name,' I said.

'That would have affected your sales?'

'A bit. Not enough to worry about.'

'But you would have seen it as a personal attack?'

'I suppose so. Yes, of course. All bad reviews hurt. But if I killed everyone who gave me a bad review . . .'

'I take your point. Mr Holiday has, however, given you some very good reviews?'

'Yes.'

'That doesn't fit in with your contention that he disliked you and was trying to frame you for murder.'

'But he had a motive of his own. Crispin and I had awarded a CWA prize to somebody else . . .'

'You failed to give him a prize?'

'Yes.'

'A major prize – like the Booker or something?'

'No . . . a relatively minor one, in fact, but—'

'So he decided to frame you for murder?'

'Yes.'

'Forgive me, Ethelred, but you are losing me here. Surely there must have been dozens of people that you failed to make an award to.'

'Yes, a couple of hundred, at least. But Henry felt very strongly about it. It's why he killed Crispin.'

'He felt strongly enough to kill Mr Vynall, but not strongly enough to give you a bad review in the *Sunday Times*?'

'I'm not explaining myself properly.'

'No, I think you've been very clear, Mr Tressider. We need to talk to Denzil at the pub and perhaps one or two other people. Then we'll run through this again. Perhaps then we'll get to the bottom of it.'

'Can I go home now?'

'I'm afraid not. Do you have a lawyer?'

'I don't need one.'

'Oh, I think you do, Ethelred. In fact, the sooner you start talking to one, the better.'

CHAPTER THIRTY-FIVE

From the journal of Elsie Thirkettle

It is relatively rare for customers to stop dead in the middle of Sainsbury's biscuit aisle and exclaim: 'Shit! I've been a total idiot!' Or at least, the reaction of my fellow customers suggested that they hadn't seen that many people do it before. But I had been just that. A total idiot.

Maybe it was the effect of the walk to the supermarket, which cannot be done without a certain amount of exposure to the fresh air, but suddenly, right in front of the Jaffa Cakes and just to the left of the Jammy Dodgers I was granted a vision and all was suddenly clear.

Of course! The death threats! There could be little doubt that these too were from Henry. The first had been intended to push Ethelred into taking the case on by appearing to warn him off – a hint of a small but manageable element of danger. The second had caused him to make an idiot of himself questioning Emma again, thus stacking up further evidence (if it were needed) of an apparent motive. They'd been effective, but Henry hadn't mentioned any of this when boasting to Ethelred about how clever he'd been. Perhaps he realised, as authors often do on rereading a manuscript, that there was a worrying weakness in their plot. And there are no second drafts in real-life murders. So he'd played that one down.

I had no doubt he'd have taken the usual precautions that people do when writing death threats. I'd already noticed the cheap paper, unexceptional ballpoint and (in all likelihood) absence of fingerprints. But he wouldn't have realised that I had taken so much interest in his grammar and spelling. Nor would he know, and this is what had caused me to freeze, hand half-extended towards a special offer on Jaffa Cakes, that I had worked out that the sender of the letters was the same person as Thrillseeker and Sussexreader. Which in turn meant that it was Henry, not Crispin, who had been running multiple sockpuppet accounts. Of course he had. It actually explained one of the many things that had puzzled me: why Sussexreader not only praised Henry but rated him more highly than Crispin. Henry's lack of interest in technology was, like his tweed jackets, a mere affectation. Nobody his age was genuinely incapable of working the Internet. I couldn't prove anything myself, but Amazon at least would know which account they had come from. They would be able to tell the police who had been a naughty little sockpuppet and, by extension, it would be possible to show that Henry had been sending Ethelred death threats, which would hardly fit in with the story he had given them.

I checked my shopping list and added Jammy Dodgers and chocolate digestives to my shopping basket. My mobile rang. For a moment I was juggling my list, my basket and my phone, then all more or less righted itself, and I proceeded on my way with my basket over my arm and the phone clutched in the other hand.

The caller introduced himself. I recognised him as being the lawyer who had, many years ago, handled Ethelred's divorce. 'Is that Elsie Thirkettle?' he asked.

'Speaking,' I said. 'In person. How can I help you?'

'You know that Mr Tressider has been arrested.'

'Yeah, yeah,' I said, surveying the shortbread selection. 'Murder. But he didn't do it.'

'He's asked me to represent him,' said the lawyer.

Well, that was an odd choice after the result he achieved in the divorce settlement, in which Geraldine had taken everything Ethelred possessed or was ever likely to possess. But Ethelred had stuck with him. Loyalty was one of Ethelred's most noted traits. Stupidity was another one.

'But he's OK?' I asked. 'I mean, he really didn't do it. Henry Holiday did.'

'That's what he tells me, but the evidence is very much against him. I wonder if you can do two things for him?'

'Absolutely,' I said, selecting the Taste the Difference shortbread rounds, which have a nice dusting of sugar – not too much but enough to give them a bit of an edge over the competition.

'First, he needs a death threat he says you have.'

'Safe at home,' I said. 'And Henry Holiday was the author.' I explained how I knew.

'Ethelred had come to much the same conclusion,' said

the lawyer. 'But we'll need at least one of the letters to prove it.'

'I can post it to you,' I added.

'Maybe bring it round yourself, if you can. We don't want to lose it. It could be critical.'

'Check,' I said. 'And the other thing?'

'It's slightly more complicated. The police seem to have got it into their heads that he might have been having . . . well, let's call it a one-night stand . . . with a young lady on the evening in question. They feel that he is being evasive in his answers to their questions. In your opinion . . . I mean, is it possible that he was with somebody and for chivalrous or other reasons doesn't want to admit it?'

'Ethelred might do almost any moronic thing for chivalrous reasons. That's the sort of person he is. He really belongs in the fifteenth century, though he'd settle for 1958, with Peter May's elegant batting securing a victory for England on a sunny July morning at the Oval.'

'So, you're saying it's possible he did have somebody with him but is not admitting it?'

'Absolutely not. I'm sure he was watching television, just like he says. He doesn't get out a lot, and I'd know if he'd got a girlfriend.' I paused recalling a certain jauntiness in his manner when he had been talking about Emma Vynall – but no, we could rule that out. 'Large or small?' I added.

'Sorry?'

'Packets of Kit Kat. Large, I think. It's always a mistake to get the small ones and run out just as you need a couple of fingers at one o'clock in the morning. But plain or milk, that's the real question? Where were we?'

'We'd more or less finished. Well, maybe one other thing . . . we seem to have lost one key piece of evidence – a CCTV recording of Henry Holiday and Crispin Vynall at a club near Chichester.'

'Apparently.'

'And there's not much else by the way of hard evidence. So, if there's anything that you can think of that would prove where Ethelred was or Henry Holiday was on the night in question, that could be very important.'

'Obviously,' I said.

The thought crossed my mind that Ethelred's lawyer had not gained any additional brain cells over the years since the divorce. Still, British justice would not condemn an innocent man, however stupid he was and however badly he chose his lawyer.

'Look, I'll get that letter to you. Then you need to get Amazon to track down the owner of the two sockpuppet accounts,' I said. 'It will prove to be Henry Holiday.'

'Fine,' he said.

I hung up.

What next? I realised that in the hurly-burly of saving Ethelred I had mislaid my shopping list. Biscuits and chocolate biscuits . . . what else? Ah yes! Chocolate! So, disaster avoided, then.

I proceeded in a westerly direction to where the chocolate bars lived happily together in massed ranks of blue and red and gold. I would adopt some and take them home.

It was as I was eating my second Kit Kat, so no more than five minutes after I had got home, that it occurred to me that it was amateur detective time again. Since the police didn't buy Ethelred's theory that Henry was the killer, they would not be looking in the right places for clues. And since Ethelred's lawyer was a dipstick, he wouldn't be either. But there might be somebody at the club who did remember seeing Henry there. And it was just possible that there was more to the Ethelred and Emma thing than met the eye. The Amazon thing should be enough, but you can never have too much evidence in your favour when it's a murder charge. I made a quick phone call to Brighton and laid out suitable clothing for a little trip to the coast.

'There's a strange sense in which death pays all debts,' said Emma. 'A couple of days ago I seriously wanted to kill Crispin. Now that somebody else has done it . . . I'd reconciled myself to being a divorcee; I just hadn't quite got my head round becoming the Widow Vynall. Now it's his killer, I'd like to kill.'

'But you don't believe that Ethelred killed Crispin?'

'Ethelred? God, no. If he'd wanted me I was there and available in Harrogate. There was no need to kill Crispin to get into bed with me or anything else. And Henry really admitted it all to Ethelred?'

'That's what Ethelred says. You'd have to be monumentally arrogant to do it, but Henry actually thinks he's been clever enough that he can let Ethelred know who's done this to him.'

'So, what do we do?'

'I'm working on it. In the meantime, can I check – there really is no chance that Thrillseeker's reviews were written by Crispin?'

'Absolutely none. I'm sure Crispin had never read one

of Ethelred's books. He tends to leave things lying around, so I know what he's reading. He doesn't read crime much at all, actually, but certainly not the sort of thing that Ethelred writes. And I'm certain he's never written an Amazon review in his life. He buys . . . sorry bought . . . all his books from an independent just down the road. And he was never that good with computers. He wouldn't know how to set up a fake account. Anyway, there was no animosity at all between Ethelred and Crispin. Well, not much.'

'And you'll say that in court if necessary?'

'Yes, of course.'

'One other thing. Where were you on New Year's Eve?'

'Since Crispin didn't come home, I went out with some friends – just to a restaurant down the road.'

'OK. My other idea won't work, then.'

'What's that?'

'If I told you, I'd have to kill you afterwards.'

'I won't ask then.'

'It's Plan C. I'm only going to try it if all else fails, anyway.'

'I'm sorry – I'm sure I've made it worse for Ethelred,' said Emma. 'With the police, I mean. But he was acting strangely. All those books. Thinking about it, I can see that it was just Ethelred being Ethelred and in a way sort of endearing. But it was still weird. Maybe if I'd slept with him in Harrogate . . .'

'He'd still have been weird. Trust me. He has towards his women a dog-like devotion of a sort that is endearing only in actual dogs.'

'Yes, I can see that might be the case. I've got some

turkey stew I can defrost, if you'd like an early supper.'

'Yes, I would like that. The place I'm going to next doesn't open properly until about midnight. You don't have any biscuits, I suppose, while we're waiting for supper?'

In fact, I arrived at about seven-thirty and had to hunt around for a way in. It was strangely quiet, even allowing for the fact that most of its clientele were not exactly early risers. I'd been snooping in a general sort of way for about ten minutes when a voice said: 'Can I help you? You shouldn't really be in here, you know. We're not open to customers. It's Sunday.'

Ah, yes, of course. Sunday. Only essential services such as the police, ambulance and literary agents would be operating.

'That's fine,' I said, 'because I'm not here as a customer.'

The young man was, if not young enough to be my son, at least young enough to be my naughty little nephew. He knew at once roughly how much shit I would take and how difficult I'd be to remove if I didn't get whatever it was I was after.

'But you can help me,' I continued. 'Were you on duty on New Year's Eve?'

'You from the police? Or are you a reporter? If you're a reporter, I can't talk to you.'

'Then it's your lucky day. I'm not a reporter.'

'But it's about the murder?'

'You could say that.'

'So you are from the police?'

My past record of impersonating police officers was mixed. Occasionally it worked splendidly. But not often.

It depended on the intelligence of the person I was trying to dupe.

'Yes,' I said. 'I'm from the police.'

'Could I see your warrant card?'

'We don't carry them anymore. It's all computerised now. I'll give you a reference number and you can verify it on the Internet afterwards.'

'OK . . .' He seemed doubtful for some reason. I couldn't for the life of me see why.

'Do you want to speak to the manager?'

'Not at the moment. You are . . . ?'

'Kevin. Kevin Smith. Assistant manager.'

'OK, Kevin. Do you remember speaking to Mr Tressider – the man now accused of the murder?'

'Yes. He came in here asking some very odd questions. Even at the time I thought it was peculiar.'

Well, that was Ethelred all right.

'But you don't remember seeing him here on the night in question?'

'New Year's Eve? No. Like I told him, there were a few old guys in, but I wouldn't have been able to pick them out later.'

'You've seen pictures of Crispin Vynall?'

'Yeah – you can scarcely miss them on the telly, can you?'

'I don't watch it much. I try to catch the book programmes, though mainly out of a sense of duty.'

'Not *Crimewatch*?'

Crimewatch? Ah yes, of course, I was a member of the police. It would probably be a good idea not to forget that.

'Can we get back to New Year's Eve, please, Kevin?

Ethelred . . . Mr Tressider . . . says that there was CCTV footage but it got wiped.'

The young man looked slightly sheepish.

'Well, was it?' I repeated.

'Don't tell the manager, will you?' he said. 'I was supposed to wipe it but I forgot. I swore to him that I'd done it too. I even swore on my gran's life, him not knowing she died when I was two.'

'So it's still there? But the manager will notice it, anyway?'

'No. A couple of days ago we got a new system in. That's the one he plays with now. He loves that new system. All the New Year's stuff is on the old one that's sitting in the storeroom waiting to be scrapped. He's getting somebody to take it for recycling. Nobody's going to look at that again.'

'You'll have to show it to the police.'

'Will I? I'll get sacked when he sees I didn't do what he told me to do.'

'But the police and I will be very grateful.'

'I thought you said you were the police?'

'I'm only some of the police. I mean the rest of the police and I will be most grateful. So will Ethelred. Mr Tressider, I mean.'

'What do you want me to do . . . ? Look, there he is!'

I followed Kevin's gaze and encountered Crispin Vynall's grinning, party-ravaged face staring down at us from a television screen on the wall. It was an old photo taken at a book launch. He had his arms round two girls, who had, as far as possible, been excised from the shot. But you couldn't excise the leer from Crispin's face.

'Can you turn the sound up?' I asked.

He fiddled quickly with the remote and we just caught the following: 'In a statement issued today West Sussex police have confirmed that a man is helping them with their enquiries. This is widely reported as being Mr Ethelred Tressider, who writes crime novels as (the announcer paused briefly to check his notes) Peter Fielding and (another quick pause) J. R. Elliott. Peter Fielding is noted for his widely praised police procedural novels set in the fictional town of Buckford. It is understood, however, that no charges have yet been made. And now I'll hand you back to the studio.'

'See,' said the young man. 'It's on all the time.'

'And do they say "widely praised" every time?' I asked.

'Yeah. I might go and buy one. I like crime. I just hadn't heard of Peter Fielding before.'

'And it's on all of the channels?'

'Pretty much.'

'Twenty-four hours a day?'

'That's how it is now. So, what do you want me to do with the CCTV?'

'Nothing at all for the moment,' I said. Because I'd had an idea. 'I'll be in touch again when we need it.'

'OK. What's that warrant card number by the way – so I can check you on the Internet?'

'B305CHB,' I said without even blushing. It had, after all, been my first car and a nice little runner. 'But I think the system's down at the moment. You may not be able to find it this evening. Don't worry, Kevin. I'll be in touch again soon.'

'And you'll try not to get me into trouble?'

'I'm sure we can just sneak the equipment away without anyone noticing, when the time comes.' It wasn't entirely untrue. I was sure the police could sneak it away quietly; it was just unlikely that they would.

'Thanks,' he said. He seemed genuinely grateful, though not as grateful as Ethelred was going to be. We'd have him sprung from the county gaol (if that was where he was) in two shakes of a lamb's tail.

Or maybe, thinking about it, six or seven shakes. After all, he was getting a plug on one channel or another every half-hour or so. His books were being mentioned without the faintest hint of criticism. You couldn't buy publicity like that. And prison was, when you thought about it, not such a bad place to write. Look at John Bunyon. Look at Oscar Wilde. Look at Cervantes. Look at Boethius. Look at Jeffrey Archer. In a day or two I'd tip the police off that the recording was still there. They'd drive down and pick it up. Kevin would get a mild ticking off, but into every life a little rain must fall.

No rush, then. No rush at all.

CHAPTER THIRTY-SIX

From the journal of Elsie Thirkettle

My final visit, on the way home, was to the pub in Didling Green. I bought myself a lemonade and had a quick chat with the landlord.

Yes, he said, he thought that one of the photos of New Year's Eve might have been taken from the board by a customer. It happened. You could never tell what customers would do. He looked at me the way I look at people when discussing the many foibles of writers. Well then, could he check his camera and see if he still had it? He shook his head in response to my question. It had not been one of his own pictures. Customers sometimes nicked photos from the board but more often they stuck up pictures of their own. He had no idea who had taken that one. There were dozens of people in. I asked him if he could find out who it was. I'd like a copy myself, I said.

He looked at me very oddly. 'You've never seen the picture?'

'No,' I said.

'And the only person you know in it is, you believe, a bit blurred and in the background, with his mouth hanging open?'

'Yes,' I said.

'And you actually want a copy for yourself?'

'Yes,' I said. 'If possible.'

'I'll let you know if I track it down, in that case,' he said.

I left my business card with him, but somehow I wasn't expecting to hear from him any time soon.

I spent the following day phoning up journalists that I knew and feeding them information on Ethelred's books. There were a couple of good reviews I wanted re-quoted (including Henry's – why not?) and I shamelessly made up details of his work in progress, saying that it would draw on his experience of being arrested for murder. It was true that, inevitably, one or two people came out of the woodwork and expressed the view on camera that Ethelred was a bit creepy and slightly wet, but on balance opinion was still very much in his favour. The overall impression was of a talented but slightly neglected author, who was well liked by his fellow crime writers. And Internet data suggested that sales were soaring. Obviously Ethelred was in a dungeon eating gruel with a wooden spoon or something, but he'd be dead chuffed once I let his lawyer know that the CCTV footage was safe and that I'd saved the day and so on and so forth. So, there was scarcely a cloud in the sky, you might say, until the second day after my visit to Sussex. My phone rang and it was Ethelred's lawyer, slightly troubled.

'When are you going to bring it round?'

'Bring what?'

'The death threat letter. It's the only concrete evidence we have.'

'Oh that old thing. Don't worry. It's there on the table. Perfectly safe. No, it isn't, it's gone.'

'Gone?'

'Well, it was there in front of me the other night. It can't have wandered very far. What did I do next? I needed food. I made a shopping list on a scrap of old paper . . .'

'Elsie? Hello? Are you still there?'

So, the question was this. If Sainsbury's found a shopping list on the floor of the biscuit aisle would they:

a) check whether it had a death threat on the other side of it and then take it to lost property to await reclaim by its proper owner

or

b) sweep it up and throw it away?

Then I noticed that Ethelred's lawyer was just saying: 'Hello? Hello?'

'Sorry,' I said. 'I was thinking . . .'

'But the death threat letter?'

'I may have left it by the Jammy Dodgers in Sainsbury's. Sorry about that. Easily done, as you will agree. I did copy it out in this notebook I have . . .'

'We need the original for it to be any use at all. If we

272

just give them a copy you made . . . you could have just made it up this morning.'

'Yes, I suppose I could. Like I say . . . I'm sorry about that. Still, the good news is that I do have a much better piece of evidence.'

'Which is?'

'The CCTV footage from the club in Chichester.'

'It wasn't wiped?'

'No.'

'And you have that safe with you?'

'Well, strictly speaking it's in Chichester. I'm going to let the police know . . . er . . . very shortly. But it's absolutely safe in the meantime. I mean really, really safe – not like the letter.'

'I hope so – but it's better we see it first, before the police. Can you get hold of it and send it to us straight away?'

'Yes, of course. No sooner said than done. I'll give you a call tomorrow. Tell Ethelred I'm on the case.'

He rang off. OK, I'd been a bit of a disappointment up to now, but I was about to make up for that. Big time.

I had the number of the club, so I rang it and asked for Kevin.

'Detective Inspector Elsie Thirkettle here,' I said. 'I'm going to drop in tomorrow morning and pick up the old CCTV equipment.'

'But you did it today,' he said.

'No, I didn't.'

'Some guys turned up, just like you said. I wasn't around at the time, but somebody told me they just took it all away.'

273

'Your boss had said the machine was going to be scrapped?'

'Yes.'

'So there's just a chance these guys had been sent by your boss to pick it up and take it to the tip?'

'Wasn't it the police, then?'

'I'd say that that was somewhere between very unlikely and completely impossible.'

'Was it important?'

'Let's hope it wasn't as important as I thought it was,' I said.

Of course, Cervantes was a galley slave for five years before his agent sprung him. With luck Ethelred wouldn't have to wait quite as long as that.

It's fortunate under the circumstances that I had a Plan C. It wasn't quite as legal as Plans A and B, but it would do perfectly well. And my first step was to make contact with Henry's mole at Francis and Nowak. I was pretty sure I knew who it was.

CHAPTER THIRTY-SEVEN

Extract from a tape recording. The two people whose voices feature on the tape would appear to be Elsie Thirkettle (ET) and Tuesday Lane-Smith (TL-S). The exact date is unclear but diary entries point to its being mid-January. The background noise and the opening conversation suggest a very cheap cafe just off Tottenham Court Road.

TL-S: Thank you so much for buying me lunch. I honestly didn't think I'd done you that much of a favour.

ET: Politeness costs nothing. Well (brief pause) twelve pounds fifteen pence, including VAT and service.

TL-S: Do you want me to pay my half?

ET: (long pause) No, no, no. (Long pause) Of *course* not. So, how are you enjoying life at Francis and Nowak?

TL-S: Brill! I'd really, really like to be an agent. I've only got another couple of weeks there, though. It's just an internship thingy. You know?

ET: I might have a permanent post coming up at the Elsie Thirkettle Agency . . .

TL-S: Really?

ET: It's technically possible. Do you like Janet Francis?

TL-S: She's a bit fierce. Except when she's drunk, of course. So, she's fine after lunch. I've never met the other partner. Nowak?

ET: He's gone. Janet ate him for breakfast in 1997. So, how did you get the internship thingy?

TL-S: Oh, a cousin of mine . . . Henry Holiday. . . he's a famous writer, you know? . . . He knows Janet Francis really, really well and he fixed it up.

ET: And does he take any interest in how you're getting on?

TL-S: Oh, yes! He's überinterested! Phones me every other day, you know? To ask about what's happening and all the gossip?

ET: And you tell him?

TL-S: In *strict* confidence. I mean, the Karen Rockingham thingy, for example – wow! If that got out . . .

ET: Karen Rockingham? She's Janet's biggest client, of course . . .

TL-S: By miles! Sells millions! I mean, the film rights alone are worth gazillions.

ET: As much as that? So the Karen Rockingham thingy is . . .

TL-S: Oh, I couldn't tell you that! I mean . . . wow!! It's really, really confidential. You won't get that out of me!!! Lips sealed!!!!

ET: But you told Henry?

TL-S: (long pause) Yes, I told Henry. But only because he got me the job and I'm certain he won't breathe a word to a soul. I mean, he knows I'd get the boot straight away. He wouldn't do that to me.

ET: Wouldn't he?

TL-S: Henry? No!!!

ET: Are you sure?

TL-S: He's really nice. A bit old-fashioned . . . but really nice.

ET: Always? Nice, I mean. I know he doesn't have any clothes designed after 1957.

TL-S: Ha!

ET: Ha!

TL-S: (long pause) You know, I shouldn't really say this . . .

ET: Please do.

TL-S: But I shouldn't.

ET: Yes, you said that and I said: 'please do'. If you were to join my agency, I'd need you to be completely open with me. And to cut to the chase occasionally.

TL-S: Is there a serious chance of that? Joining you . . .

ET: Simply regard this as a sort of interview with a small hummus salad thrown in.

TL-S: Well, it's just that it was Henry who got Mary Devlin Jones dropped by Francis and Nowak. That wasn't nice, was it? Janet told me one of the times she was really, really, really drunk? Henry told her how Mary had sort of copied somebody's book?

ET: Crispin Vynall.

TL-S: That's right! You knew about it! So it was true?

ET: Just because things are generally known doesn't make them true. But that's certainly interesting. Very interesting. Now, tell me about Karen Rockingham.

TL-S: I said, I can't. That's all there is to it.

ET: But you've already leaked the information to Henry. Janet will find out.

TL-S: She may not.

ET: She will if I tell her. So you'll be sacked and have no references. No agency will look at you. Ever. You'll have to go out and find honest work.

TL-S: But you wouldn't . . .

ET: Of course, if you join me, you won't need a reference from Janet Francis.

TL-S: So, you're definitely offering me a job?

ET: Tell me about Karen Rockingham. Then let's have a look at the pudding menu. Mmm, look . . . lemon sponge and custard.

TL-S: This is horrible! You invite me out for a nice lunch, then get me to tell you things I shouldn't tell you, then you blackmail me into telling you more. Is publishing always like this?

ET: No, there are bad days too. What's Karen Rockingham done?

TL-S: (very long pause) She's written a detective novel.

ET: OK. Well, that's pretty shocking, but I'm not sure it will completely destroy her reputation . . .

TL-S: No, no. She's done it under an assumed name so nobody will know it's her. She wants to see if she can make a success of it without her real name being on the cover. We're all sworn to secrecy. She'll be furious if it all gets out.

ET: But Henry knows?

TL-S: Yes.

ET: And if he leaked it to the press, Karen would be annoyed?

TL-S: Really, really, really mad.

ET: And she'd leave Francis and Nowak?

TL-S: If she knew we'd leaked it . . . She'd leave and then sue us for absolutely squillions.

ET: Is a squillion more than a gazillion?

TL-S: I think so. I'm not that good at maths. Oh my God! Is that what Henry's planning to do?

ET: He hates Janet Francis.

TL-S: But Janet gave me the job . . .

ET: She doesn't know Henry hates her. It's his little secret.

TL-S: So, I'm going to get sacked?

ET: Yes.

TL-S: But you'd give me a job?

ET: Quite possibly.

TL-S: On what terms?

ET: Well, without wishing to commit myself . . .
Hold on a moment. I need to get something
from my handbag.

TL-S: Is that a tape recorder in there?

ET: Only a little one. OK, that's it . . .

RECORDING ENDS

CHAPTER THIRTY-EIGHT

From the journal of Elsie Thirkettle

The police arrived mid-afternoon. One convention of amateur detective fiction is that the police blunder around and ask only the obvious questions. These two, however, a detective inspector and a sergeant, seemed bright and on the ball. They questioned me about Ethelred generally. Since they weren't critics for any of the major papers, I didn't bother with words like 'gripping' or 'innovative' or even 'reasonably well written'. I just said he was a mid-list author who did mainly police procedurals and a bit of historical, with the occasional slice of romantic fiction thrown in when all else failed. No chick lit and sadly no best-selling blockbusters optioned for Hollywood.

I told them a bit, of course, about what a tosser Henry Holiday was and about how I was certain he had stitched Ethelred up, but they seemed less interested than they might. They wanted something they called 'firm evidence', not 'baseless speculation bordering on slander'. I told them they could suit themselves.

We talked about Amazon reviews. I explained that most writers didn't give a toss, except for sensitive little souls like Ethelred, for whom any criticism was a cut to the quick. Not that he'd kill anyone for that, of course. Did I think that Crispin had written the reviews? No, I said, I knew that Henry had written them, I just couldn't prove it. But Amazon would tell them for sure.

Then we got on to what I had been expecting. Was it likely, they asked, that he was alone on New Year's Eve, watching David Attenborough? Well, yes, of course it was, because that was roughly what he'd done for the past two or three years – unless he was teaching on some creative writing course in Caithness or Anglesey, designed to attract other people with nothing much to do over the holiday period. So I said: 'Alone? Oh dear, officer, I'm not sure I should say . . .'

'You do realise that if he was with anyone it would be critical to his defence? We just got the impression—'

'Then you may not be wrong,' I said. 'But I couldn't possibly comment.'

'Henry Holiday thought it likely.'

'But Ethelred wouldn't have told Henry who it was,' I said. 'What you have to understand about Ethelred is that he's an old-fashioned gent.'

'So, if he had been with somebody that evening he might not tell us? Even at the risk of harming his defence?'

'His lips would be sealed,' I said. 'If there were still gallows, he would probably go to those gallows without breathing the name of his beloved to a soul.'

'No shit?' said one of them.

'No shit,' I said.

They nodded thoughtfully and made notes.

'But he fancied Emma Vynall?'

'He fancied her rotten,' I said. 'Would you like another biscuit, Inspector?'

Some of the interviews I had to conduct I rather looked forward to. One I didn't. But I needed to test the water. So I made the call.

'Henry Holiday speaking.'

'It's Elsie Thirkettle here.'

'Ah, Ethelred's agent.'

'Just a courtesy call to say I'm onto your game, punk.'

'That won't help you. In the game you refer to, I happen to hold all the cards, you see.'

'I know you are Sussexreader and Thrillseeker.'

'No you don't. You are guessing I used both names but you don't know and have no way of finding out.'

'The police can get Amazon to identify you. I've already told them to check.'

'You haven't heard of using false identities on the web, then?'

'I bet Amazon have a way of telling.'

'Perhaps they do. Thank you for alerting me to that possibility. Very well, if it pleases you, let's say I wrote reviews on Amazon under both names. It isn't against the law.'

'But you claimed to be Crispin Vynall in one post.'

'Oh, I don't think so. Thrillseeker may have said he was going to some conference or other and it may be that

Crispin Vynall did attend that conference. But I don't think he said specifically that he was Crispin Vynall.'

'You aren't as clever as you think you are, Henry.'

'Aren't I?'

'You created this image for yourself as somebody who had no idea how the Internet worked. In the meantime you were creating false identities and laying a trail of clues to incriminate one of my writers.'

'Perhaps. In what way does that make me less clever than I imagine?'

'Because I know you're Thrillseeker.'

'Do you? I can promise you you'll have a great deal of difficulty proving it, even with Amazon's help, and it won't save Ethelred even then. He thought Thrillseeker was Crispin. The fact he was mistaken doesn't change a thing. It was still the reason why he killed him. There's no law saying I can't set up accounts on the Internet. I might have just posted the reviews for fun. How could I possibly know that Ethelred would resent them enough to kill Crispin – I mean, it's not as though I ever claimed the reviews were by Crispin. That was just your vivid imagination. Proving I am Thrillseeker won't help you at all.'

'What if I've recorded this conversation?'

'But you haven't.'

'How do you know?'

'Because you wouldn't have told me that was what you were doing. You'd have kept going until I said something incriminating.'

'I might already have all I need.'

'No you don't.'

'You can't be sure.'

'Yes, I can.'

'No, you can't.'

'Elsie, I do not have all evening to engage in witty banter with you. And don't tell me I can't be certain about that. Do you have anything new to say?'

'Not really,' I said. Then I added: 'Yes, actually, I do. You may have won this round, Mr Holiday, but you are still a slimy little toerag. Ethelred's sales may be a fraction of yours, but he is a gentleman, whereas you are but a pale imitation of one. You lack his compassion, his generosity, his integrity and a good six inches of his height. Even if he goes to prison he will still have all those, but you will just have the mossy stone that you have crawled from under. I despise you utterly.'

Or at least I would have said all that if he hadn't hung up just after I said 'not really'. Still, I could always say it some other time.

Anyway, what Henry didn't know was that I'd done my groundwork for Plan C. Nothing could stop that one. Time to close the deal.

CHAPTER THIRTY-NINE

Extract from a tape recording. The two people whose voices feature on the tape would appear to be Elsie Thirkettle (ET) and Mary Devlin Jones (MDJ). It must have been recorded a day or two after the lunch with Tuesday Lane-Smith. The meeting clearly took place in a branch of Café Nero, possibly in Kingsway.

MDJ: . . . . shopping in Oxford Street later.

ET: You can cut through Covent Garden or High Holborn. Not bad here, is it?

MDJ: No. Of course, my last agent always took me to the Groucho Club.

ET: Your last agent dumped you.

MDJ: Dumped? You might say that.

ET: I did say that. Anyway, there's nothing wrong
     with Café Nero. Just drink your skinny latte
     and shut up and listen. I have something to
     tell you. Mainly about your last agent.

MDJ: Do you treat all your authors like this?

ET: Yes. I also make sure you get published by
     proper publishers who pay proper advances,
     like they did in the olden days. Look at
     Ethelred. If it wasn't for me he'd be self-
     publishing postmodern novellas written
     entirely in blank verse.

MDJ: Rather than on remand for murder?

ET: That's not my fault. Well, not entirely. The
     point is that I've discovered what happened
     at Francis and Nowak before you left.

MDJ: Relations just got a bit difficult . . . I mean,
     after the Crispin Vynall business . . .

ET: Do you know who started the whole plagiarism
     rumour?

MDJ: No.

ET: Well, I do.

MDJ: You've found out? How?

ET: I have an informant at Francis and Nowak. It would seem that Henry Holiday told Janet Francis that Crispin had written the thing for you. I have little doubt that he leaked it onto the Internet for general consumption too.

MDJ: Henry Holiday? Why?

ET: Because he was one of the losing authors in the CWA competition.

MDJ: When I won?

ET: Yes.

MDJ: Just that?

ET: No, there's a bit more – about a lost master-piece and a life utterly destroyed, blah, blah, blah – but that's the short version of the story. You don't want the full one. He stitched you up, Mary.

MDJ: The bastard.

ET: Then he stitched Ethelred up. Henry Holiday killed Crispin Vynall and incriminated Ethelred. We just need to produce the evidence that will prove his innocence.

MDJ: Wow! This is just like a genuine murder mystery! But why can't the police do it?

ET: The police might not go along with what I'm going to suggest. It's not quite as legal as they usually like it to be.

MDJ: But there *is* evidence to clear Ethelred's name?

ET: There was a video recording of Crispin with Henry Holiday but it got . . . lost.

MDJ: So, there's other evidence?

ET: I can prove that Henry impersonated Crispin in writing really evil Amazon reviews for Ethelred's books. That meant that Ethelred seemed to have a motive for killing Crispin. I also know Henry wrote death threats and sent them to Ethelred.

MDJ: So, Henry's right in the middle of it.

ET: Yeah, but Henry is going to say that he did the reviews as a joke – he never dreamt Ethelred would see them and go off and kill Crispin. If he had his time again etcetera, etcetera, etcetera.

MDJ: But you're certain about the death threats.

ET: I'm certain because I know Henry's a nasty little toerag. Sadly the police haven't yet reached the same conclusion. Mainly because Ethelred gave one death threat away and I lost the other one at Sainsbury's.

MDJ: So what are you planning to do?

ET: What were you doing on New Year's Eve?

MDJ: Me? Nothing. I stayed in, opened a bottle of Pinot Grigio and watched some programme on television. Meerkats, I think.

ET: Did anyone visit you, phone you or anything?

MDJ: My mum phoned me on my mobile around midnight, just to wish me happy new year.

ET: So, if you'd had a man in your flat all night, making passionate love to you, nobody would know? Or indeed, a man in somebody else's flat.

MDJ: I wouldn't necessarily have told my mum, if that's what you mean.

ET: And you say you've always been very fond of Ethelred?

MDJ: He wasn't with me, I promise. I went to bed alone.

ET: Let's not be too hasty in reaching that conclusion Mary, have you ever committed perjury? For the best possible reasons, of course. To ensure that good triumphs over evil. And to screw over a slimy scumbag.

MDJ: Excuse me, Elsie, but is that a tape recorder in your bag?

ET: Sorry, force of habit. I'll switch it off now. Don't worry. I'll be careful to wipe the tape. I'll do it the moment I get home. Nobody will ever . . .

RECORDING ENDS

CHAPTER FORTY

From the journal of Elsie Thirkettle

There was one other call that I needed to make. Janet Francis's PA was reluctant to let me anywhere near her but I persisted and was told that I could have five minutes – and no more – with the great agent in person. But I'd need to come round straight away.

'I hope this is as important as you claim,' said Janet. She was putting papers in a bag, preliminary to departing for some Important Meeting. 'I'm already late.'

'You'll want to hear this,' I said.

I produced a piece of paper and placed it on the table. She picked it up.

'What is this exactly?

I, Janet Francis, declare that I was told in December by Mary Devlin Jones that she was in a relationship with Ethelred Tressider, also known as the author

Peter Fielding, and that she was looking forward to
spending New Year's Eve with him. She later told me
that she and Mr Tressider had been at Mr Tressider's
residence for the entire night of 31 December/1
January.

Then for some reason there's a space for my signature.
I'm not signing that! It's not true for one thing – it
cannot possibly be true – and even if it were, why on
earth would I sign? I'm well aware that Ethelred is
under arrest for murder and I'm well aware that New
Year's Eve is supposedly when the murder took place.
Why would I sign something I know to be a lie?'

'Because I'm asking you to perjure yourself. You may
later have to swear to this in court, but I hope not. I
think all charges will be dropped the moment the police
interview Mary.'

'I'm sorry, but I really have to go. I don't have time for
some elaborate joke at my expense.'

She stood up.

'I know about Karen Rockingham's detective novel,' I
said.

She sat down.

'You can't! I mean, there's no such thing.'

'Yes, there is. I know and others know too.'

'Who? What are they planning to do about it?'

I pointed to the note on the table.

'You can't expect me to sign that in order to find
out . . . You *do* expect me to sign that to find out, don't
you? Oh my God – this is blackmail, isn't it?'

'Yes, it's proper blackmail. The leak comes from this

office. If it reaches the press it will ruin your agency.'

'Then you have to tell me.'

I tapped the note on the table.

'Do you know what the penalties for perjury are?' she demanded.

'Less than what will happen if news of the Rockingham novel hits the press. Anyway, read the note in front of you: all you're saying is that's what you believe you were told. It would be difficult to prove that Mary didn't say that to you. It would be even more difficult to prove that you didn't think that's what Mary told you. I doubt you'd even get a custodial sentence.'

'I'd make sure you went down with me.'

'It's a deal. We'll share a cell. I bag the top bunk.'

Janet's eyes shot daggers at me across the table, but I was dagger-proof. She took out a very expensive fountain pen and scratched her signature furiously on the page.

'Now, who leaked what to whom?'

I told her.

'And there's no point in sacking Tuesday,' I added. 'I already have her under contract to me, as is Elisabeth Söderling, interestingly.'

'Elisabeth Söderling?'

'Maybe I'll need to explain that one some other time. I'm sorry you've lost Crispin too as a client – though I guess that the estate of Crispin Vynall is almost as valuable.'

'Value? That isn't a consideration,' she said.

Then I remembered something Mary had said about Janet fancying Crispin – or perhaps I had said it to Mary. Either way, it could well be true. Maybe it wasn't just the commission that she would miss.

'I suppose,' I said, 'that you get closer to some of your authors than others.'

'Meaning what exactly?' Janet was haughty but very much on her guard. I could tell there was something she was holding back about Crispin – or maybe one of her other male authors. Well, I could get Tuesday to relate all of the gossip to me at leisure. I didn't need to know at this precise moment.

'I've had my five minutes,' I said. 'I'd better be going.'

'But what do I do now? I've signed your damned note, but as far as I can see there's no way of stopping Henry Holiday going to the press.'

'These things always depend on how they are done,' I said. 'Henry would leak it to the journalist who would put the least favourable interpretation on it all – a trashy novel that had been largely ignored and sold few copies. You, on the other hand, can select your own journalist to leak an exclusive story to – you might let their paper write a very favourable review a week or so prior to the leak so that they can boast they spotted the exceptional quality of the novel even before they knew who had written it. Most papers like an exclusive. They'll be eating out of your hand. You'll know how to handle it from here without advice from me – now I've told you what's going on and you have time to ensure things happen your way rather than Henry's.'

Janet was nodding thoughtfully and looking at me almost with respect. Her nimble mind was planning each step. She knew I was right. As long as she could control it all, she could turn this to her advantage. The publicity would be enormous. At the very least she could massively increase the sales of Karen's book.

'I'd better let you go to your meeting,' I said.

'Meeting? That wasn't important. I have calls to make.'

I left her dialling furiously. She hadn't thanked me in so many words, but deep down I knew she was grateful.

Of course, I hadn't told her my whole plan. She'd learn that later. I folded the signed perjury note carefully and put it in my bag. Then, thanking her secretary profusely, I went on my way.

CHAPTER FORTY-ONE

From the journal of Elsie Thirkettle

'I have,' I said to Ethelred's lawyer, 'some good news and some bad news.'

'Do you have the CCTV footage?'

'That is the bad news.'

'There is a delay . . . ?'

'It's gone to the rubbish dump.'

'How did that happen?'

'I don't know. I wasn't there. By dustcart, probably.'

'So, our last piece of evidence has gone?'

'Yes, but I have an even better plan.'

'Which is?'

'I have established that Ethelred spent the night with another writer. She is willing to give evidence that she did so.'

'But Ethelred says he didn't. He was alone.'

'Well, that's Ethelred all over, isn't it? He'd go to the gallows before he besmirched a lady's name.'

'Elsie, we are living in the twenty-first century, not the nineteenth.'

'But Ethelred is still living in the nineteenth century, isn't he?'

'You might say that.'

'There you are, then.'

'And this is true?'

'It's as true as it needs to be,' I said. 'You lawyers spend all day saying, "I put this to you" or "I put that to you", and you know damned well that you're just on a fishing trip. I bet fifty per cent of the things you say in court are less than half-true.'

'I don't say things in court that I know to be lies,' he said.

'You don't know this is a lie either,' I said. 'Anyway, you won't be saying it. Mary Devlin Jones will.'

'How do you spell that?' he asked.

I told him. 'Don't worry if Ethelred acts a bit surprised when you tell him,' I added. 'That's just his way.'

'Is there any danger he will deny it?'

'Yes, because he is noble and chivalrous and, frankly, a bit of a plonker. The police suspect that there may have been somebody because Henry told them there might be, but that subtle little double bluff is about to rebound on him. We're pushing at an open door.'

'And will there be any proof that Ms Jones was with Ethelred? Just in case the police think that's it's slightly too convenient that this evidence has shown up when it did?'

'Yes, I have a signed note from a very well-respected agent, saying that Mary told her some time ago that that was what she had done.'

300

'Any other evidence like that?'

'How much would you like?'

'I'm not asking you to fake witness statements.'

'OK. We'll have to do it your way, then. That's all I have. Is it enough?'

'Do you assure me that what you have told me this morning is the truth?'

'Yeah, yeah, whatever.'

'Based on that assurance, I'll let Mr Tressider know, then.'

'Just make sure he doesn't screw it up.'

'If you don't mind me saying so, Elsie, coming from you that's pretty rich.'

He had a point. Still, what on earth could go wrong with a plan like mine?

Later I phoned Ethelred's editor.

'Hi, Will, you'd better start reprinting Ethelred's books. He's about to be released from custody and there's going to be massive interest. I'm going to arrange for him to sell his story to one of the big Sunday papers. His books will just be flying off the shelves.'

'We're already reprinting. Sales have rocketed in the last few days. Being arrested was the best career move Ethelred's made for some time. Just so long as he is found not guilty.'

'Strictly speaking he hasn't been charged yet. Nor will he be. Fact.'

'You sound very confident.'

'Oh, I am, Will. I so am.'

* * *

But the next day came, and the one after and Ethelred had not been released. The story had, to tell the truth, faded a little from the front pages. Other stories had taken its place. Book sales were still good, but Ethelred's face no longer featured on the news programmes.

I tried phoning his lawyer a couple of times, but on each occasion I was told that he wasn't available but that my message would be passed on to him.

Doubtless it took time for the police to conduct their interviews with Mary and Janet. Soon – tomorrow if not today – I would receive a call from Ethelred, thanking me profusely for springing him from his dungeon and expressing admiration for my strategy in delaying his release to ensure maximum publicity and book sales. Well, something like that, anyway.

And I had plenty to do. Tuesday had started work at my office, which involved finding her desk space and a computer and a phone and paper and pens and paper clips and showing her how a very old photocopier worked and discussing why we didn't have a nice coffee machine like Janet's.

I put her straight onto the recently acquired Söderling account. But I was expecting to land a much bigger fish very shortly. I put through a call to Karen Rockingham, and explained one or two things to her.

I also sorted out things with one of my contacts at the *Sunday Times* – Ethelred would write them an exclusive account of his unjust incarceration for a fee to be agreed, once it was clear he was actually being released.

I was in fact so busy that three days passed before I actually started to worry. I mean, had I underestimated not merely his chivalrous nature but also his honesty? He would obviously have worked out what was going on. Would he have decided he would rather go to prison than lie? It was unlikely but then . . . and, holy shit! If he said it was untrue and the police believed him, that did not look good for Mary or Janet or me. I wasn't sure whether my offer to share a cell with Janet was in any way legally binding, but I didn't want to go to gaol anyway.

I was, of course, still hopeful my plan would work, even after the call from Mary.

'The police interviewed me yesterday,' she said.

'And?'

'I told them what we agreed. That I had arranged to spend New Year's Eve with Ethelred.'

'And what did you say you did?'

'We watched the programme on meerkats.'

'Nice touch. And absolutely true. You did both watch it – at precisely the same time, only not in precisely the same place.'

'They seemed very suspicious.'

'That's their job.'

'They seemed to know I wasn't telling the truth.'

'It's just a way they have.'

'I hope so.'

'Trust me. I'm your agent. Would I allow you to get into some stupid mess?'

All week, I've had *BBC News 24* running constantly in my office, volume muted, just in case there was the merest hint that Ethelred was about to be freed or, conversely, that investigations had taken a more serious turn, with other arrests expected. Possibly that the police were hunting for two literary agents and one author of books about a cat detective. But there has been nothing at all.

So, I have decided to drive down to Sussex, with this notebook and my tape recorder. I shall visit Henry Holiday and see what more I can get him to tell me. Because it is just possible that there is more evidence that I have missed and it is just possible that he is so conceited and arrogant that he will tell me. But before I do that, I shall drop in on Ethelred's house, because I know his neighbour has a spare set of keys, and I shall check that all is well there and nothing is malfunctioning. Ethelred and I go back a long way. If he does go down for thirty years, less time off for good behaviour, I'll at least need to know how his boiler works.

CHAPTER FORTY-TWO

It had been a long day. When the police finally said that I was released and could go, I felt an immediate flood of relief, tinged almost with disbelief.

My lawyer had kept me well informed, of course. I'd heard with despair of Elsie losing the death threat letter and then, disaster piling on disaster, how she had also failed to obtain the CCTV footage when it was available. Then, when her Great Plan was revealed to me, I almost gave up on the spot. Fortunately it had all worked out in the end. I had been driven back to West Wittering and had just made myself some tea when I heard the key in my front door. It was only a mild surprise when Elsie marched in to the sitting room.

'Bloody hell, Ethelred! What are *you* doing here?'

'It's my house,' I said.

'That doesn't mean you can just barge in whenever you like, frightening the shit out of me.'

'Yes, it does.'

'But you are supposed to be in gaol. I still haven't got the *Sunday Times* deal in place yet. They'll want pictures of you leaving Paddington Green police station. We need to get you back there and—'

'There's a police station at Selsey, if you'd like to get a snap of me outside one. I've no plans to go inside a police station for some time.'

'So, Plan C worked, then? I mean you're free?'

'Elsie, shall we run through your contribution to my freedom? First, you encouraged me to start this stupid investigation on Henry's behalf.'

'A bit,' she said.

'Then you allowed yourself to be fooled into believing that Crispin was Thrillseeker . . .'

'You'd never have worked it out.'

'. . . thus providing one of the key pieces of evidence against me.'

'Your infatuation with Emma Vynall was good evidence too.'

'I was never infatuated with Emma Vynall. But you still told the police that I fancied her rotten.'

'Well, you did.'

'Once, perhaps. But you didn't have to say it. It wasn't helpful.'

'Still, it was me that got you off. I mean, if I hadn't got Mary to say that she'd slept with you . . .'

'That was a complication that I would prefer to have avoided. It could have ruined my defence and led to Mary being convicted of perjury. But never mind. In the end it left the police bemused but they won't be pursuing that line of inquiry further. It did no harm.'

'So, the police haven't released you because of the watertight alibi I constructed for you?'

'I've *always* had my own watertight alibi. And it was a real one – not an invention. I just preferred not to use it unless I absolutely had to.'

'What was that, then?'

'I spent New Year's Eve in bed with somebody.'

'Not Mary Devlin Jones?'

'Clearly not.'

'Emma Vynall?'

'No. Even though I apparently fancy her rotten.'

'Who, then?'

'I'm coming to that. Fortunately I never needed to tell the police who it was.'

'So, if the police *didn't* believe you were in bed with Mary, and you wouldn't say who you were really in bed with, how did you get out of gaol?'

'The CCTV footage.'

'But it was thrown away.'

'No, the police picked it up. My lawyer told me what you'd told him. You thought, and Kevin may have thought, that the old machine had gone for recycling. All that had happened was that the police had contacted the manager – the proper manager, not the idiot boy you spoke to. The manager said that he still had the machine in store and the police came and took it away. He hadn't told Kevin because it was none of Kevin's business. The police went through the footage for New Year's Eve. It was clear that Henry had lied to them and that he and not I had been with

Crispin shortly before midnight. He has now been arrested. Henry's problem was that he was just a bit too clever for his own good. He'd forgotten, on the night, that there might be CCTV in the car park, but when I told him that the recording had been wiped he felt completely safe. Hence his willingness to taunt me with the details of how he had done it all.'

'So the police have identified him from the CCTV?'

'Yes, and from the photo in the pub.'

'They found it? But the landlord said he had no idea who took it.'

'People put pictures up in all sorts of places these days. The police searched Facebook for "New Year, Didling Green". It came up straight away. Then there were the sockpuppet accounts. They were just the icing on the cake, but it was helpful in proving my contention that Henry had been trying to frame me.'

'The police traced them to Henry? I told them they might be able to but they didn't seem that interested.'

'They were already onto it. Amazon were apparently very helpful. They wouldn't say exactly how they had done it, but they identified Henry as the originator. One of the problems with crime writers is that they don't keep up to date with the technology. Their apparently watertight plots are blown wide open. Thus it was with Henry.'

'Wow. So that's Henry put away for a few years. He'll have time to reconstruct his great literary crime novel then.'

'He doesn't need to. It was never destroyed.'

'But he burnt the paper copies, wiped the discs,

shredded the notes and then shed genuine tears into an empty glass . . .'

'The CWA had sent a copy to each of the judges. Crispin and I had destroyed our copies years ago, of course, but Janet Francis has an army of efficient helpers and a well-organised paper filing system. Some intern had filed them in boxes in the storeroom – all two hundred of them. If Henry had asked her, he could have had it back any time.'

'And it is a great literary masterpiece?'

'I haven't had a chance to read it yet. Janet has – she says it's a pretentious load of crap. We were quite right not to shortlist it. Of course, following Henry's arrest, and the publicity that will certainly follow, some publisher may now be interested . . .'

'Well,' said Elsie, 'Janet may have the manuscript but she no longer has Karen Rockingham. I signed her yesterday.'

'So I heard. But you let Janet know about Henry's plot to reveal Karen's crime-writing activities, and she was working on releasing the news to the press. All should have been well. So why did Karen switch agencies before the news was even out?'

'Because,' said Elsie, 'I then phoned Karen and explained that the only reason Janet was able to rescue things was that I had found out what was going on. If she wanted to avoid screw-ups in future, she'd better sign up with an agency that was slightly more on the ball.'

'And she did?'

'And she did.'

'You explained, of course, that the person who leaked the information was now working for you?'

'I may not have mentioned it yet.'

'Well, you haven't done too badly out of my incarceration, have you? You've acquired three new writers: Mary Devlin Jones, Elisabeth Söderling and now Karen Rockingham. And you got yourself a new assistant in Tuesday Lane-Smith, though you'll probably need a couple more just to handle the Rockingham account.'

'It would be a sad world if good deeds went entirely unrewarded.'

'By good deeds, you mean the way you almost got me twenty years in gaol by interfering and faking evidence?'

'That's slightly uncharitable but yes, if that's how you want to describe it. Anyway, how do you know all this? You've been in a dungeon with just a meagre streak of daylight providing enough illumination for you to be able to see your bowl of gruel. You won't have been able to talk to anyone except your lawyer and maybe the gaoler when he came to refill your jug of putrid ditchwater and plump up your straw pallet for you.'

'Janet drove me back to West Wittering,' I said. 'She gave me a full account during the two-and-a-half-hour journey. She is not happy.'

Elsie looked at me. I'm not sure at what point it had dawned on Henry Holiday that he had not been quite as clever as he had thought, but my guess was that his face at that point looked much as Elsie's did now.

'*Janet* drove you back?'

'Yes, Janet drove me back.'

'Janet *Francis*? Not somebody else, coincidentally called Janet, who happens for unrelated reasons to be a bit unhappy about something – the death of a pet hamster, say, or Ed Milliband's latest opinion poll ratings?'

'Yes, Janet Francis. She doesn't have a hamster, as far as I know.'

'Ethelred, when you said that you were in bed with somebody on New Year's Eve, you couldn't have possibly meant . . .'

'Janet and I have been friends for some time. Neither of us had anything to do on New Year's Eve so I invited her over. One thing led to another. The morning after, we both agreed over hot coffee and croissants that it had really been a bit of a mistake. Not that either of us regretted it . . . it had been fun . . . but all the same . . . We're at an age when one-night stands feel a bit . . . juvenile. So we promised each other that we would stay friends but would never mention New Year's Eve again.'

'Even if the alternative was going to the gallows?'

'That was not an eventuality we foresaw, even if there was still any such thing as gallows in this country, which there isn't.'

'So you always had a fallback if the other evidence failed?'

'Not one I wanted to use.'

'And the police were right. You were concealing the fact that you'd had somebody with you. I just thought they were being stupid.'

'The police aren't stupid. Not in real life. Fortunately I never had to tell them about Janet because they came up with the other evidence. Which meant I also never needed to deny Mary's touching but completely untrue statement about what she was doing on New Year's Eve. That was fortunate for a lot of people.'

'Well, how right you were to end it amicably over coffee. I mean, I realise that you *thought* you were attracted to Janet. And I suppose, now I think about it, that she is precisely the sort of bossy, upper-middle-class, school-captain type that you go for. And she's as old-fashioned as you are, in her own sweet way – I mean, those Filofaxes and card indexes she so loves. She probably enjoys country walks and the Last Night of the Proms and the Chelsea Flower Show and wet Labradors slobbering over her. But you were *so* right to dump her. She'd have bullied you mercilessly, Ethelred. She'd have organised your life for you down to the last detail. She'd have . . . *Why* did she drive you home?'

'I phoned her as soon as I was released.'

'Not me?'

'No.'

'But—'

'You've treated Janet very badly. Do you realise how humiliated she felt having to sign that ridiculous piece of paper saying that I'd spent the night with Mary Devlin Jones?'

'But you'd agreed to remain just good friends . . . Oh, no, don't tell me . . .'

'We're not going to move in with each other . . . not yet. But I think we'll be meeting up from time to time. As often as possible, in fact.'

'But I'm still your agent . . .'

'That might be awkward. You really have upset her. And taken her biggest client.'

'But the story for the *Sunday Times* . . .'

'Janet has organised something with the *Mail on Sunday*. Then I'm going to work on the book about it all that will come out later this year. Janet thinks we might sell a couple of million. She says you always undervalued me as a writer.'

'No more than you deserve.'

I said nothing. Elsie was right. All of those put-downs over the years – hadn't I somehow invited them? I'd got what I deserved. It had just taken me a long time to realise that there was an alternative. I could have what I didn't deserve.

The silence lengthened until eventually even Elsie realised that something was slightly amiss. 'You're a bit cross with me, then?' she asked.

'What do *you* think?'

'I could apologise to Janet.'

'Thank you. I'll pass that on. But it wouldn't really change things.'

'Is it because I lost the evidence that would have cleared you of a murder charge?'

'No,' I said.

'Is it because I ate your chips?'

'No,' I said.

'So, that's that?'

'Just leave the keys on the shelf in the hall.'

'Bye, then.'

'Bye.'

Just as she was leaving the sitting room, Elsie turned. 'I bet Janet wouldn't have faked evidence for you or blackmailed people or got half the crime writers in the country to commit perjury.'

'Hopefully not,' I said.

A bit later I heard her car engine cough into life and a bit after that I heard her turn the corner at the bottom of the road. Then there was silence.

POSTSCRIPT

I'm not sure people read postscripts that much, either. I mean, you've found out who committed the murder or whether Elizabeth Bennet married Mr Darcy. They were popular in the nineteenth century, of course – a whole chapter or two on what each character did next, whether they got their just deserts, whether they were happy, how many children they had.

But the story's finished when it's finished in my view. There's the final tableau, then the curtain falls and the audience goes out into the cold night, turning up their collars against the rain.

I have not lost touch entirely with Elsie. Twice a year an A4 envelope still arrives with the accounts for the earlier books that are still under contract to her. A short time afterwards, a payment is made into my bank account, less fifteen per cent commission. And every now and then her assistant, Tuesday, phones with some query about a request for a book signing or new large-print rights. She is always very bright and cheerful, and seems unaware that my new books are all contracted to Francis and Nowak.

When Elsie departed, she left behind her a Sainsbury's bag containing two Kit Kats, a leather-bound notebook and a tape recorder. She has never asked for them back. The notes, though purporting to be a diary, increasingly took the form of a first draft of a book about the Vynall murder. I have therefore felt free to draw on them in producing this account of my last ever case. I did write and offer to share the royalties with her if I found a publisher, but I received no reply. Karen Rockingham's sales as a crime writer are enormous and she is doubtless very busy. When I last heard, the agency was about to move into new and much grander offices.

I was called as a witness, of course, at Henry Holiday's trial. He cut a very sorry figure in the witness box – the round, red face just peeping over the rail, the old-fashioned waistcoats, the slightly grubby paisley bow ties. Everyone agreed that he was an improbable murderer. The second death threat letter, which he had carefully preserved, simply provoked mirth when produced in evidence – it was, with hindsight, a ludicrous fabrication. So, indeed, was the entire story he had spun to incriminate me – it was as crooked and full of holes as any of his plots. Henry produced the occasional flash of the old arrogance, but the main question on everyone's lips was how he thought he would ever get away with it. It's strange how, for a while, I actually thought that he might. But that's what we writers do all the time – suspend disbelief for a short while and tell a story.

Then the curtain falls.

ACKNOWLEDGEMENTS

Many writers like to state in their acknowledgments that they could not have produced their book unaided. Obviously I could have done this one on my own, but it would have probably consisted of some A4 sheets of paper, badly stapled together, full of typos and with a number of holes in the plot. The version you have here is better in all respects. My thanks are therefore due to everyone at Allison and Busby and in particular to Susie Dunlop, publishing director, Sophie Robinson, Lydia Riddle and to Fliss and Simon Bage. I am also grateful, as ever, to my agent, David Headley, and to my family for their continued support, without which even the stapled A4 version would have been a challenge for me.

I must also take this opportunity to apologise to the people of West Wittering for dumping another body on their doorstep. I would like to reassure potential visitors that on most days in West Wittering nobody is murdered at all. I should also like to apologise to the City of Chichester for suggesting that it is not as exciting or dangerous as Raymond Chandler's Los Angeles. Anyone who has negotiated the bypass at 8.30 in the morning will know that is untrue.